LEIGH RIVERS

SATANIC SHADOWS

SATANIC SHADOWS

Book 1 of the Broken Realms series
Copyright © 2024 by Leigh Rivers

First Edition 2024
Edited by Laura at Ten Thousand Editing and Book Design
Proofread by Lauren at PSR Editing
Cover by Ashes & Vellichor Designs
Formatted by Jen Stevens

ISBN 978-1-7394330-8-6

CONTENT LIST

Compulsory sexual contact, memory tampering, threats of violence and murder, blood, degradation, choking, attempted drowning, shadow play, kidnapping, bullying, and attempted assault.

For all the good little humans with a shadow kink.

CONTENTS

PROLOGUE

"Did you count the register?"

Pulling off my apron, I nod. "Yep. Fifty short. Maybe we need to keep an eye on the new girl."

Clarissa sighs then goes to the cash register to count, just in case I've made a mistake. Not that I have. I counted that thing three times before I came to the conclusion that our new waitress has been dipping her hand.

"I'll see you in the morning," she calls to me.

"Can't wait for twelve more hours of hell."

The bell of the diner rings as I pull open the door, finally at the end of my day. My feet hurt, my hair's a mess and hanging out of its clip, and to make things even better, rain is pouring from the sky and I don't have a jacket.

My car beeps as I unlock it—it's old, rusty, but gets me from my apartment to work five days a week. As I drive the fifteen minutes down the interstate, I yawn and refuse to check my phone. No doubt Grayson will be filling my DMs demanding to know when we're meeting up tonight.

Clarissa thinks he's my boyfriend, and no matter how many

times I correct her, she never understands the friends-with-benefits set-up.

But even though we planned to do something, I'd rather go home, walk my dog Toodles, and curl up on the sofa and watch movies until I fall asleep.

It's night by the time I reach my apartment, climbing four floors until I get to my door. Toodles is barking, jumping up on me when I get in. He's chewed up my mail but otherwise doing well with his housetraining.

The Labrador sits nicely while I grab his leash and harness, but I pause when I hear a light knock on the door.

Frowning, I peek out the eyehole, my shoulders slouching when I see Grayson. His shaggy blonde hair hangs over his forehead, his hood's up, and he stands back as I abruptly swing open the door.

"What are you doing here?"

He shrugs. "You never replied to my messages, and we had plans."

Don't get me wrong, there's nothing wrong with Grayson. He's sweet, funny, and he knows how to keep my bed warm, but there's never been a spark that pushed us to go further. We've never even discussed dating. We've been friends for years, since we were both placed in the same orphanage and somehow ended up with families in the same town. When we both turned eighteen and found ourselves homeless yet again, we helped each other get back on our feet. It just so happens that one of the times he ended up staying over, we slept together. It's just been a thing since.

Toodles jumps up on him, and Grayson grins down and starts to babble to him like a baby. "Are you just home? Do you want me to come for a walk with you both?"

"Sure." I hand him the leash. "Hold, please. Give me two seconds to find my raincoat."

He crouches down to Toodles, giving him an ear scratch

while I hunt for my coat, but when I step into my bedroom, a hand presses over my mouth.

A large, cloaked, masked person keeps their hand on my mouth as they use the tip of their finger to trace something on my wall. My eyes widen as the wallpaper burns, a symbol appearing, and I try to kick my legs out when the middle of the symbol starts to swirl. Terror takes over me as my wall starts to twist, my heart rapidly beating out of my chest in fear when it grows into a dark hole.

Grayson is standing two seconds away with Toodles, yet he can't hear my muffled screams or when I kick over my bookcase trying to get away from another of the masked beings, who shackles my wrists together with metal cuffs.

The room grows so cold I can see their breaths through the holes of their masks, and when the wall opens to a whirl of darkness, I'm sucked into it with my kidnappers, and everything spins, my insides knotting and coiling as my vision vanishes, and the shriek I let out is silent as I feel myself falling.

Falling and falling and falling.

Until my knees clash with something hard, my hands now free of the cuffs, and I gasp air into my lungs as my fingers dig into sand.

Water laps at my feet, and I shiver in the coldness, choking as a pair of black boots appears in my line of vision.

Taller than anything I've ever seen, someone who wasn't there in my bedroom crouches down, his face covered by the same mask as my captors. Large, warm hands grab at my face, forcing my head back so my eyes clash with green ones. It feels like they're searching my soul before the person pulls away like the touch alone burns them.

"She's human?"

"It seems so."

The voice, a man's voice, is muffled beneath the mask as he curses under his breath. "How is this possible?" When no one

3

replies, he shakes his head and turns around. "Take the human to her room."

I'm yanked to my feet, my eyes lifting to the canopy of trees hiding the sky until my breath is knocked out of me by the sight.

A castle. A fortress. The kind I've only seen in history class or in ruins. Towers take each corner, so high my neck hurts to look at them as I'm dragged up the stone steps to the entrance.

"You have no idea how long we've been looking for you," the muffled voice says as they pull me through the doors and down a corridor lit only by candles lining the stone walls.

The place is empty, cold, dark, and when I reach what they call the dorm rooms, I'm thrown inside.

My lungs squeeze as I hit the ground, my body shaking, and when I look up at the fireplace, the dresser, and the four-poster bed, my eyes land on a school uniform neatly placed on top of the mattress.

1

The reason I'm here is because the headmistress decided I was to be collected from the Mortal Realm and brought to this deserted island. In the middle of nowhere. Surrounded by a sea that seems to stretch to the end of the world. The past week since being brought to my room, I've stood by my window and watched the sun rise and set, the moon taking over the scene, and the way the water meets the beach.

To the right of a vast forest is a lake that nearly takes up the entire island, and I swear I've spotted something extremely large swimming around in it.

This place isn't normal. These people—things—aren't normal.

The school uniform is tight on my body. The black shirt buttons up to my throat, there's a black tie with an academy crest, and a matching pleated skirt sits high on my thighs.

I feel like I'm in a dream. A nightmare. Today is the first day of classes, and I've already been denied a meeting with the headmistress to get answers. Everyone is taller than me. Freakishly taller. Some don't speak my language, and I'm sure they're not human.

I know they're not. No one on this island is except me.

I jump as a knock sounds at my door. My blood runs cold as the knock sounds again, and as I smooth down my uniform and slowly open the door, I stare at two girls.

One grins at me. "Hi, I'm Poppy."

The other, evidently Poppy's identical twin, seems bored. "Mel," she greets, popping her hip out. "We have our first class, and Mrs. Dalton told us to collect you, so you know where you're going, since you missed the introduction day. Grab your satchel."

"I..." My voice shakes and stops, my hand rubbing up and down my arm. "Can you help me get home?"

"No," she replies, while the cheery one slides past me and into my room, picking up my satchel and slipping it over my shoulder. "Let's go, Sera."

"How do you know my name?"

Mel nudges Poppy when she fails to respond. Her smile falters, but she paints it back on. "Mrs. Dalton told us. We need to go now, or we'll be late for our first class."

Against everything telling me to slam the door in their faces and hide in the bathroom, I take one last look at my dorm room and follow them into the corridor—stone walls lined with candles and paintings and a pinned piece of paper that explains the rules of the girls' dorm rooms.

I don't bother reading them. It's a mistake that I'm here. And as Poppy starts to talk, the more I realize how true that is.

"So, the first class is mortal studies. We all need to learn the ways of humans so we can pass through the realms to their world. Tomorrow, we'll be covering combat, so we know how to fight like humans." She tuts. "Rather annoying that we can't defend ourselves using our powers. What do you wield?"

I frown. "I don't wield anything."

She giggles. "We all hold some sort of power. Mel and I are twins, so our powers are the exact same. We control water, and we don't feel pain."

I gulp. "I'm... I'm human."

Mel and Poppy both stop walking and turn to me. "What?"

Pulling my satchel up my shoulder, I chew my lip. "Some people showed up at my apartment and brought me here. I'm from Earth."

Mel looks at Poppy. "Earth is the Mortal Realm."

"Oh," she replies, confused. "You're probably going to die here then."

My eyes widen, and I take a step back. "What do you mean?"

"Well, if you fail classes, you get taken to the dungeons. Most of us don't get back out of there. We have a year to pass all of our classes and prove we can pass to the Mortal Realm, but if you're already human, I don't see why you're here. They'll probably get rid of you as soon as they find out."

Mel elbows her. "You idiot."

But I've already dropped my satchel and turned on my feet to run down the spiral stone stairway, nearly slipping when I reach the bottom. Students who tower over me stare at me as I run through the main corridor to the exit, and no one stops me as I push open the doors and desperately try to reach the pier off the side of the beach, needing to get onto the little boat and get the hell away from here.

As soon as my feet carry me down the path towards the water, a large mass appears in front of me out of nowhere, and I collide with their chest so hard, I'm thrown back, hitting the back of my head off the ground.

My vision blurs, and I groan as I sit up, the shadow standing above me shading the sun and turning everything around me dark.

I note hair as white as snow, almost silver, with the greenest eyes I've ever seen as he comes into view, a desperate look in his gaze.

"Who the hell are you people?" I shout, pushing to my feet. I barely reach his chest.

7

At my words, the worried look vanishes from his handsome face, and his jaw sets, his eyes darkening. He steps forward, and my neck aches when I try to hold eye contact.

"Dane," he says. "Ever heard of me?"

Trembling, I shake my head. "Never."

The concern vanishes from his face entirely, anger replacing it, and he grabs my chin in a firm grip, drags me towards the pier, and whispers in my ear. "You don't belong here, human. You'll be ripped apart by the end of the fucking week."

He shoves me forward, and instead of falling onto the start of the pier, pressure encases me, everything spins, and I drop onto the floor of my dorm room.

2

The grandfather clock that echoes throughout the entire castle begins to strike, telling me it's ten minutes until class. I've been staring at my reflection in the bathroom mirror for the past ten minutes while Mel and Poppy argue about their hair.

Mel leans on the sink beside me, twirling her black hair around a finger while glaring at her twin. "I still don't think you should have cut it," she says, using one extremely long, sharp nail—which could pass for a dangerous weapon—to flick her sister's short curls just above her shoulders. "Why did you dye the ends pink? You look like... What is it the humans call it? A Barbie doll."

She glances at me for confirmation, and I give a short nod.

Poppy scowls at her sister, eyes glowing yellow. "Mortals dye their hair, and the professors want us to be capable of living amongst them come graduation. You grew your nails to resemble blades, so what's the harm in me coloring my hair?"

"You look ridiculous. Sera has brown hair and she's human. And what are you doing with your eyeliner? You're not a cat," is her twin's reply.

Ignoring Poppy's building rage, she turns to me. "We'll meet you at class, Sera."

"Try not to kill each other on the way."

My forest-green eyes stare back at me as I finish washing my hands. My friends have changed their appearances a lot in the past four weeks. Being around me definitely doesn't help their new obsession with looking human—every day, they ask me multiple questions about what it's like to be powerless and if I'm scared to die of old age.

I've grown used to their questions though. At first, the whole immortal aspect of the students made me uneasy, but now, although some of my classmates are terrifying, I'm just focused on getting the hell off this island.

A month. An entire month of this and I still have no answers as to why I'm here.

The halls are busy when I exit the bathroom, students making their way to class in a rush, some glaring at me as I try to get through the crowd.

Someone materializes in front of me, and a solid shoulder hits mine. The abrupt collision is hard enough that I fall to the ground, a rush of air escaping my lips and my books scattering across the floor.

The same person who appeared in front of me a month ago on the beach is staring down at me—dark brows, white hair that falls over his left eye, tall enough to make me crane my neck.

I scowl at the large presence as he squats closer to my level, elbows resting on his thighs. His eyes dance at the sight of me on my knees before him, trying to gather my things.

"You should watch where you're going. This seems to be a daily occurrence now."

He moves a few strands of hair covering my eyes and face, tucking them behind my ears. Although the act is soft, the expression and the way he's looking at me tells a different story.

"See you in class, mortal."

I seethe, slapping him away and gathering my things as he straightens his spine, smirking down at me. "Stop touching me. And I already told you to stay out of my way."

He looks down at me, eyes flashing from green to silver, the way they always do when he stares at me. His teeth are clenched —I can tell from how tense his jaw is.

I've still to find out what type of immortal he is. Regardless, he doesn't scare me.

As if he's read my mind, he lets out a soft laugh and glances over his shoulder at the incoming professor. The corridor empties as she approaches.

"Seraphine Winters!"

She waves her hand, and invisible fingers wrap tight around my throat, yanking me to my feet as I choke.

"Stop causing trouble and get to your class!" Her voice lowers as she turns to face my bully. "I can only apologize for her clumsiness, Mr. Dalton."

"No apologies needed," he says in a deep tone, dragging his gaze up and down my body while I struggle. Dimples dent deep as he smirks. "I think the human likes being on her knees for everyone. Maybe she should stay there. It seems to be the only place she belongs."

Dane Dalton is his name. He's the son of the headmistress and the biggest dickhead in the academy, and if I had the chance, I'd kill him with my bare hands. As if being trapped here isn't bad enough, Dane has some unnecessary rage towards me, like I've ruined his entire life just by breathing the same air as him.

He laughs down at me before fixing his crisp white cuffs and vanishing on the spot, taking his friends with him.

The teacher grimaces at me then releases her invisible hold. I drop to the ground once more—painfully. I try not to say a nasty comment as her heels click away from me.

Welcome to Quarrierton Academy, where violence is praised, and the weak and mortal are punished.

3

The mortal studies class is giving me a complex. I'm obviously going to pass this module, but sitting around everyone belittling everything about humans is making me feel small and useless.

Not only have I had zero sleep from the harrowing screams keeping me awake all night, but someone also stole my books, so I needed to borrow paper and a pen, which earned me a scowl from the professor.

She's green. With scales and eyes too big for her head, to go with the tail that keeps hitting stuff off her desk.

"I thought humans have no magic?" Orsen, Dane's best friend, interrupts Mel mid-question, making her glare at him. She looks like she wants to stab him with her long nails.

Mel isn't a fan of him, like I'm not a fan of his far-too-tall-to-be-normal leader.

The professor huffs out a cloud of steam from her large nostrils. "They do not."

She raises the mobile phone above her head. I wonder if I should tell her that no one uses black-and-white phone bricks anymore? "This gadget is how mortals communicate. If and when you are granted permission to leave the island, students will be required to know how to use one."

"What does it do?" someone asks. "What are its powers?"

"For the tenth time, it doesn't have any powers." Staring at the stapler she just knocked to the ground, she snaps the pencil in her hand. "I've already explained the satellites and messaging service. Does anyone need me to explain these again?"

Annoyingly, someone says yes. The professor dives into how the numbers on the keypad also have letters. Some of the students take notes, and others pay no attention, but Dane Dalton mutters under his breath how ridiculous and weak mortals are before leveling his gaze on me.

He's goading me to react, but instead, I pretend he doesn't exist.

He flicks his finger, and all my notes fall to the ground.

"Sera Winters!"

I roll my eyes at him as the professor throws her chalk at me. It bounces off my desk and rolls across the ground.

"Dickhead," I snarl in his direction as I reach for my papers. "Grow up."

A gust of wind whips at my hair, and she bellows, "Language, Miss Winters!"

After nearly twenty minutes of everyone in denial that there are satellites in the sky and the internet is a thing, the professor sits at her desk. "Any questions before we move on to the next subject?"

A hand raises, and the entire class groans. "To sum it all up," a student says, "mobile phones are a form of magic."

She rolls her lizard-like eyes. "You are all insufferable mutants."

Never in my twenty years have I ever witnessed a teacher speaking to their students like this. They'd be kicked out and never allowed to teach again. But all the professors are like her.

They throw around their powers for punishment and talk down to each and every student.

The professor walks to her desk and pulls out a second phone. "You will have one mobile, and the individual you are trying to contact will have the other. Each one has a unique number. You dial it into the keypad and..." She does this as she talks, and the other mobile begins to play a polyphonic ringtone.

"Can mortals be any more pathetic?" I hear Dane mutter to one of his friends. "Unnecessary technology, and for what? If you need to speak with someone, go see them."

I contemplate slapping him. All these little comments are aimed at me. He knows he's doing it, and he knows I know. It only pushes him to piss me off even more.

Yet, other than being a human with no powers, he has no reason to actually dislike me. But no matter what, every day, he'll throw me a nasty comment, call me disgusting, and act like I have a disease. He's lucky I haven't kicked him in the balls by now.

Poppy asks an insane number of questions, which I end up having to answer because the teacher doesn't know. I even inform the class that mobile phones are more advanced than the brick she's holding, that they have color touchscreens now.

We haven't even started on social media yet. Imagine trying to explain that to eighteen confused immortals? Let's just say I'm glad next week will cover how human education works compared to what they were taught in their own realm as children. Because if they were catapulted into my world tomorrow, they'd stick out like sore thumbs and probably get arrested within the first hour.

If they graduate.

Failure means restarting from the beginning and resitting all exams. It's the only way to escape their crumbling realms.

I haven't learned much about the other students and their history yet, but I have some details. There are a vast number of realms, and apparently, mine is the safest and not currently being overtaken by a curse. I've learned about three so far. Water, air, and fire.

And then there's my realm. The Mortal Realm.

We've yet to learn of the other fallen realms. I think it might be a hard subject and unnecessary information. I still have no idea why they need to know their own history when they came from these places. Why sit exams on their own realms' history to be granted entry into my realm?

I've been walking the earth for twenty years, and not once have I come across an immortal trying to blend in, though I guess being a bunch of creatures who can make themselves look human, it'd be easy to pretend to be like me.

"Are you going to partner us up now?" Poppy asks, tapping her pen on the table. "Or do we find our own partners?"

"No, I'll put on the board outside who you'll be partnered up with for the rest of the year. This means all of your assignments will be a joint effort." And she vanishes with a puff of green smoke just as the grandfather clock sounds, indicating the class is over and the next is due to begin.

Some students disappear from the room, vanishing on the spot like magic.

Even though I've only been here a few weeks, I've already adjusted to how things work here. The first time I saw a professor disappear into thin air, I nearly had a panic attack. Then when I walked into the human relations class—a way for the immortals to learn about the human body and the emotional connections we form—I nearly sprinted back out when I saw the board and the multiple positions the stick people were in.

Poppy and Mel tap my shoulder and tell me they'll catch up with me later since most of the students have left the classroom.

Dane's voice shatters my peace and quiet. He hovers over my desk, and I spot a ring on his middle finger with a carving that represents a realm, but I don't know which one. His black suit is fitted, and his eyes shift to a light silver as he talks.

"I thought mortals were pieces of shit, but now, being in this class, I realize I was wrong."

I raise a brow, crossing my arms. "Great. And you're telling me why?" I try not to gulp as the last student exits, leaving the two of us alone.

The door slams, and Dane, without moving an inch, locks it. "You are all worse than shit. I hope I never pass these classes, so I don't need to be stuck with your kind."

"You wouldn't last a second in my world." I stand, but he still towers over me. "Get fucked, Dalton."

I swipe up my new mobile phone, turn my back to him, and make my way to the door. But although he's a few steps behind me, something wraps around my arm and drags me to sit once more.

Then two shadow hands grab at my thighs, pressing me to the chair.

"Pathetic," Dane spits. He takes slow, careful steps towards me as the shadow fingers tighten. "You can't even push against me, can you? I'm using the most basic of my powers, yet here you are, trapped."

I swallow as he gets closer. "You use your powers because you aren't brave enough to do it yourself."

He hums, stuffing a hand into his pocket, the other twirling a pen between his fingers. "Humans carry enough diseases that I know never to touch you directly. And I imagine *you* are riddled with more than enough." He grimaces. "Disgusting, really."

Funny. He's touched my hair on multiple occasions mid-mockery, but instead of mentioning that, I hold in a smile.

"I've read about your kind," he continues, to my dismay. "You're dying from the moment you're born."

My eyes roll to the back of my head in annoyance. "What's

your plan if you do end up graduating and need to live among us?"

His devilish smile makes him more annoyingly handsome. "I'll burn you all to the ground."

I giggle at the absurdness. "Right. Can you take your little ghost hands off me now? As much as I love being held down and degraded, I have a boyfriend, and I'd like to go to my next class."

Dane doesn't let me go. In fact, those ghostly hands are firmer now, his jaw tight, and if this wasn't a horrible situation and he wasn't dropping to a crouch in front of me, this would be a turn-on.

Grayson would be ecstatic if he heard me call him my boyfriend, but Dane doesn't need to know that I just lied to his face.

"I bet you do like being held down. I couldn't imagine anything more repulsive. Seeing you beneath me." With his bright eyes, Dane studies me—from my long, brown curls, to my face and chest, all the way down to my black heels. "You are repulsive, mortal. If I ever get out of here, you'll be my first target." The shadowy hands part my thighs slowly. "I'll rip these legs off, and when you beg for mercy with tears in your eyes, I'll snap each bone in your body, if only to hear the way you scream."

The image in my head has sweat building on the back of my neck. I can see him doing something like that.

His eyes flash to a brighter silver. "I'll make it slow of course. I want to feel how your body breaks. How your lungs burn when you're desperate for oxygen. The last thing you see before I take your sight will be me. When you plead for me to end it all as you lose feeling in your entire body, I'll heal you, only to start all over again. Do you know why?"

I just stare at him blankly, waiting for him to continue.

"Because you are a human. Useless, already-dying creatures who depend on ridiculous things like mobile phones to live."

"Are you done?"

My toes curl as he tightens his invisible hold on my legs again. "You'll know when I am. Right before the soul leaves your body for good—only then will I be done with you."

My blood runs cold, and instead of giving him what he wants —to see me squirm from his threat—I tilt my head. "That was poetic. Did you rehearse that?" A breeze hits between my legs, and I battle against shifting. "What's your deal anyway? The fuck did I ever do to you?"

"You merely exist."

"Great," I retort. "Can you release me now? You're kind of creeping me out, not scaring me."

Dane stares at me, his eyes darkening. "You mean nothing here."

I scoff, trying to shift away from his hold when a faint pulsing begins, which only grants him more power to grip me. "Let me go."

"You. Mean. Nothing. Here."

"You should work on your tone. It's getting scary, but not enough to make me beg you to stop. Maybe you should abra-cadabra back into your real form and fuck off?"

My legs part further, and I don't fight it, even though I know he can see my panties. The feeling rushing through me has me gulping and heavily breathing through my nostrils.

The grandfather clock sounds again, and the hands stop pushing my thighs apart, but Dane doesn't move, his second set of hands still keeping me pinned to the seat. His pupils have dilated, nearly taking over the shocking silver.

"Why are you here?" he demands.

I shrug, holding on to the sides of the chair. "Ask your mother. She's the one who had me kidnapped from my life and thrown onto this island and won't answer a single one of my questions."

His jaw tenses, and the hands vanish from my skin. He

stands tall, wiping invisible dust from his sleeve. "Leave the island. You have no place here."

I get to my feet and quickly fix my skirt. "I don't know if you're aware of this, *Einstein*, but there's a spell on the island. No one can leave without graduating. Have you not listened to a thing in mortal studies? No wonder you're still stuck here."

His eye twitches, but with one more glance down and up the length of me, stopping on my reddening cheeks, his irises shift back to his usual green, and he rapidly disappears from the room.

I finally breathe. My lungs were struggling for a beat there, but now he's gone, I can let my thoughts run wild and my fear sink in. He's an asshole, one who needs a good slap across the face, but he's also undeniably hot, which makes him even more annoying.

He knows all the students in the academy want him, but I don't. I'll never fall to my knees and suck his cock like everyone else in this place wants to do. He can take his threats, his second set of hands, and his moodiness and go back to whatever realm he came from. Most likely the Fire Realm. He's a hothead, angry all the time, and thinks he owns everyone. I bet if he shapeshifted back into his own form, he'd be a snake or a dragon.

Either way, I've failed at dodging him yet again. Daily, this happens. I wonder if he'll ever grow bored of materializing in front of me or knocking me over? Or will I be forever cursed to listen to his fantasies of killing me?

My traitorous thighs tingle with the aftermath of him pinning me to the chair. I blame the fact I've been stuck here for weeks with no attention.

He's just trying to scare me. He doesn't really want me dead. Right?

I pack up my papers and walk out of the classroom, stopping when I see him staring at the board with a deep grimace. It looks like the professor has already placed students into pairs, and when he glares at me over his shoulder, I know who I'm part-nered with.

"This is your fault," he snaps before disappearing again.

*It is compulsory for this module that students complete **all** assignments. The first one is due in two weeks, and you are both, as a TEAM, required to show that you understand the system on mobile phones by using the text messaging service at least once. No abuse will be acceptable.*

On the board are names side by side. At the very bottom, I find my own with my new partner.

Seraphine Winters and Dane Dalton.

How many times should one knock on the door of the headmistress's office before giving up? I've reached ten so far, but I don't have anywhere else to go on a Sunday night. If she doesn't eventually open it, I'll resort to kicking the thing in.

Maybe not. I like my shoes. And I'm not that strong.

Mel leans against the wall while I continue bruising my knuckles against the wood. "Have you ever considered that she may be in her room, sleeping? Not everyone sits in their office after hours."

"No." I continue knocking. "She's probably standing opposite the door, trying not to laugh. Mrs. Dalton knows how much we hate each other!"

She rolls her eyes. "She's not going to change partners for you. Dane already tried, like, a million times."

Even his name makes me mad. "He set my papers on fire when I told him to help me with the project. Do you know how much work that was? A lot! I'm telling her I'm either going to kill her son, or she needs to give me another partner."

My friend inspects her nails—still long and sharp like blades. "You need to start fighting back."

I sigh and drop my forehead to the door. "And what exactly am I to do? I'm certain he can read my mind, for God's sake!"

"I hate when you say that. We don't have the same god." Then she shrugs. "The mind reading could be fun. Throw him off with some sex thoughts."

I groan. "He's powerful. I'd be toast before I could even blink if I attacked him back."

"Humans are very dramatic. I have no idea how I'll ever fit in with your kind." She pushes off the wall. "Come. She's not in her office, and the castle guards are probably on their way with all the noise you've made."

"Fine."

Just my luck—Dane and his friends are in the courtyard as we make our way to our dorm. I can feel his deathly stare on me as I try to ignore him, my fists tight and itching to smash into his face.

But Orsen, his little sidekick, appears beside us, giving an unimpressed Mel his best smile. "You haven't replied to a single message. Care to explain?"

She crosses her arms and blows a strand of hair from her face. "Go away."

His laugh is deep as he shakes his head. "Come on, ice queen. Either reply to my message or let me fuck you. I'll make it worth your while. We are partners for human relations after all. Either way, my dick is going inside you. Let's make it fun."

Dear God.

She smiles the fakest smile I've ever seen. "I'd rather fuck myself with my fingers, but thanks."

I stare at her blade-like nails in horror.

Orsen, with his charming smile and blacker-than-black eyes, goes back to stand beside Dane, who hasn't stopped glaring at me.

"The offer stands!" Orsen calls to Mel. "And message me back!"

"The offer can fuck off," she mutters, taking my arm and pulling me away from the courtyard. "I swear, ever since I've been partnered up with him for nearly all my classes, he's gotten clingier. I say we kill them both in their sleep."

I manage a laugh as we step into the castle. "All your classes?"

"Five so far. Who are you with?"

Confused, I shake my head. "Only mortal studies with Dane."

"Hmm," is her reply as we walk into the ballroom, a shortcut to the dorms.

The students being punished are setting the room up for a dance that I unfortunately have to attend. Big chandeliers line the ceiling, and the students are busy scrubbing some graffiti away and polishing the floors. Apparently, most of the students have been in the dungeons for years and haven't yet earned their freedom.

Some are killers, and others have committed some of the most heinous crimes possible on the island over hundreds of years.

My friend smiles at the view. "It's going to be the best night, right? Have you picked out your dress?"

I look at her in mortification. "It's not for another two months. And where the hell am I going to find a dress?"

She tuts. "Humans."

"You're probably going to have sex with a human one day. Maybe you should get used to us?"

Mel couldn't look more disturbed if she tried. "I most certainly will not."

I smile. "Unless you want Orsen?"

Grimacing, she ushers me out of the ballroom. "Stop. We have human relations tomorrow, and the last thing I need is a tired human by my side."

We stop at the dorms, and she waves her hand, opening my door. "Sleep. We'll speak tomorrow."

As soon as I'm in my room, the wood in the fireplace ignites and the candles flicker beside my bed. I'm showered and under my duvet within ten minutes.

And I'm annoyed again.

Dane doesn't plan on lifting a finger for this project, so neither will I. If we fail, so be it. He can go take a flying fuck for all I care. After all, I'm the only one who knows everything we need to know in order to pass that class.

The following week comes and goes, and I think I might throw myself out the window of the tallest tower. Head first, just to make sure I don't survive. Though knowing my luck, someone will just revive me and send me back to class.

All Dane's doing is scowling at me in the corridors, knocking my food off my tray in the canteen like a teenage schoolboy, and making me trip up in the courtyard.

What can possibly be worse than being partnered up with Dane Dalton for one class? Being partnered up with him for *four* of my classes!

Mortal studies.

Communication and socialization studies.

Combat and weaponry studies.

Cult studies.

All four classes I have to sit beside him. And in all four classes we don't speak a word. He makes me do all the work—because why would someone who needs to learn to adjust to live around humans do the work when the human can do it all for him?

I've not yet been partnered up for human relations, but I know that'll happen tomorrow. If I need to work with Dane, I might actually cry. So far, from what Mel and Poppy have told me, the professor wants all the students to know how to form romantic connections, how to kiss and touch and care, and as soon as that part is established, she wants everyone to move on to more intimate forms of contact.

We haven't used the mobiles yet. He has no idea how to use his, and I refuse to help him. I don't think he's even taken the phone out of its case. Meanwhile, Poppy is having a blast with her partner, and Mel has done nothing but complain about Orsen, saying he should be expelled for sending her pictures of his cock.

It's big, to be fair. In my world, he'd be considered an extremely large eggplant, though apparently Mel has had bigger dicks inside her. Given her slim yet freakishly tall frame, I'm mentally questioning how she hasn't been split in half.

She's learned how to forward messages, much to my own misery, so as I'm her friend, she thinks it's perfectly fine to send me every single one of Orsen's penis pictures, with the horrifying bonus of a two-minute video clip. With audio. I've never witnessed so much sperm in my life.

I've also never deleted something so fast.

The professor upgraded everyone's mobile phones a few days ago, which is a relief yet a curse because as much as they appear as something we mortals use, they never lose battery.

This entire school is full of firsts for me, so I guess the shock value of being surprised when powers are used, or when my bed randomly shakes while I'm trying to sleep, is fading.

Dane and his little gang don't have that issue, I'm sure. They sleep in fancy rooms—probably have their own ball washers too.

They get special treatment here, being the offspring of the teachers and all.

I lie in my four-poster bed, situated in the middle of my dorm room, listening to the rain smack against the window and the whistle of the wind through the trees, which must be close to being ripped out of the ground. My room falls into darkness then fills with moonlight every few minutes. It storms a lot here, and every time it does, I can't sleep.

The crack of thunder and the flash of lightning seems to awaken the lost souls stuck in the walls, and shadows dance on the bricks while I watch. A silhouette of a woman holding a child's hand, running from a large mass. A man sitting down and reading a newspaper while someone cuts his hair.

Sometimes they wave at me. And sometimes I light a candle and hide under my duvet and wait for the storm to end. The shadows like me; they enjoy me watching them move across the bricks. I feel them when I wake, when I walk into the room, and I also feel them trying to comfort me when I'm sad.

When I'm anxious, or debating if I should just jump from my window, or smash a glass and take myself out with a shard, the shadows shiver, and the entire room grows cold, as if they're warning me to stop.

The phone on my bedside unit vibrates then starts to ring, and I frown. It's the middle of the night.

I roll my eyes when I see who it is. Nearly two weeks of silence and now he wants to contact me?

I busy-tone him and lie back in bed. It rings again, and again, and again, until even the shadows in my walls tremble in annoyance.

"You want to deal with him?" I ask the gathering masses. "Go. Be my guest."

I throw my phone at the wall, but it materializes above my head.

"Ow!" I rub my scalp, glaring at the swirling darkness of laughter trailing to my ceiling. "Stop doing that!"

It rings once more, and my patience has vanished.

"What do you want?" I snap as soon as I answer. "It's three in the morning, Dane."

There's ruffling then a scoff. "Ridiculous piece of technology. How can I hear you?"

"If you paid attention in class, then you'd know. Really, what do you want? I'm trying to sleep."

"We have to hand in our first assignment tomorrow and I..."

He stops, and I know he's gritting his teeth. "How do I send a message to you?"

I huff. "I'm not telling you. Read the manual the professor gave you. I already covered my part when I texted you. Learn something for once."

"Listen here, mortal. If I don't pass, neither do you. And we both want you off this island."

"Sure. So you've mentioned, like a million times. It's getting old now. Just open the app called *Messages*, then click new, then click on my name. Or reply to the one I sent."

I messaged him when we got the newer phones and knew he'd never respond. If you class a middle-finger emoji as a message.

"What do you mean?" he asks, confused. "How do I search for that app?"

Groaning, I bury my face in my pillow. "Figure it out, Dane. Like everyone else in the school, you need to actually work to pass this."

"Oh, fuck off."

It's obvious that he thinks the call has ended. Faintly, I hear him muttering that I'm useless and that he wants to strangle me. His phone is far away from him, but I can tell he's getting dressed. Metal—I assume a belt buckle—knocks against something, and Dane swears to himself then continues to ask himself where he put his shoes.

"Fucking mortals and their idiotic ways."

I try not to laugh, but a smile breaks out across my face. I wipe it away with my palm and narrow my eyes. He doesn't deserve anything of the sort directed at him. "I'm still here. You didn't hang up."

Nothing. He runs the tap in his bathroom, brushes his teeth, then there's more ruffling.

I can hear footsteps on his end, then a heavy fist against a hard surface, and to my absolute horror, I realize I can hear it happening twice.

"Are you at my door?" He knocks again. "No! Go away!"

He can't hear me because I'm in his pocket.

In my short nightdress, I hunt for my robe, falling short just as he opens my locked door. "Dane!"

Blank faced and monotoned, he says, "Mortal," as he struts in, waving his hand to close the door behind him and lock it. His gaze lands on me, and he stops walking. "Please don't make me bring up my insides." Dramatically, he covers his eyes with his hand. "Dress—before I intentionally blind myself."

"I wish you would." I glare, secretly wishing I had powers to set him on fire. Who the hell wears a crisp white shirt and dress pants at this time in the morning?

At least he hasn't done his hair. It looks disheveled, as if he's run his hand through it one too many times. Little curls fall over his forehead, and I want to pull one to watch it ping back into place. They're kind of cute.

"Please keep your childish thoughts to yourself," he says, and I feel all the blood draining from my face. "Touch my hair and I will hex you."

Finally finding my robe, I pull it on and wrap it tight. "Why are you here?"

He parts his fingers to see I'm decent enough for him to look at me. "Much better. I need you to show me how to send a message then I'll never set foot in your..." He grimaces as he glances around my room. "It even smells like humans in here."

I raise a brow. "And how do you know what humans smell like if I'm the only one you've met?"

"Vile. Sour. Like stale sex." Dane waves off the subject. "Back to the main issue." He tosses his phone at me—it's still connected to our call—and clasps his hands behind his back. "Send a message so I can get the hell out of here."

I end the call and open a new message, send myself one that says, *Humans rule,* and give him it back. "There. Now leave."

He stares at the phone. "Can you show me how you did that?" Then he brings the screen to his face and squints at it. "Remove this. I don't want such messages to be connected to me."

I sit on my bed. "I'm trying to sleep."

He frowns in confusion, like my words have no meaning to him.

I screw my eyes shut and cover my face with a groan. "Dane?"

"Mortal?"

I remove my hands. "Get out of my fucking room."

He sneers. "Watch your tongue."

I raise a brow. "Or what? Are you going to use your ghost hands on me again?"

Just as I expect, something wraps around my throat, like an ice-cold snake twisting around my neck. I can breathe perfectly fine, but I can feel the faint press of its tongue against my hammering pulse.

"I have a number of powers," he says, still standing at the opposite side of the room. Then he takes slow steps towards me as the invisible snake tightens around my neck ever so slightly. The hissing tongue slides across my cheek then to my ear. I shiver, tingles traveling down my spine. "But I can tell you like this one. Will I use it when you meet your end?"

Another step, and the snake tugs at me, so I lie back on the bed and stare at the ceiling. The silhouettes are hiding now. In the corners, in the designs of the bricks—anywhere Dane can't see. I fist at my bedcovers, trying to control my breathing.

Shakily, I say, "Am I supposed to be afraid?"

I should stop. But he pisses me off to no end and is still in my room, even after I told him to leave. He's got what he came for, so why is he still here?

Dane walks until he's in front of me, looking down with a curled lip. My robe has fallen open, and my nightdress is very, very revealing. He allows his gaze to trail down the length of me, and behind him, the shadows come out of hiding. They start to move slowly, silhouettes of a man and woman dancing, a dog barking as it chases a ball.

They must be trying to distract me.

Dane's eyes turn silver, and his white hair ruffles as random wind whips around my room. "If I ever see you dressed this way again, I will personally drown you in the castle's lake."

I drop my gaze to the obvious—large—tenting in his pants. "That must explain why you're hard."

The oxygen to my lungs cuts off, and my eyes widen with the pressure as the snake tightens around my throat until I'm unable to breathe. But as quick as my air supply stops, the snake vanishes, and Dane steps back.

I cough, trying to fill my lungs.

Dane shoves his hands in his pockets, probably to try to hide himself. "Why do you keep trying to provoke me?"

"Me?" I sit up and rub my throat. "You're the one who won't leave me alone. You're like a child. Who acts this way? How old are you?"

Dane's entire expression changes as he backs away from me, and he appears to be thinking. When he doesn't respond, realization hits.

"You don't know how old you are?"

"That is none of your concern," he replies. "Age is a number. You are born to die, whereas I am born to live. I don't need a number."

"You can just say you don't know. Unless you're two hundred years old, then it would be weird that you keep targeting someone a hundred and eighty years younger than you. You say humans are pathetic, yet you're acting like one by bullying me. You, Dane Dalton, are the pathetic one."

31

As his eyes darken, so does my room. My walls turn to black, the floor crawling with swirling, angry shadows, the ceiling full of them. The happy silhouettes are gone now, replaced by evil. He takes a step forward, and although I feel trapped in place, a force shoves at me from behind, as if it's pushing me towards Dane, and suddenly I'm standing.

My bed creaks before it slides backward and hits into something.

A wind builds, and my chandelier swings, the room turning cold enough that I can see my own breath.

Two more steps and Dane is right in front of me, his eyes narrowed, his jaw tense. "Do not speak to me like I'm beneath you."

He's fuming with rage as he glares at me. Something presses down on my shoulders, and my legs give way until my knees crack into the ground. I look up at him, my hair a mess over my face, and watch his eyes flickering to a bright silver.

Now I'm scared.

I think my heart might beat out of my chest as my things start to fly off the units and pictures crash off the walls. The rug in front of my fireplace is thrown across the room, and flames swirl out of the hearth.

As if something slaps him across the face—maybe the realization that he was about to destroy my room with me in it—he looks around us, eyes wide, noticing all the mess and the gathering shadows on the walls, the ceiling and slowly crawling towards us on the floor.

I can feel them too. They're excited; they want Dane to keep going, to let out all that power.

No. They aren't excited. They're... aroused.

He realizes the same time I do, or he reads my mind. He doesn't walk out; he vanishes in a swirl of darkness, and I let my lungs fill with much needed air as my room falls silent, as all my things return to their rightful places. The shadows vanish, and the silhouettes are back, watching me.

Dane is powerful, but I don't think he realizes just how powerful he is.

5

"Tell me, human girl," Mel begins while brushing Poppy's hair, "what does an orgasm feel like to you?"

I sigh, looking up from my papers. "Really? Why would it be any different from yours?"

"She has a point. We take a human form now," Poppy says, wincing when Mel hits her head with the brush. "Ow! You bitch."

Mel ignores her twin. "Have you nearly died from one?"

I choke on air. "What?"

"I take that as a no. Then it's clear you have the worst sex life in the universe."

"Nearly dying from an orgasm sounds horrific, so maybe yours is the worst."

"I cannot die," is her reply.

"Then you can't *nearly* die," I retort. "And I used to have a great sex life, I'll have you know."

Humming, she continues brushing for the next few minutes, and I continue writing notes for my next class. After vanishing the brush from her hand, she starts to braid Poppy's hair to her scalp.

She doesn't continue the subject, so I quickly finish my notes, close my book, and pick up my sandwich. We're sitting in the food hall. We usually sit in the courtyard, but the weather is bad, so given our short skirts and the fact we have no protection against the rain, we hide in here.

Dane and his group of hooligans are a few tables over, and I can hear Orsen speaking about Mel and how nice her ass is.

In the last twelve hours, he's sent her ten messages, a video of him showing her his bed, and asked her to her face if she wanted to go for a quick round before class.

He's ruthless.

"Oh fuck!" Orsen yells, quickly getting to his feet and jumping as water pours from his pants, coming from over his waistband.

Smoke pours from his skin to heat himself up, and he glares up at Mel while she whistles, continuing to do her sister's hair. He isn't going to retaliate—he wants her too much to get mad at her. Instead, he chuckles, wipes himself with napkins, and winks at her.

This is a regular occurrence now. The pair are brutal. She's either torturing him with her powers, or she's complaining about his dick pics. I think she secretly likes it too. It's not that Orsen isn't hot; he is, but he's a little out there for me. Boisterous, wild, loud. Plus, he's dead set on having my friend—who just happens to be the total opposite of him. The only thing they have in common is that they seem to enjoy sex. Not the vanilla kind, but the kind that makes me want to put on a chastity belt and claim innocence for the rest of my life.

I can feel Dane's eyes on me as I put my books into my leather satchel then fold my paperwork to add it to the bag. It's weird that I can suddenly sense him everywhere. He could walk into the room, and with my back turned, I'd know he was there. It's like the energy changes around me, but only I can feel it. When he left my room last night, the silhouettes in my walls wouldn't stop dancing. The shadows shuddered across my floor, and my bed shook when I told them to get a grip.

I don't look at him as I get to my feet. "I'll see you both at class? I need to use the bathroom."

Lie. I need to get away from him.

"Don't be late. We're practicing emotional kissing today."

I groan. "Awesome."

"Hopefully the professor partners you up!" Poppy yells as I walk away from the table. "And I hope, for your sake, he's hot!"

Dane's stare follows me out of the room, and I fight the urge to give him the middle finger like the mature adult I am. An adult who somehow has to study how to be a human for the next year.

I dodge students as I make my way to the bathroom. I lock the cubicle, sit on the pan and relieve myself, then drop my head into my hands. It's been weeks, and I still haven't woken up to my work alarm, in my bed, wrapped up in blankets with Toodles pawing at my face.

So many times I've talked myself into believing this is a dream—a long, terrible nightmare that I need to wake from.

I pull out my phone, dial "911," and press it to my ear. But the line is dead. It's the same when I call my work's head office, and again when I try to call my old mobile number.

I stupidly click on Dane's to see if it's maybe the signal in the bathroom, and it rings.

I freeze and hang up.

Idiot. Absolute idiot.

I clean up, wet my face in the mirror, and ready myself for my next class. The one I've been dreading. Because there's no chance I'll get away without being partnered up for this one.

When I woke up this morning, I thought my week couldn't possibly get any worse. Another day in hell, even if I'm one day closer to graduating and getting off this goddamn island.

However, the universe seems to be playing a joke on me.

When I make it to my human relations class three minutes late, I try not to look at the two students on the bed in the middle of the room. Fully dressed but groping each other over their clothes.

The professor sits at her desk, arms crossed, appearing bored and more human than anyone else here. At least she doesn't look like the mortal studies teacher, with a tail sweeping everything off her desk.

"What did I tell you? You need to kiss her with tongue, and stop acting like a statue. I scanned you—you are no virgin."

He turns a deep shade of red all over, and his partner winces from the heat. He quickly cools down, apologizes to her, and does as he's told.

"Great!" She stands from her desk chair, leaning over to get a better view. "Yes, good! I can sense the emotional connection strengthening. Trust and comfort are massively important when it comes to intimacy in humans. You cannot go out into their world and expect to be brutes like you are in your own. Humans are delicate and need to be treated as such."

I groan inwardly and drop my gaze to my lap, to the book hidden in my bag. Reading helps pass time, but the only books here are educational, guides to torture, and spell books. I accidently took one back to my room and read it while I was bored, and now I know how to summon a demon.

The library here is full of strange stuff. The books aren't even half of it. Safe to say none of them are to my liking, but I'm settled reading a story about crimes committed in the Fire Realm, and I'd rather read about dragon laws than watch two students slowly falling in love with each other. Or whatever it is the professor wants from them.

"In this semester, we're going to learn about the emotional side of sex. As I said before, humans need gentle and caring partners. If you wish to leave this island and somehow form a connection, then the last thing you want to do is hurt them."

Students grimace, and I keep reading.

"You have your partners, and I have all of your logs, including activities outside of our lessons. To pass this class, your score needs to be above seventy percent. This will be shared between you and your partner."

The twins are sitting with their partners, and Orsen keeps whispering in Mel's ear. I can tell she's getting pissed off—she's got this demonic look in her eyes every time she glares at him.

He might wake up dead tomorrow, immortal or not.

Dane must have ditched class because he's not here, and of course the professor doesn't mind. He was with his friends before the lesson, so he's obviously intentionally skipping.

Not that I care. I'm just glad I have one less person planning my murder today. With everyone focused on everything else, I have fewer haters, and fewer scowls aimed at me.

Unsurprisingly, they aren't a fan of me, but I've yet to wake up with only one nipple or half a heart. They'll get to me eventually, and I hope by then, I've either sprouted an immortal life, or I get good enough with a sword to defend myself.

They aren't going to survive a day in my world. If they can't stand me for being a human, how the hell will they be able to live with billions of them?

My phone buzzes in my bag, and I look over at Mel, knowing it's her. She and Dane are the only ones with my number, and hell will freeze over before he willingly messages me.

Poppy wants to stick to the rules of only having contact with her partner, the little do-gooder. From what I've heard this morning from her sister, Poppy's been having a wild time with her partner, and poor Mel has had to cast a spell to sound-proof her side of the room, so she can get some peace and quiet.

"More tongue!"

Someone giggles, and I go back to reading my book.

My phone buzzes again, and I finally give in and grab it.

Under the desk, I unlock the screen and see two messages from Mel.

> Mel: Orsen said Dane was in your room last night. If I don't receive details, I will pull that chair away from under you without lifting a finger.

> Mel: Don't ignore me!

Instead of replying, I look up at my white-haired friend. She's currently having a silent argument with Orsen. He seems mesmerized, unable to take his eyes off her face.

She is beautiful, to be fair. His only request since partnering is that she cut her nails because he doesn't want her to carve his organs out while he's, and I quote, *"hammering into her."* I think Orsen will fit in with humans easier than he thinks. He certainly acts like one of us.

The entire class goes silent as the door flies open. Dane, with a deep scowl and raging eyes, walks in, ignores everyone staring at him, and takes his seat across the room from me.

He crosses his arms, leans back in his chair, and parts his legs under the table. "Sorry I'm late," he says, his gaze flicking to me momentarily. "I was sidetracked."

"That's okay, Mr. Dalton. I was just explaining to everyone the importance of trust and connection when it comes to intimacy with a human."

He couldn't look more disgusted.

"And for the first part of this semester, you'll be working with your partner endlessly to gain both of these." She goes on to explain the scores, how she tracks everyone, and that they'll be joint tasks.

His brow raises. "And who am I partnered with?"

The professor stares at him before pressing a hand to her chest. "I didn't pair you with someone already? My apologies,

Mr. Dalton!" She rushes to her desk, flying through paperwork before her eyes find me. "Miss Winters also doesn't have a partner."

Dane's spine straightens. "No."

"Yes. You will be a pair. Please sit together."

My eyes go wide, and my mouth drops open. "Excuse me? Why?"

"You. Are. Partners."

Dane's hand slams down on the desk as he gets to his feet, and all the windows burst open, papers flying everywhere. "Do not insult me by assuming I'd engage in sexual activities with a human."

"Sit down, Mr. Dalton."

Orsen picks up Mel's paperwork while the biggest smirk ever plays on his face.

Dane refuses again. "Absolutely not. How dare you partner me up with this... this... human?"

The professor clicks her tongue. "A perfect match then. It seems you need this lesson more than anyone, to get over your opinions on human beings. How do you expect to have a relationship once you leave the island?"

"I'm the most powerful creature on this island, and you want me to do these tasks with..." He grimaces at me. "She's nothing but a warm body."

Ouch.

I shake my head. "If it makes you feel any better, I'd rather kiss a dead frog. You repulse me just as much as I repulse you."

"Silence, mortal," Dane snaps. "You were not asked to speak."

I stand and pull my bag up my shoulder. "I can't wait for the day someone knocks you off your imaginary pedestal. Go fuck yourself, Dane."

"Get back here, Miss Winters!"

The professor might kill me, but I'm walking out of here anyway. I hate her and everyone in this school.

I'm the only human here, and that makes me a target. Yet, in every class, they're learning how to adapt and act around my kind for a chance at survival. If they can't handle me, a twenty-year-old girl with no family or close friends who works in a diner, they're screwed.

I barely make it to the entrance to the girls' dorms before vines break out from the walls and I'm dragged into a dark room. A candle lights as Dane walks in, the door closing behind him.

I roll my eyes. "You're becoming obsessive now. What do you want, creature?"

The vines tighten around my waist and wrists.

"Obsession is a persistent need to know someone, to not be able to stop thinking of them or to control them. If I were obsessed with you, mortal, you would be chained to a wall in my room where I could keep an eye on you." He takes a step towards me as the tight restraints pull me to him. "I merely want you to refuse this partnership."

"I've refused each class we've been partnered in. It won't work," I reply, tugging at the vines. "If you don't release me, I'm going to make this class ten times worse for you."

"Your threats are weak."

"So are you," is my immature reply.

"You're not special. If I killed you right now, no one would miss you. No one would look for you. I'll get a new partner, and you will be buried in the dirt where you belong."

"You try so hard to be the bully. It's getting tiring and predictable now. If you were going to do something, you would've by now. Why don't you just leave me alone? And go fuck yourself while you're at it."

The vines vanish, and Dane has me pinned to the wall. Bright silver eyes stare at me with rage. "I will not take part in these ridiculous classes."

I smile, even though he's so close, so close I can smell his manly scent, the cedarwood and spice and everything that would usually be my go-to in a guy. "Enjoy the dungeons then."

He smirks as his hand slides up to my throat, and his thumb presses against my pulse. Dane had said days ago that he'd never physically touch me, yet here he is, skin on skin. "If I go, so will you. And I'll gladly watch you being ripped to shreds by the immortals down there."

He shoves himself away.

"You will refuse our partnership, little mortal. Because if I ever have to fuck you, I'll make sure it kills you."

Dane vanishes, and so does the tension on my shoulders, the air returning to my lungs as I slouch against the wall.

We'll both be punished for walking out of class. I will be anyway. He'll get off easy and probably get praised for trying to go after his human relations partner.

What the hell have I done in my life to deserve this? Of all the people here, I get paired with him in most of my classes. It's not fair.

When I reach my room, Mel messages me to say that she finally gave in to Orsen, and that they're going to sit by the waterfall near the forest full of secrets. She tells me to come with, and she'll invite Dane, and I politely tell her to shove it.

I shower, get into my bed, and pull out my homework. It takes me hours, but I finally close my notebook. The candles flicker, the walls calmer than usual, and as I lie under my duvet, my phone dings.

> Dane: I spoke with my mother, and she said it was important that we stay paired. Congratulations, mortal.

I pull the covers over my head and reply.

> Me: You can't threaten my life and text me like you haven't. You are by far the weirdest dude I've ever met. Psychotic behavior. You really won't last in my world. They'd make a documentary about you before giving you the lethal injection.

He's going to give me a rundown of my death again, I can just tell. He'll use excessive amounts of detail and make out that I'm a vile creature he'd never touch.

Yet he was hard as a rock last night. Unless arousal or getting a hard-on is a side effect of his anger. After all, I don't know what species he is.

> Dane: What is a documentary?

I'm never getting off this island.

6

Everyone is to be seated and silent in the canteen by noon. At the strike of half past the hour, I think my professors might blow the entire castle up given how noisy and late people are. Chairs are kicked over, groups laugh and chatter between them, and someone is smoking what I can only assume is the Quarrierton Academy version of a cigarette.

The lights flicker. "Silence!"

No one listens as I rest my elbows on the table, my chin in my palms. Apparently, being powerful will not grant you power over fifty-odd magical students. Well, magical bar one. Me.

Dane and his group of hooligans walk in, or more like swagger, and the hall falls into a still quietness. It irks me that they're praised for no reason. They have the looks, sure, and the shitty attitude to go with them, but being the offspring of professors shouldn't make them so special.

I might bring up my lunch—everyone is ogling them like they're fresh meat and they're all starving for a piece. Dane does look good, in all fairness. His hair is a curly mess on his head, his shirt is partially unbuttoned—no tie—and his hand is tucked into his pocket.

The rolled-up sleeves draw my attention to his forearms, and I gulp away the irritating notion to watch the way the veins bulge through his tanned skin.

I look away as his gaze finds mine. Hopefully his mind-reading weirdness can't reach away over here. If so, he just got an eyeful of his own hand around my throat.

Smooth, Sera. Smooth.

Annoyingly, Orsen notices the table the twins and I are sitting at, points in our direction, and smiles at Mel. We all groan in unison, and Poppy's head connects with the table dramatically. She hates them all, and Orsen tends to tease her about her partner. He also tells her that he's her future brother-in-law.

"Whatever he says, it's a lie."

I give Mel a look. "What did you do?"

"Nothing," is her reply. "Whatever Orsen says, don't believe him. I didn't kiss him outside of the class tasks, and I definitely did not feel his fingers inside me in the middle of the forest."

Poppy grimaces.

My eyes narrow. "I thought you hated liars."

She glares as he reaches us, leaning his freakishly large hands on the table. "Good morning, ladies." Orsen tilts his head to me. "Human."

I roll my eyes then avert them when Dane sits directly across from me. His foot hits mine, and I tense all over, like his black vines are wrapping around my body again. Instantly, my heart rate speeds up, and I need to clear my throat to stop any sounds from forcing their way out.

"Go away," Mel says, but Orsen sits beside her, nudging her shoulder with a wink.

"You weren't saying that last night, ice queen."

Dane scoffs. "Please don't go into detail again."

I'm extremely grateful I haven't had much in the way of detail yet.

Mel shakes her head, but I know she enjoys this. She looks at Orsen, fights a smirk, and slaps his leg under the table.

I want to laugh with them, something to lighten the mood. It's been nothing but doom and gloom the past few weeks. Bad news after bad news after bad news.

Stuck on an island with magical, mythical creatures. A bully who's told me on more than one occasion that he wants to kill me—who follows me around the castle, breaks into my room to ask me how to use a mobile phone, and gets hard when he sees me in my sleepwear.

I can feel Dane's eyes on me, but I don't look his way. Nerves consume me, but not the terrifying kind.

The feeling vanishes, as does every voice in the hall, and the history professor clicks her fingers. "When you are asked to be silent, you will all be silent!"

I try to mutter under my breath, but no words come out. One of the professor's strengths is that she can remove everyone's voice. We can all breathe and give each other looks of confusion, but no sound can be heard throughout the hall.

If a handful of pins were to drop, I'd hear them hit the ground.

Dane seems unbothered. As if he's used to this behavior.

She smiles. "Great. Thank you for giving me your undivided attention. Shall we begin?"

For the next few minutes, she walks around with a scroll, calling out names and marking them off the register as hands raise to show their presence.

"Seraphine Winters."

Involuntarily, my arm snaps up. Pain snakes around my bicep and wrist, burning, and settles when she sees me.

She nods, smiles, and marks my name off.

Once everyone's names have been called out, Headmistress Dalton rises from her chair, addressing us all as her wonderful students.

She walks to our table, and Dane ignores her as she rests her hand on his shoulder and speaks about safety measures within the academy. He tenses under her firm grip, his cheeks turning red, and for some reason, I feel the tension of his muscles in my own, the embarrassment, the need to get away.

I frown, and he glances at me, shaking his head slightly, as if to stop me from making it obvious I can feel what he feels.

I want to mouth, *What was that?* But I know not to. She'll see, and knowing her brutality, she'll demand to know what's such a secret.

But how did I feel all of what he was feeling? And how did he know?

Mrs. Dalton clears her throat, releasing Dane and folding her arms in front of her. "Most of you are aware of what happened this morning. I want you all to know that we are taking action and putting security measures in place."

I tilt my head, looking over at the twins. Words don't work, but I mouth, *What happened?*

Poppy graciously slices her finger across her neck, tilts her head, sticks out her tongue, and crosses her eyes.

Gosh.

In the short time I've been here, a few people have been murdered in the most barbaric of ways, so what's different this time? I guess their immortality only goes so far if people can be killed on this island.

"I will be questioning each student who attended the history room, and if I find you suspicious, you will be sent to the dungeons. Death here is a consequence of bad behavior, not a hobby to keep you busy when you're bored. If I find another butchered student, I will punish each and every last one of you."

Professor Mallory, head of martial arts and weaponry training, gets to his feet. Every girl in here instantly drools at the sight of him. In all fairness, he's a tank given how muscular he is. Tall.

With the brightest, bluest eyes ever. And he's handsome. Really, really handsome.

But he'd snap a neck without even blinking.

I'm a tad scared of him. He's asked me a lot about being mortal, and sometimes, when he's teaching me a fighting stance, his hand lingers far too long on my hip. He always partners with me, saying that I'd be snapped in half if I were with someone else.

Also, he and Dane don't get along, which makes him my favorite person. From afar, at least.

"I will be leaving a magical signature around the island. If someone steps out of line, I will be notified."

Gentle pressure releases from my neck, and I cough, hearing a few others do the same. Some students are mumbling words, and someone lets out a sob.

Mrs. Dalton speaks again. "From now on, you will have a designated partner. You cannot walk the grounds without them by your side." Dane's mother watches me as she adds, "No one will refuse their pairing."

Kill me. Now.

Dane and I requested we be paired with other students for our classes but were denied. This is definitely aimed at me.

Her eyes stay on me as she moves across the hall, then she looks at her son. "Your partner will also be the only student permitted to be in your dorm room. On weekends, you will decide between the two whose room to sleep in together."

Orsen whispers into Mel's ear, and she elbows him in the ribs.

Mrs. Dalton goes on to explain the new rules around the castle.

One student is killed, and we all need to suffer like this? No, there's more to this story. Something else must have happened for the teachers to go to such extreme lengths.

Mrs. Dalton then excuses us all, telling us to check the scroll hovering by the door on the way out.

Dane is walking behind me. I nearly trip up as he leans down to whisper in my ear, "I need to talk to you."

"Then talk."

"Not here," he replies as we wait in line to exit the room.

Students have stopped to argue about their pairings, but no one is paying them any attention.

"Nope," I respond. "Talk here or go away."

He growls, and something warm slithers up my spine before disappearing. "Stop being difficult. I know you can feel me."

"That sounds wrong."

"I don't care. It's true."

I continue to ignore the person who wants me dead. When I reach the door, I glance at the scroll, roll my eyes, and turn to Dane. "I'm going to slap your mother."

He goes to retort but then sees the scroll. Our names are side by side. His teeth grind as he glances back at me.

I shake my head. "Deal with this."

And I follow the twins out of the room, away from the glaring man with shadows pouring out of him, twirling around him like a tornado.

We're screwed. I already knew who I was going to be paired with. But seeing our names again, I'm more than pissed off. He won't be setting foot in my room, and we definitely won't be sleeping in the same dorm on the weekends, and that's a promise.

It's getting out of hand now. Why do they keep partnering us up?

He mentioned his mother said it was important. But why? He even went as far as writing to the professor of human relations, asking her to change the pairing without informing his mother.

Denied.

7

Professor Mallory, who tells me to call him Valin, is circling me while I stand with my fists raised, my elbows tight against my ribs for protection.

"You are quite weak, little Seraphine." He inspects my posture, flattening his hand on the small of my back. "Straighten your spine and try to relax."

I don't relax at all. He's everywhere.

He lets me punch his side, but I might as well have punched a wall.

"Good, now use more power." He smiles when I groan and laughs every time I hurt my fist. "Come on. Harder."

I throw my fist.

"Harder."

I throw it again, missing him.

"*Harder.*"

Dane is watching us as he spars with Orsen; they're both punching each other and using their powers to battle. Orsen whips him with a wave of water, and Dane nearly burns him to a crisp before a black mass of shadows shoves his friend to the other side of the arena.

Typical that he doesn't follow the rules. We aren't to use powers, since everyone is training to fight as a human.

We have our fighting uniform on. The girls are wearing shorts and tops with the academy logo, and the boys are wearing black sweats with tanks. Everyone is sweating, and the space around us is full of trees and buildings and objects to mimic a battleground, despite being a class where students must learn how to fight without powers.

For some reason, the teacher wants to work with me again. I initially thought he was taking pity on me for not having powers and all, but the attractive man has done nothing but put his hands on me, floor me, and grab at my hair.

My back slams into the ground, his hand pushing on my chest. "Focus."

I blink away the shock and windedness.

After getting back to my feet, I take a blow to the ribs, then something shoves me to the side. Valin's fist misses my face by an inch, and I glance over at the twins to thank them, but none of them are looking at me.

But Dane is watching us. So much so that Orsen gets a good hit in.

Valin continues his lesson, and by the end, I've been pinned beneath him more times than I can count. There's growing frustration, but not on my part. It's almost suffocating.

"Who is your partner?" Valin asks while we pack up our weapons and head for the changing rooms. "For the security measures."

"Oh," I say, capping my bottle of water. "Dane."

He flattens his lips. "That's unfortunate."

"Yep."

"A beautiful woman like you shouldn't be around the likes of him."

I stop walking. "Should you be speaking to me like this? I'm a student."

"There are no rules, little Seraphine."

My cheeks heat.

A wave of annoyance hits me from behind, and I already know who it is, even as he says, "The mortal is needed at the main office. Perhaps try to fuck someone else you're supposed to be teaching."

Valin smiles, but it's fake. "Of course." His blue eyes find me again. "No rules. Remember." And he winks before walking off.

He even has power over the teachers.

I watch Valin's muscular back then spin to glare at Dane. "Really?"

Dane crosses his arms. "We have a lot of work to do, and I refuse to sit in your room while it smells like him. He's fucked half the students here. He's just flirting with you because he knows you're easy."

"I want to slap you."

He chuckles deeply. "You would only hurt your hand."

I sneer. "Fuck you."

"Unfortunately, you might have to."

I pause, staring at him, before I shoulder into him and get the hell away before he sees how red my cheeks are.

He doesn't follow me into the changing rooms, or when I march past him to my room.

This is the only time we've conversed properly, and it's him interrupting a teacher flirting with me.

———

By the time Friday comes, I'm excited to have some peace, but when I get to my dorm after class, a checklist is sitting on my bed.

Ten assignments for our human relations class. Not one or two, to break us into the strange and new set-up of a mixture of sexual and emotional tasks.

Ten.

And the first one needs to be completed by Monday morning.

I sigh and drop down on my bed, pulling out my phone and opening our messages.

Dane Dalton is an asshole, and quite frankly, I'd like to avoid him in every way. Then I can focus on passing and getting the hell off this island, but unfortunately it seems he's going to be key to making that happen.

> Me: Did you get the list?

An hour later, he replies. A small miracle. Maybe Orsen helped him.

> Dane: List?

> Me: You take too long to reply. It's like texting a ninety-year-old grandpa. Come to my room. Easier to talk, it seems.

There's a knock at my door the second after I press send.

I open the door an inch. "You're fast."

He looks bored. "Speed is one of my powers. What list?"

"Yet it takes you an hour to type one word."

I let him in, ignoring the silhouettes around the room dancing and becoming excited in his presence.

"This," I say, handing him the scroll. "It's for our human relations class."

He grimaces as he starts to read the first one then stops. "Task one is due on Monday morning."

"I know," I reply, snatching the list and reading it aloud. "Ask your partner five questions to get to know them. You cannot lie or skip. The task will be recorded automatically and sent to me."

"I don't want to know anything about you," he kindly tells me. "You're as boring as any human."

I'm pretty sure I'm the only human he knows, which makes that statement invalid.

"Great, then this will be quick. Ask me something."

He huffs, hands gripping the frame at the foot of my bed. The wood cracks under his grip, and I shouldn't be concentrating on his fingers flexing around it. But I'm staring.

"I can't stand you," he says. "And being forced to be around you makes me sick."

"Then quit. Go back to your own realm and stay there."

He waves me off. "It isn't that easy, or I would."

I guess I'll start off task one. "My first question..." I flap the list above my head. "What realm are you from?"

"The Shadow Realm."

I tilt my head. "There isn't a Shadow Realm."

Silence, and Dane lowers his gaze to the ground. "I'm aware."

Nodding at the meaning behind his quietness, I take a deep breath. "Now you ask me something. We need to get this task out of the way."

He pays me no heed as he paces the room for far too long. Stops. Paces. Stops. And I want to throw my phone at his head.

"I don't know what to ask you."

I huff as Dane leans against my dresser in his dress pants and shirt, the top two buttons still undone, his tie resting across his shoulders. He's rolled up his sleeves again, and to my dismay, I allow myself to look at the veins on his forearms.

He shoves his hands into his pockets and pushes himself away from the dresser. "This is ridiculous. What am I supposed to ask you? Your fucking favorite color? I can't stand your presence, and now I'm stuck with you. What I want to know is why?"

I roll my eyes. "I can't answer that. Ask me something else or leave. I don't have time for your dramatics, Dane."

He sighs, chewing on his bottom lip. "If I were to cut you, what color would your blood be?"

I drop my back to the mattress and stare at the swirling shadows, calm and free. The opposite of how I feel. "I hate you."

"The feeling is mutual. Answer the question, mortal."

"Red. Happy? My turn. Why are you such a dick to me?"

He shrugs. "You shouldn't be here, and I simply don't like you." He turns and studies the papers on my dresser, then looks at the pictures on the wall as he asks, "Are you a virgin?"

He spins to face me when I don't give him a response. I scowl before giving in. "Obviously I'm not."

His eyes take in the full length of my body, clad in my uniform. There's a hint of anger in his tone with his next words. "Yes. It is obvious."

"Because I'm nothing but a warm body?"

He hums. "Yep. Yet you did mention having a boyfriend before." He grits his teeth as he says the word "boyfriend," like the mere thought of me having a partner makes him sick.

I don't show any emotion on my face that shows the last part isn't even remotely true. "Are you a virgin?" I ask, already knowing the answer.

He smirks. "By far the opposite." Then he wipes the smile off his face. "What sad excuse for a human would ever fuck you? Who is he?"

I could explain my last encounter with Grayson, if he wants the details, but it would sound extremely boring. Instead, I pace. "My next question: why don't you know your age?"

"It was my turn to ask something. Age is just a number and unnecessary." He suddenly winces in pain, folding forward, and I look at him in confusion. "Fuck. The questions are spelled. I can't lie."

"What did you lie about?"

"I don't know my age because..." He grits his teeth, gasping. "Fucking hell. I don't know my age because I don't fucking know." The pain stops, and he catches his breath. "After a while, we lose track. I don't know how old I am."

Oh.

"That's quite sad actually."

His eyes darken, and the shadows on my walls gather. "Do not pity me. I am, and always will be, above you."

"Great. Next question."

He closes the distance between us, until I'm nearly snapping my neck to look up at his towering form from my bed. "Why are you here?"

I stand, so we're nearly head to chest. "I already said I don't know! Do you want to kill me?" I counter with my last question, desperate to end this. I should ask why I can feel him, his emotions and his presence, but these are the first questions that come to mind.

I'll ask later.

"Yes," he says, and when no pain comes his way, I clench my jaw and fists.

"Don't look at me like that, mortal. I've made my feelings towards you very clear. I want to watch you suffer, hear you beg, and feel you take your final breath with my hand around your throat. *That* is not a lie."

I do the only thing acceptable at my height—I knee him between the legs, satisfied when he drops down to my feet in agonizing pain.

I should be scared, running, begging for my life, but I hum in contentment as I sit back down on my bed, reading the list once more as he tries not to burn down the castle with fury.

"As soon as you stop crying, get the fuck out of my room."

A gust of wind swipes the list out of my hand, and Dane is on top of me in a blink. He straddles my waist, rage in his eyes, pinning my hands above me.

His ghost hands take my throat. "Do not ever hit me there again."

Instead of wincing or flinching, I smirk. "I hope it hurts."

"Shut the fuck up. I have two questions left. Would you fuck your teacher?"

I shrug. Might as well be honest. "If you mean Valin Mallory, then I probably would."

His grip tightens on my wrists and throat, but not enough to cause pain. Dominance—that's what he's trying to prove.

"Last question." He lowers his face until his cheek grazes mine and whispers against my ear. "Do you want to fuck me, mortal? Do you want me to slide my cock between your legs and make you forget your precious professor?"

My eyes widen as he lifts his head to look at me. Silver eyes with dilated pupils stare back.

"Absolutely not!" But as the words fall from my lips, so does a loud scream as invisible nails stab into my brain.

8

I'm starting to think I've made the wrong friends here in the academy.

While all three of us sit on a log in the middle of the forest, the twins discuss between themselves their favorite childhood memory. How they killed their father, and the way he squealed like a pig when they ripped his eyes from their sockets and made him choke on his own skin. From what I've heard from them, he was an evil individual, so I find his death acceptable to an extent. What I don't agree with is that they feel absolutely no remorse; that they find it funny that they *killed* their *father*.

Poppy giggles when Mel tells me they were wanted from then on, and that their mother sent them here to not only escape being killed as a result of the laws in their realm but to protect them from the destruction of their world.

At least their mother seems nice.

"What's task two again?" Poppy asks, trying to catch raindrops in her palm.

I pull the list from my satchel and clear my throat.

"Task two..." I begin reading out the scroll in my hand while we wait for our next class. "Physical touch is important to humans, and one of the ways to demonstrate and sense a person's trust is through touch. For this task, you will be spending time with your partner and getting used to how they feel. A minimum of six hours is expected. I suggest sharing a bed or holding hands to make up some of this time. This task will be recorded and sent to me."

Mel scoffs. Poppy plays with an orb she's made from gathering drops of water, which is floating above her head, and I shift on the log so I'm lying on my back.

"So we need to... what? Just touch each other?"

"She has a point," I say. "It does build trust to be comfortable with someone touching you." I nod, rereading the task. "I think it's so task three is more straightforward."

Poppy pops her bubblegum. As soon as she found out it was a type of human candy, she became addicted to blowing the biggest of bubbles. "I don't mind two. I quite liked task one. And three looks fun."

"It looks horrific and boring," Mel says, rolling her eyes. "Did you both do task one too?"

We both nod.

Mel inspects her nails. "Orsen's questions surprised me. I expected sexual and rude ones, but he genuinely asked questions about me and my life."

"Brandt asked me all my firsts," Poppy says, blushing the deepest shade of red. "What about you, Sera? I'm shocked that you and Dane haven't killed each other yet."

I tell them, dodging any mention of the last question. It resulted in me covering my face in embarrassment and Dane disappearing into thin air as he got the hell out of my room.

The pain I felt when I lied was brutal, but it eased off as soon as Dane vanished.

And now he thinks I want to sleep with him. It was an in-the-moment rush of desire from being pinned beneath him. Nothing more. Nothing less. Dane isn't ugly, and he's muscle upon muscle all over. He smells good. His eyes are mesmerizing. And he's tall. Really tall.

Who wouldn't want to fuck him while he's on top of them?

Regardless, he probably thinks I have a crush on him, or that I'm pleased to be partnered with him.

I'm not.

And now I can't face him.

I saw Dane walking to the canteen this morning for breakfast, and before he could notice me, I barreled into an empty classroom and waited a full hour before going back to my dorm.

How the hell am I going to look him in the eye and touch him for hours for task two? He can barely stand the smell of me, so how will he touch me without a spark of rage that results in me being pinned to something by the wrists or throat?

We're screwed.

But I refuse to fail.

I pull out my phone and open our messages.

> Me: Don't make this awkward. It must've been a glitch in the magic because the last thing I want is to sleep with you. But we need to do task two, and if you mess it up, I'll knee you in the balls again. Harder. Got it?

> Me: I look forward to your one-worded response in two working days.

"What are you smiling at?"

I click my screen off and put away my phone. Flattening my smile, I say, "Nothing."

———

During cult studies, I focus on the book in my lap instead of the floating head talking to us about rituals and prophets and ways to be accepted.

Teachers are supposed to be in their mortal forms, just like the students, but I guess some just don't follow the rules and get away with it. If this were weeks ago, I'd have thrown my book at the head and run from the class screaming, but I guess I'm adjusting.

Usually, Mrs. Dalton takes this class, but she's not here. Neither is her son.

It's been four days, and either Dane is still struggling to work his phone, or he's ignoring me. Either is fine. But that doesn't explain why he's been absent from classes. Poor Orsen seems like a lost puppy without his leader.

He isn't following the rules. We're supposed to be together for security reasons, so instead of me hunting for him, I've kept close to my friends.

Perks of being the son of the headmistress. He thinks he can break rules and not get any form of punishment. I'm dreading the next meeting about it all and having a public shaming.

Although, what I thought would be a week of dealing with Dane's insufferable self has turned into me being a nervous wreck for a totally different reason.

A deep need to know where he is.

It's almost consuming me. I've been constantly fighting the urge to sneak out of my dorm after hours to hunt for him.

I haven't.

However, I did have a nightmare last night. Heat. Screams. Fire. A lot of it. Then someone had lifted me from the flames and carried me to safety as two people I assumed to be my parents had wailed in agony while they burned.

I'd tried to get to them and failed.

And before I'd woken from the dream, green eyes had stared back at me, and there had been so much panic in them, anguish, desperation as the deep voice muttered my name.

Seraphine.

I'd let out a scream and sat up in my bed, covered in sweat. The silhouettes on the walls had just stared back at me.

Now I'm researching what dreams mean while the freaky head hovers near the main desk, asking students about prophecies and why they're important to the realms despite being irrelevant to how we can pass our classes and get to the Mortal Realm. Some answer, but most look bored out of their minds.

I keep reading my book to figure out what my dreams mean.

In the human world, they can have a lot of meanings, but here, within these castle walls, I don't trust that they mean nothing. There must be a reason why it felt so real. Like a memory more than a fucked-up scenario my mind concocted.

Some dreams I like to stay in, but this one felt like a trap.

The book I have now explains that they may be memories from a different life. Or a desire to have that life.

Burning to death is definitely not a life I want, and I don't know who my birth parents are. As far as I'm aware, the system raised me. I jumped between the orphanage and foster families and eventually found a home that gave me everything I needed. But then they died in a car crash, and since I was classed as an adult, I had to fend for myself.

Maybe that's why I'm having these dreams. Or maybe I'm just stressed with my position. I'm frustrated because my needs aren't met, and I'm lost, trying to find a way out.

Either way, I'm still in a magical school full of killers and bullies and creatures who want me dead.

I nearly jump out of my skin as my professor's floating head appears in my lap. "Miss Winters! Pay attention or you'll be given detention!"

I slap the book shut on the head. He vanishes and pops up at his desk.

"We do not tolerate laziness and immaturity in this academy. Tell me, little girl, what exactly is a prophecy?"

Little girl?

"You are aware that I'm twenty, right?"

His lips pull into a smirk. "I am four hundred and eighty years old. You are a *little girl.*"

I look around the room, swallowing harshly, before leveling my bodiless teacher with a glare. "It's just another way of saying something is a prediction," I answer.

"A prediction of what?" he asks.

I shrug. "The future."

"Wrong."

A few students giggle, and my cheeks heat with exasperation. "No it isn't. And cult studies have nothing to do with divination."

"Wrong again. A prophecy is a forecast of events that are yet to happen. Something solid. Predictions are not accurate. In this world and every other. You are human. Tell me prophecies that have been true to *your* god."

I shake my head, silent. And extremely confused.

"I have no idea what's happening right now," a student says. "What are we talking about?"

The teacher grits his teeth. "Be quiet, Quigley." He settles his head on top of his desk. "We're going off-topic. The reason for bringing this up is that there is a prophecy about a being who will end the war of the worlds..."

I stop listening. Not because he's speaking far too fast and what he's saying is far too complicated to understand, but because there's a coldness wrapping around my leg, up my thigh. It weaves around me like a snake until it reaches my throat. Invisible, so no one can see.

And then there's a quiet whisper in my ear. A lifeless hiss. *Death to her. Death to all.*

I spring to my feet, gathering my books and grabbing my bag, ignoring the professor as I run from the room. My feet take me out of the castle completely, as if they know where to go, and I only stop when I reach the barrier line next to the water.

I try to put up a facade that I'm fine, but I'm far from fine.

63

I'm in a school full of creatures and paranormal entities. With someone who wants me dead yet has been partnered up with me for multiple classes.

As soon as the opportunity arises, as soon as he knows he can get away with it, he'll come for me.

I can't breathe. I press my palm to my chest, count to five, ten, fifteen, twenty and close my eyes. Lowering to sit on the ground, I inhale and exhale, my vision blurring.

The air shifts, cold and wet, and someone sits down beside me. "Are you okay?"

I don't look up at the familiar voice. "No."

Valin, hushed and present, doesn't speak again until my heart rate decelerates and my sight gradually clears. We listen to the water lapping the shore, the wind gusting, and the trees nearby shivering as the leaves rustle.

Finally, he talks. "You seem down. Anything you want to get off your chest?"

Shaking my head, I hug my knees. "I don't belong here. That's all."

"None of us belong here, little Seraphine."

I raise my head to look at him. "It doesn't matter anyway. My partner seems to have vanished into dust, and my second task is due tomorrow. You know more than most that every single part needs to be completed." I nudge him with my shoulder, trying to lighten the mood. "You're going to be stuck with me for an extra year."

"I can't help you with Dane. He always disappears for weeks at a time. Show me your list," Valin says, reaching out his hand.

I sigh and pull it from my satchel. "Everyone has the same. Task two is to be completed by noon tomorrow."

"I could help you with some of them, if he doesn't make an appearance." He stares at the scroll, eyes flitting from side to side as he takes in each line. "I'd be more than happy to assist."

I frown. "But you're a professor."

He winks. "An off-duty professor. Besides, as I've pointed out before, there are no rules."

"Did you even read task two?"

He nods, blue eyes flashing. "I certainly have."

"I'm only twenty."

He grins. "And I'm only thirty-four."

I stare at him. With his young features, the thickness of his hair and the contours of his cheeks and jawline, he could pass for a model in my world.

But he's a professor.

"You wouldn't get into trouble?"

He laughs, standing and reaching his hand out. "Come. Let's go to your dorm."

Despite the uneasy feeling rolling through me, I take his outstretched hand and follow him. Something within me is telling me to get away. To run. But I can't let go. Something is wrong. Something doesn't feel right.

He knows where my dorms are, the exact corridor, and ignores the stares from students as he walks with the mortal.

His thumb rubs over my skin, and I frown because I don't feel anything. Before, when we were sparring and he was teaching me fighting stances, I was affected. Yet now, as he unlocks my door and ushers me inside, I feel nothing.

He looks around as I close my door; I lean against it while he touches everything. The silhouettes on my walls are hiding, nowhere to be seen.

Valin turns to me, a twinkle in his eyes. "Come here."

I take a few steps without meaning to.

His fingers trail up my arm, and he studies me, the bare legs and thighs revealed by my uniform, and his Adam's apple bobs. "You are fascinating. You always have been."

Unfastening the top button of my shirt, he carefully keeps his eyes on me. Another. And another. Still, there's no rippling need to rip his clothes off. When he does the last one, he slides the material over my shoulders, and the shirt pools on the ground.

I tense all over as he reaches for my bra strap. "What are you doing?"

Softly, like a purr, he replies, "Task two."

"It states not to do anything sexual."

He tucks his finger under the strap, hooking it then snapping it back against my skin. "I'm simply removing your clothes. They're dirty, and I can't touch you while you're wearing them."

As soon as he steps into my breathing space, I feel uneasy and uncomfortable. A voice in my head tells me to run, to shove him away, to yell at all the professors to remove him from my room.

Dane.

Where the fuck are you?

The second voice didn't come from me.

But instead of reacting, I'm frozen as Valin grabs my shirt from the ground, caressing the material between his fingertips, then bringing it to his nose and inhaling.

"Ahh. What a wonderful scent." Another sniff. "If your shirt smells like this, I can only wonder..."

I stand back, hitting my hip on the bed frame. "I think that's enough."

Tilting his head, Valin looks confused. "What is?"

"I want you to leave." I try to sound intimidating, but my voice shakes.

His eyes are shifting to a deep red, transforming into something... immortal. His teeth lengthen, sharp and terrifying.

He takes a step, but before he can reach me, the entire room erupts in an explosion of smoke. Everything catapults around us, yet I'm still, something encasing me, like a forcefield shielding me from danger.

Papers and splintered wood and stones fly around me. The

flames of my candles snuff out, and the windows smash, sending fragments of glass all over my floor and destroying the bed.

It's not smoke at all; shadows. Lots of them. Circling. Dancing. Screaming as they twirl and twist around a dark figure. Voices—deep voices. Chanting something I can't quite make out.

But I'm not scared. I feel somewhat safe.

A black mass surges towards Valin, flipping him to the opposite side of the room, where his back smashes against the wall.

He groans, pushing himself to his knees and wiping his nose with a chuckle. "Just couldn't help yourself, huh?" He tries to move towards me, but the room erupts like a volcano once more, and flames burst across my ceiling.

I don't feel blistering heat, or scared for my safety, or anything.

Dane, dressed in nothing but a pair of dress pants and a half-buttoned shirt, materializes in front of Valin like a vortex, rage and fury and death in his eyes. "Get the fuck out," he roars as the shadows rush back to him, right into his chest. "Now."

"You should be in the dungeons," Valin seethes as he struggles to get to his feet. "You should be in the dungeons! How did you escape?"

Dungeons?

He said he didn't know where Dane was, that he always vanishes for weeks at a time. That's why Dane hasn't been following the security rules.

"Do not insult me by thinking a few spells and a prison will keep me locked away." Dane flicks his hand, and my door is thrown open, the wood cracking, nearly breaking at the hinges. "Don't push me. I'm in no mood for any more of your bullshit."

Valin looks at me then at Dane before he straightens his collar and walks to the door.

He stops and growls at him. "You cannot keep her."

Dane just gives Valin a dark look, his brows narrowing, and

without him saying a word or moving a finger, the professor is shoved out of the room before the door slams shut.

Dane wipes his palms on his pants before waving his hand at the door, locking it.

"What was that about? And why were you in the dungeons?"

"That's no concern of yours. He was trying to take advantage of you. And you were going to let him?"

I cross my arms. "No! You blew in here like Peter Pan with your shadows before I could stop him!"

Dane stares at me for a long second. "Who?"

"You have no chance in my world."

He mutters something under his breath before the room starts to rearrange, all my things repairing and settling back into their rightful places. My duvet flattens on my mattress, and my candles, windows, and books repair themselves.

"Valin is not good. He's a power hungry monster and shouldn't be trusted," Dane says, not once looking at me. Probably because I can't seem to move and I'm standing in just my bra and a short, pleated skirt.

I watch as he studies my room, grimacing at my shirt on the floor.

"He said he was in his thirties," I reply, his presence cracking the energy in the room, in my core.

"He lied. He wants you." Dane rubs his large hand down his face, looking exhausted. His shirt is a mess with soot, and his hair looks like he's been running his fingers through it for days. "I hit him," he explains. "He demanded I leave..." He pauses. "Leave the island. But I said no obviously."

"Why does he want you to leave the island?"

Dane's jaw tenses. "We're from the same realm."

I raise a brow, waiting for him to elaborate.

"I'm the heir to the Shadow Realm, and he doesn't like that. Never has."

I whistle. "Wow. You're an heir, yet you're here, acting like some bratty teenager and fighting with your professor."

"Shut up. As I said, he wants you."

I fight a laugh. "And that's an issue because...?"

His now silver eyes snap up to my face. "Did you not just hear me? He's a monster."

"So are you, and so's basically everyone else here."

His gaze falls from mine, stopping at my exposed collarbone. "Put your shirt back on. I don't want to have nightmares from seeing you like this."

I scoff. "And that's why you just exploded into my room."

"You are my partner in this school. If you fail, I fail. That means if either of us dies or becomes bewitched, we're stuck here for even longer. I don't need you drooling over the professor while we're both trying to pass each class."

"Fine."

He snarls, trying not to glance below my throat or at the fluttering pulse on my neck. "Fine. You'll keep your distance from him. And you'll train with me from now on."

"If I'm training with anyone else, it's definitely not with you. And remember the security measures too."

We stare each other down until he groans, bends at the knee to gather my shirt in his fist, and throws it at my face.

"Dress, mortal."

Once I'm covered, I imagine myself slapping him. Hard. So hard that his face bleeds.

With a grimace, Dane runs his thumb across his lip. "You'll only hurt yourself if you do that. But, please, do try."

"We have to do task two." I change the subject because, for some reason, I'm feeling less annoyed with him and more... needy. Like I don't want him to leave. "Have you read it yet?"

"I've been in the dungeons for days. What do you think?"

I roll my eyes.

"Stop rolling your fucking eyes at me."

"Okay, *Peter*," I reply, walking to the desk and collecting the list. "Read it."

"Do not call me by another's name." He snatches it from me and reads each word of task two with a deepening scowl, then squeezes the scroll in his fist. "No."

I raise a brow. "No?"

"I will not touch you for six hours. What kind of challenge is this?" He rips and tosses the paper, but with the magic the professor cast on it, it just unravels and floats back to us.

"I'll make task three easier."

He glares at me. "And what is task three?"

"You need to kiss me."

Dane looks like I just killed his mother.

He turns and walks towards the door.

"Where are you going?" I call.

"To hang myself."

"Stop being dramatic. Just..." I bite my lip, unsure how to word this. "The professor said we can sleep in the same bed and it would count. We're supposed to share during the weekends anyway."

"Is this your way of seducing me? Because it isn't working."

I snort. "If I wanted to seduce you, I could."

His eyes flicker from green to silver then back to green. "I will not fornicate with a human."

I just roll my eyes again because I'm sure he has no idea what that means. "I'm going to shower and get ready for bed. If you're serious about these tasks, come back here in an hour."

Dane looks at me.

I pull my shirt off, throw it at him, and head for the bathroom.

By the time I'm washed and in my nightdress, he's gone. I tuck myself into bed, blow out my candles, and melt into my pillow.

The door creaks hours later, but instead of barreling in and demanding boundaries, I hear him mutter to himself that he can do this followed by the sound of fabric hitting the floor.

The mattress dips behind me, and I hug the duvet to my chest as Dane settles into my bed.

His shoulder is to my back. "Is this good enough?" he asks quietly, a whisper in the dark. "For the task?"

I nod once. "I think so."

"Goodnight, mortal."

I flatten my lips. "Will you ever call me by my name?"

"No."

I huff, and the bed shakes. He's... laughing?

"I hate you," I say, battling a smile. "I really hate you."

"That's why you want me to fuck you."

I turn to face him, not realizing how close we actually are. "If you got my text, I said it was an in-the-moment thing. I'd rather fuck a cactus."

He grimaces. He's so, so close. I can feel each breath between us. "You humans are strange."

I turn away from him again. "You're about to be surrounded by billions of us. Get used to it."

"I can assure you that I will *not* get used to it. Now, tell me. Who is Peter Pan? Does he wield the power of shadows too?"

Fighting a laugh, I tighten my fist in the duvet. "Go to sleep, immortal creature."

He chuckles deeply, and it rushes straight down my spine and gathers between my legs. He might as well have run his tongue against my core before plunging it inside me.

"Please keep your thoughts to yourself."

I pale, all the blood draining from my face. "It was—"

"In the moment. Yes, you seem to have that a lot."

Blushing, I bury my face in the pillow.

And for the first time in weeks, I fall into a peaceful sleep, where I dream of myself dancing in the rain and laughing with friends; a young man with dashing green eyes introducing himself in my diner as he orders a milkshake and waffles. He hands me his bank card to swipe his order, and the spark is instant when our fingers touch.

When I wake through the night, a heavy arm is snaked around my waist. Our bare legs are intertwined, and Dane Dalton, in only his briefs, is attached to me like a sloth to a tree.

The shadows and silhouettes swim around my room, but instead of searching for something, looking for their source and savior, they're calm.

At peace.

9

I try to push the duvet off me, but it seems to have gained a few pounds overnight.

I shove it again, but nothing happens. My eyes are closed, my brain foggy from just waking up, and I'm hot. Really, really hot. A thin layer of sweat covers my skin, and when I try to sit up, so I can go wash my face in the bathroom, an immovable object stops me.

Said object being the heir to the Shadow Realm. No age. No patience. Someone who doesn't know when to leave a woman's bedroom.

His arm is heavy, and I turn my head to find his face is relaxed, lips slightly parted as he sleeps. Cute yet handsome. From this angle, I catch a glimpse of a scar on his neck, as if someone once tried to cut it open.

Knowing him, he probably can't die. Or won't.

I scowl at him before shouldering into his chest.

He groans, his already closed eyes screwing tight, but his face relaxes and he's asleep once more.

I do it again. Harder.

"Insufferable," he mutters. "We have eighteen minutes left. Stay quiet and pretend I'm not here."

"Pretend you're not here? You're like a man-sized heat pack!"

He groans again. "Stop yelling."

There's silence for a beat, then he lifts his head. "Is a heat pack something I should be aware of in your world?"

I try not to giggle, my body trembling when I fail. "What do you do if you have a stomach ache?"

"Pain is a sign that I'm alive. When one feels such—"

"Oh my God. Stop. Let's go back to being silent."

He drops his head onto the pillow, getting comfortable behind me. The duvet shifts, then Dane, being the pain in the ass he is, yanks it off the bed completely.

The fabric lands on the other side of the room.

"Was that necessary?"

"Very."

I note that he doesn't move his arm or the close proximity of his chest to my back.

I can feel him breathing on my neck, and I'm confused as to whether it's turning me on or if I'm slowly losing my mind by even thinking that this feels intimate.

"Nine minutes left," he says. "I've never wanted time to pass so badly. I don't know how Orsen can do this with your friend every night."

I narrow my eyes into the morning sunlight shining through the window. "He sleeps in her dorm every night?"

Dane nods behind me, and the stubble on his chin grazes my ear.

A pulse between my legs has my eyes widening.

My body needs to stop. Now.

"Seven minutes. And please, for the billionth time, keep your thoughts to yourself."

"If you keep reading my mind, I'm going to hurt you. It's weird and creepy."

"I can't help it," he replies. "It's intrusive."

I try to sit up and fail. "You're intrusive!" Childish response, but oh well.

"For a weak human, you are incredibly rude."

Against my better judgment, I somehow smile. "Thank you. Except for the weak part. That's getting a little overused. Get a better vocabulary."

"The human vocabulary makes me question life itself. Your dictionaries are even worse."

"Get used to it all, or you'll perish."

"The latter seems the best option." He inhales. Holds it. Exhales. "Five minutes, mortal."

"Sera."

"No."

"Yes."

"Grow up," he mutters under his breath.

I sigh.

So does he.

"Do you still want to kill me?"

I can sense his smile as he replies, "Very much so. Don't get confused by me sleeping in your bed. This is a task." He stops, waits a few heartbeats, then adds, "I'd rather fuck a cactus."

"You'd rather feel excruciating pain?"

"How so?" he asks as he dips his chin, his cheek against my hair.

I imagine falling down the stairs dressed as a clown so he doesn't see that I'm absolutely dying for his touch right now. If he were to reach into my panties, his fingers would end up soaked.

Is this normal? To lie in bed with an enemy who wants to kill you and to be... sexually frustrated?

To ease the tension between my thighs, I rub them together and say, "Explain to me how you'd even do that?"

"Explain to me what a cactus is and I will."

I purse my lips. "You don't have them in the Shadow Realm?"

"No." His response is blunt and bored and full of tiredness. He's falling asleep again.

I laugh. "You are doomed. It's basically a penis-shaped plant covered in spikes."

Dane doesn't respond; I can feel just a slight shake of his head behind me as his breaths grow heavier, like the arm still bracketing my body.

Three hundred seconds drag in, and neither of us speaks; neither of us mention the silhouettes waking up within the walls and watching us. A little dog wags its tail and shows us a ball. A little girl waves, and when I unravel my arm from beneath Dane's, I wave back.

The motion must wake him.

"Time's up," is all he says.

My heart stops, and I have no idea why. I don't like Dane. I hate him. And he wants me six feet under or tossed in a river somewhere. But a huge part of me wants to stay like this a little longer.

Dane doesn't move, and neither do I.

"Has it definitely been six hours?" I ask, trying to turn my head to look at him.

He tightens his hold around my body, stopping me. "Yes. I believe so."

"Then you should probably go."

He hums. "I should."

A calm silence falls between us.

But then he loosens his hold; however, the touch of his skin against mine doesn't vanish instantly. My nightdress has danger-ously hiked up, bunching at my hips. And with him slowly putting distance between us, the heated area of my back turns cold.

I almost reach for his hand to keep him there.

Almost.

Dane sits up; runs both hands across his jaw and into his hair, messing it even more. "It's five in the morning."

"Are you so magical that you have an invisible watch?"

The confusion on his face makes me giggle, and I cover my mouth with my hand as I turn onto my side to watch him.

"What is funny?"

"Did you have anything in your world? You have no idea who Peter Pan is, or the Teenage Mutant Ninja Turtles. What did you watch growing up? Wait. No TV, I'm guessing. No phones or internet. No plants apparently. And you don't have goddamn hot-water bottles! What did you do for fun?"

"We aren't doing task one again, human."

My mouth opens. Closes. "Oh."

He looks at me as if he wants to speak some more, yet neither of us bother, and, right now, I can't avert my tired gaze. Dane has sleepy eyes all the time, even more so when he just wakes. I would say he was cute if it wasn't for the personality transplant he needs and the obvious darkness in his soul.

"Stop looking at me," I say. "It's creepy."

Dane groans and lies back down, his strong shoulder right there, in my line of sight. And my God is it a nice shoulder. The arch of his neck makes me want to dig my nails into it, my teeth, to mark it by sucking on the skin.

Dane grimaces, and I fight a scoff before turning away from him to face the wall. "If you thought task two was bad, we'll never survive the rest. They get more intense."

"Elaborate."

"I'd rather not. Go read the list."

He yawns and replies, "I'd rather not."

I grunt, but my eyes close once more.

For some reason, he isn't leaving, and I'm not telling him to.

A few moments pass, then I'm pulled against him again.

"Just to be sure we did the full six hours," he whispers against my ear. "Okay?"

I nod. "Okay."

We fall asleep for what feels like hours, but in reality, going by the sunlight still barely lighting up the room, it's only been about twenty minutes.

But his hand is on my hip, and the electricity strumming between us is intense and indestructible.

Like two magnets, stronger than anything I've ever come across, our bodies press against each other. A force not even Dane can fight. It's not uncomfortable or sickening. It's the total opposite.

A steady calm of two heartbeats.

Blood pumping through veins.

Lungs expanding and contracting.

Each breath from Dane fills me, and the touch of his hand on my bare skin isn't burning like my dreams but like ice melting on a hot day.

I could lie here forever, if the world allowed me to.

When I shift, my eyes ping open at what I feel.

He's hard as granite. Long. Big. There. Pressing against my ass, only my panties to create a barrier, because my nightdress has risen up even further. But instead of tensing or wincing or trying to pull away, if only to stop embarrassment on his part, I stay still.

His arm—which is still on top of me—is in full view now that the room is brighter. Naked. There's no shirt to hide the tanned skin, or the strange writing and symbols that are tattooed on his forearm.

I've never been able to make out his ink before, but now that he's all over me, I allow my eyes to explore what I can.

The hairs on his arm stick up as I trace the black writing, the symbols I don't recognize. An immortal who gets goose pimples across his skin seems bizarre.

As if my touch has woken him, his fingers bury into my skin as he yanks me against him.

He's still hard; still pressed to my ass. The impressive rigidness could likely rip through my panties, if he really wanted to go there.

Against my better judgment, for the hundredth time in the past six hours, I arch my back and push my ass into his erection. The groan that leaves his throat vibrates all over me. From my chest, down my spine and right between my legs. Deep. Dangerous. Deadly.

The walls are empty of shadows as Dane reaches down and grabs my inner thigh, the other hand pushing under my pillow and snatching my throat. Firm, yet gentle—enough to show he can dominate me without even trying.

My erratic pulse is thudding against his palm.

His fingers dig into my flesh as he dips his face to the space between my shoulder and neck.

"Do that again," he orders quietly through gritted teeth.

I do as I'm told. I arch my back, rubbing my ass against his hard cock. I can tell by the thickness that he's considerably larger than a human. Quite frankly, I reckon he'd snap my body into pieces if it went anywhere near me.

He exhales through his nose, each breath harsh and forced out as I move against him again and again.

A sound vibrates from his chest once more, making me close my eyes as he yanks my head back by the throat, so we're cheek to cheek. He grips my thigh harder, lifting it so he can thrust between my legs from behind.

Slowly, we both move our hips. The coiling deep within me starts as a dull pulse, and it's as if one of Dane's shadows is snaking up my spine, wrapping around each vertebra and whispering sweet nothings to my soul. Promises to seek revenge.

On what, I don't know.

Again and again, the concealed length of him rubs against

my ass, pushing between my legs to run over my soaking pussy. And the urge to turn and face him so I can feel his cock from the front is unbearable.

But I won't turn.

It might break whatever spell we're in. Need. Desire. Black liquid lust injecting into our veins until we both peak, and I realize the sunlight is no longer shining through my window.

The room has fallen into darkness, and neither of us has noticed until now. We both freeze. Our orgasms are fading.

We look up to the ceiling. A black vortex filled with flashes of lightning swirls above us.

Dane removes his hands from my throat and thigh.

We swallow, gulping down the need to continue. We breathe in unison. When the warmth between us dims, the moment is gone, the veil of black is lifted, and the sun shines once more.

The vortex shimmers to nothing until it's gone. Everything is. Even the tenderness of Dane that comforted me all night. It felt familiar somehow, as if I've been in that position a thousand times before. I look over my shoulder to my school bully. Half-lidded eyes are on me.

"What was that?" he asks, running his hand through his unruly hair. "Fuck, where are my clothes?"

I shake my head. "I don't know what that was. I thought your shadow pets were getting excited again."

He pulls away from me completely, breaking our touch and connection. And instantly, everything feels different. It feels wrong.

"They are not pets. They are the only shadows that remain from my realm and will be treated with respect."

He gets to his feet and pulls his shirt on, keeping it unbuttoned. His abs strain, and my gaze fixes on the prominent V leading down to his boxers. Without sparing me a glance, he shoves his legs into his pants.

Eventually, his eyes meet mine then trail down the length of me before he shakes his head and mutters deeply, "Fuck."

"It was a pleasure doing business with you, Mr. Dalton. I'll see you soon for task three. Wear some ChapStick."

He narrows his eyes. Then the air shifts, taking all the energy with it, and Dane is gone.

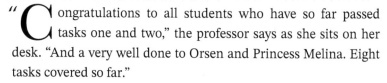

"Congratulations to all students who have so far passed tasks one and two," the professor says as she sits on her desk. "And a very well done to Orsen and Princess Melina. Eight tasks covered so far."

I look at my friend. "You have some nerve to complain about me keeping secrets."

She shrugs. "I got bored and he was there."

"No. Since when are you a princess?"

She shrugs again, scribbling on her paper.

"You're a princess too?" I ask Poppy, who nods with a grin. I stare at my so-called friends. "So you're both technically royalty and you"—I nudge Mel—"are sleeping with Orsen."

"I'm not sleeping with him," she drawls.

"Oh, sorry, I must've gotten the part where he's been sleeping in your bed for the best part of two weeks wrong," Poppy adds, leaning forward on her desk. "He made himself invisible when I came in to speak to her about homework. What if I farted? Like, what the hell, sis?"

Mel rolls her eyes. "Stop trying to speak like a human."

"Stop sneaking around like one then! You know everything about me and my partner."

Mel begins writing down notes from the chalkboard. "And that has been a horrifying experience."

I have no idea how these two are sisters. One is moody and scary, and the other looks like she'd climb a tree to save a kitten before handing over every bit of money she had to a homeless man. Kindness drips from her.

Across from me, Dane sits with his legs parted wide. His pencil twirls around his fingers. Not once has he looked at me in the six days since leaving my room.

We passed each other in the hallway and neither of us paid any attention to the other. I could sense him behind me while waiting to get my lunch, and when Valin took me aside in class and apologized for his behavior, especially when he told me to be careful who I'm friends with.

In classes where we've had to sit together, we've stuck to solely focusing on the work. If words were used, they were short and necessary. In mortal studies, he had to show he knew how to call me, so that night, he rang once and hung up.

The communication between us is limited, and it's weird, to be honest. I'm used to him firing rudeness in my direction or tripping me up, knocking my work from my hands or turning my food into dead animals.

That seems to have stopped, along with everything else.

It's like I'm a stranger to him now.

Which is fine. I can't stand him either.

It seems having his dick rubbing against me is a forgotten dream. Just to play tricks and piss him off, and to see if he's trying to pry into my mind, I think about Valin and I training as he holds a sword to my throat. He tells me that Dane isn't good enough before bringing his lips to mine.

Dane's shoulders tense, and I try not to chuckle.

Slut.

My pencil falls from my fingers, and I glance back over to him. Did he say that out loud? No one bats an eyelid in our direction, and the teacher is still writing on the chalkboard.

Well, drawing several stick figures in different positions of giving oral.

Dane continues to write, and I glare at the back of his head. *Asshole.*

He stops and looks over his shoulder at me. We both frown, and slowly, he turns to face the front of the classroom.

He... heard me? And I heard him? What kind of weird witchy crap is this?

Then I remember the voice in my head when Valin was in my room. I had involuntarily wanted Dane, and the distinct deep voice had said, *Where the fuck are you?*

Oh God. Is this a paired-up thing? Can Orsen and Mel talk to each other?

I go to ask my friend, but the sound of the grandfather clock halts me.

It's the end of class, and I aim to drag him into an empty class with my nonexistent vines and demand answers. But when I get into the corridors, he and his group of friends are gone.

I walk to the food court with the twins, holding my leather satchel against my chest.

Can you hear me?

Nothing.

Dane?

Nothing.

I guess that's good. Maybe I imagined it, imagined it all, or it was just a coincidence that he looked at me after I called him names in my mind.

Once I've eaten, I excuse myself and make my way to the bathroom. I freeze as Dane turns a corner, nearly smashing into me.

Our eyes lock, and I wait for it. The name calling. The

bullying he's put me through since I got here. But no vines snap out to restrain me, and no black masses of shadows try to swallow me into an abyss.

Your hair is stupid.

Dane wets his lips and tucks his hands into his pockets. Waiting. He's waiting for me to say something.

I want to punch you.

"Why are you staring at me, mortal?"

I cross my arms, acting as indifferent as he is. "Task three is due by Tuesday."

His half-lidded eyes drop to my chest for a split second before looking to the side. "I'm aware. It's Friday."

"I'm aware."

Dane snaps his gaze to me. "Do you always act like a child?"

"You know, I may be older than you, or I could be a baby compared to you. What if you're like a thousand years old? I like older men, but not that old." I raise a shoulder. "Unless you're Valin."

"The monster who tried to fuck you. Of course you're fine with him. A few apologies and you forget the way he approached you?"

I smile. "Apparently so." Lie. Valin gives me the creeps, but I like to push Dane's buttons. It seems he doesn't like Professor Mallory too much. "Was that you who spoke to me before you blasted into my room and wrecked everything?"

"What would your boyfriend think of you being so open about fucking someone else?"

My brows narrow, and confusion sets in before I remember I lied that I had one before, so I tip my chin and stay silent.

Dane stares at me for a long moment before scoffing. "I'm needed elsewhere. Be gone, human. I don't need people seeing me conversing with you."

I raise a brow. "Because you're the prince of shadows and I'm a mere mortal?"

"No. Because I'm the heir to an entire realm and you are nothing."

I smirk, spinning on my heels and walking away from him. "One day, you're going to realize repeating yourself gets you nowhere."

I'm away from him as soon as I turn the corner, and I press my back to the brick wall to catch my breath. Something was tugging on me when I was in front of him, like I needed to touch him, to run my fingers through his hair and feel all of him against me again.

The rush to approach him was like bad adrenaline.

That's new.

Maybe as the tasks are completed, the magic that was cast for our pairing grows stronger? If so, I'm not sure what things will be like in a few tasks' time. It would explain Orsen and Mel jumping from hatred to barely being able to take their eyes off one another.

As I head for my dorm, I stop near the library. It could be a good idea to know more about Dane. His powers and history and what caused his world to perish.

Each realm has a different story, but they're all linked to one source of power. Poppy once explained to me that it was like a missing piece of a jigsaw. One broken element, and the worlds are slowly falling apart.

I rush to the library and hunt for a book on the Shadow Realm. He said he was the heir, so surely there will be information on him? His family?

It takes me nearly three hours, but I eventually find one. It's at the top of the shelf, so I grab a ladder, slide it over, and settle my bag at the bottom of it.

The book is heavy and full of dust, but I manage to carry it down to the bottom. I drop to the floor, crossing my legs and leaning my back against the bookshelf.

The hard cover cracks as I open the front page. I cough into my sleeve and screw my eyes up from the dust. The smell is rancid, like it's been through wars and drains and death. The writing is in a different language altogether, but there are some illustrations.

I skip pages until I reach one that looks familiar. A symbol, similar to the yin and yang yet distorted. The lines of the shape are written words. Handwritten. These symbols have been drawn into the book instead of being natural to the edition.

Dane has this one on his wrist. The exact same. I try to read what it says beneath, but it's not a language I've ever come across in my world.

I flick more pages, until I see another symbol, another Dane has on his skin. There's the tiniest line of words beneath it.

The divine darkness does not exist without her.

It's handwritten in English. A language some creatures here are still learning. I frown at it before turning the page to an animal, like a bull. A snake wraps around it, with two broken hearts trapped between its horns.

And handwritten again is, *The heir of all the realms will wield the power of darkness until its love returns. Death to her, death to all.*

11

Dane Dalton doesn't know what ChapStick is.

The message that probably took him all day to type stares at me as I sit in the library.

> Dane: Where do I find ChapStick and what does it look like?

To annoy him, I've so far waited three hours since receiving the text. Instead of going to combat training with the twins for some extra credit with Valin, I came back to the library to read more of this book. Well, read what I can. Basically, none of it makes any sense to me. I've even hunted for books to help translate certain words and phrases and symbolic meanings, but it seems it's a dead language of which there's absolutely no trace in the history section.

That's strange. All the other realms have shelves upon shelves of research, yet I have one tattered book that better not give me a rash.

I scratch my arm impulsively and chew my lip.

Surely there must be more? I could ask our history professor, but I fear being trapped in a room with him. He reminds me of Slenderman and, from what I've heard, is a cannibal.

The librarian also looks like she wants to eat me, so I don't bother asking for any assistance, even though she's been watching me for the past hour.

I sip on my fruit juice while I flip through pages and take notes—mostly scribbles of faces and three-dimensional houses as I try to figure out what the hell certain equations mean.

Eventually, I give up and slam the book shut with a loud thud, pushing it across the table.

I cross my arms and ankles before slouching in the chair. Annoyance and something similar to deflation have me sighing and huffing as I stare at the papers before me.

"There you are! I snuck away from combat class to come sit with you," Poppy says with a huge grin. It falters when she sees my expression. "Cheer up. It's Wednesday."

"Although it's Friday, there's nothing good about Wednesdays, Poppy." Her smile drops completely, and I instantly regret my words. "I mean..." I sigh and lean forward. "In the human world, I used to hate mid-week. It dragged in, and all I wanted to do was go out on a Friday night, get drunk, and dance until my feet fell off."

The smile thankfully returns, and she's intrigued. I know for a fact that she'll fit in so well. She's mesmerized by everything human.

Sitting across from me, she rests her chin in her palm. "Your feet fell off when you danced?"

I can always count on Poppy to cheer me up. "It's a figure of speech."

She giggles. "Humans are so different from us, so I never know what's serious and what's not. I know my sister can be moody with it, but can you tell me more about your kind?"

"What do you want to know?"

Her eyes light up, bright and alive. "Everything."

My plan to message Dane back with some snarky response floats from my mind and takes flight out the window as I go into hours upon hours of details. From being young and playing in the yard, to going to a normal school and experiencing life as a teen. Poppy listens to every word as I tell her about high school, about sneaking out of the house to get drunk with my friends and then sneaking back in. She gasps when I tell her about the game of dares that landed me my first kiss with the school's bad boy, and that he turned out to be a terrible kisser.

Blushing through each story, Poppy stays with me until it's dark outside, and she has more than enough to keep her fascination with humans at bay.

She even asks me how she would be able to have a relationship with a human and tells me she wants to have a family one day. Her partner, she explains, is fun, but she can never see a future with him.

She wants happiness and peace and love.

Without thinking, I tell her all three of those exist—an instant thought that makes me question myself. I've never once found happiness. As I said, I grew up in the system. Peace is make-believe in my world, and love... I can't imagine being in love.

But telling my friend that she could have all three puts a huge smile on her face. It has her clapping and laughing and getting excited about graduating.

She has a pure heart.

When Poppy and I finish up, she eyes the large, tattered book. "What's this?"

I shrug. "I wanted to know more about Dane." When she gives me a knowing look, I sigh. "For educational purposes obviously. I should know who I'm partnered up with, right?"

"You have no idea who he is, do you?"

"Of course not," I reply. "Tell me. Please."

"Dane's from an extinct realm. He was the heir, but some

people now know him as the Prince of Darkness. When their world perished, most of them lost the ability to contain their power, but somehow he kept all of his. Dane doesn't have full control. But yeah... It was pretty nasty from what I've heard."

I tuck the heavy book back into the hiding spot I chose on the third row of shelves. "Can you tell me what you know?"

She bites her lip. "It's not my story to tell. All of them... the survivors, they lost a lot. I'm surprised Dane got out before the explosion."

"When?"

Poppy glances behind me then around us, making sure no one is near. "A long time ago. He's been searching the realms ever since."

I frown. "Searching for what?"

"I'm not sure how much I'm allowed to tell. Some things are kept secret for a reason."

The line between my brows deepens. "I don't understand."

"Keep this between us. I'm sure I overheard him talking about a blade. Him and Orsen were looking for it. That's the only information I can give you."

My brow furrows even further. "A blade?"

Poppy blows a bubble with her gum, pops it on her finger, then rips it off with her teeth. "I need to go. Speak to you later?"

I nod, confused. "Sure."

She skips out of the library.

I turn back to the table, drop my bag, and go for the book again.

Hours later, no further forward with my research, I'm woken by the librarian slapping me hard and telling me to get out before she turns me into a puddle of vomit.

A shiver wracks through my body as I stare her down, paper stuck to my cheek. She eventually straightens her spine and goes back to her desk to stamp floating books.

As I check my phone on the way to the dorm room, I notice

it's two in the morning, and I received a message from Dane half an hour ago.

Dane: C109

That's all.

I stop walking and stare, unsure of what this means.

The classrooms are all labeled like that, or maybe he sent it by accident?

C stands for the cult studies corridor, and the *1* stands for the first floor, door nine.

Me: ???

I know he'll take forever to respond, so I click off my phone and make my way to the cult studies corridor. It's late. Dark. The usual harrowing screams are silent, but I can feel eyes on me. I'm being watched as I walk through the darkness.

I grab a candelabra from a table sitting outside one of the classrooms, using it to guide me. The soft glow from the flames licks the walls, and if it wasn't for the eeriness of the entire situation, I'd say this was a nice aesthetic.

If Wi-Fi were a thing here, I'd take a picture and post it to one of my socials.

I'll make do with seeing it and living in the moment.

Something moves in the distance then, and I stop in my tracks.

"Dane?"

No response.

A hiss of a snake comes from behind, but as I gasp and spin towards the sound, there's nothing there.

I gulp down my fear. I should be asleep or heading to my bed, not hunting down Dane Dalton of all people. This could potentially be a prank he's pulling, where I step into the class and he and his friends do something to me.

I think I'll slap him if he's messing with me.

My nerves catch fire as another hiss sounds, further down the corridor, straight towards door nine. I want to turn and run, to get away from the potential threat, but I don't. My feet move without thinking, the clicks of my heels filling the still silence of the corridor.

I'm a little scared, but I'm also intrigued to keep going.

It's like something is drawing me in. Like I'm being lassoed down the corridor. The candelabra is heavy, and my bicep burns, but instead of placing it down, I tighten my grip on it.

My unsteady breaths echo through the pin-dropping quietness. A chill creeps up my arms, coldness encasing me, and the faint sound of a piano playing has me stopping outside C102.

I push the door open, and a box sitting on the professor's desk glows brighter than the candles in my grasp. It rattles on the desk, but the only noise that comes is the keys of the piano.

Around the edges of the box, a bright glow of a white light beams through. Then the box rattles hard. A slam. No—more of a smack against a skull. The thud of someone's head hitting a hard surface. Again and again. *Crack. Crack. Crack.*

The closer I get, the more my heart races. I'm terrified but can't stop my hand reaching out for the lock.

"Mortal."

I nearly drop the candelabra as Dane appears in the doorway, holding his side, black blood oozing between his fingers.

"Do not open that, or we're all dead."

I step towards him, away from the screeching screams. "What happened to you?"

He doesn't shove me away as I close the distance and take in his appearance. I set the candles aside, their glow highlighting the side of his face. A fresh bruise sits on his cheek.

"I'm fine. I just need assistance." The words are shaky, and his voice is off.

Dark liquid drips from his nose.

A lick of rage has my teeth gritting together. The words, seethed, are out before I can stop them. "Who did this to you?"

"It's amusing that you think you can do something I'm incapable of." He gestures to the doorway. "And you're in the wrong room."

"I heard something," is all I reply as I follow the Prince of Darkness, leaving the candles behind.

Dane doesn't reply to me, but I keep right behind him, looking around us for the hissing snake or the singing killer. The closeness—I'm nearly stepping on the back of his shoes—is unnecessary, considering I'm not actually scared.

Yet here I am.

We reach C109, and before he opens the door, he glances over his shoulder. "I needed someone with no powers. Don't think I'm bringing you here for a repeat of what happened the other night."

I hum. "And here I thought you were surprising me with roses and chocolates."

He rolls his eyes, holding his side as his blood drips down his pants.

Screw him—he can lick his own wound.

He opens the door to reveal numerous weapons sitting in the middle of the room and scattered across the floor. The place is destroyed.

"What happened?" I ask as Dane closes and locks the door, trapping me in here with him. "You're not one of those kinky demons who like dub-con, right? My safe word is not pineapple."

"I've no idea what you're talking about." He winces as he lets go of his side, leans down to grab a large diamond, and places it on the professor's desk. "I need you to open this, that's all."

94

"You want me to open a diamond? Are you for real? They're specially made by pressurized—"

"Stop. Speaking." Dane rudely slams his hand on the table. It's covered in blood. His blood. "Do you take anything seriously? You do all that research on me and still try to provoke me? Do you have any idea what I could do to you without even blinking?"

I straighten my spine, attempting to make myself seem taller, confident, and hopefully a little intimidating. "You don't scare me."

"Then you're as dumb as I assume all humans to be."

"Hey, have you forgotten we're partnered up for everything? Stop treating me like I'm worthless and show me some respect."

Dane looks bored as he shoves one hand into his pocket. "No. Can you open this or not?"

I cannot believe this guy.

"Tell me how you got hurt and I will." I have no idea why I said that, or why I have the urge to know, to hunt down the person responsible and rip them to shreds.

Sighing, he pulls his hand out of his pocket, takes his other hand from his wound, and begins to undo the buttons of his stained white shirt. I feign indifference, but the sight of him stripping down his top half with only the moon shining through the window is fascinating. I allow my gaze to trace his chest, the powerful muscles there, the ridges of his abs and his hips, coated in blood.

"Why is your blood black?"

He freezes as the shirt slips from both arms. "Because it is. Why is your blood red?"

"Because I'm normal."

"Nothing about you is normal, human." He leans against a student's desk, showing me the deep gash at his ribs. "I tried to open the diamond and it sensed my magic, so it struck me. It has information I need."

"A diamond beat you up, and you think I'm the weak one?"

His patience is nearly nonexistent. Good. "It won't be able to trace any power from you, and you'll be able to pull the scroll free."

I stare at the diamond, which is no bigger than my palm. "And how do I do that?"

In a foreign language I can only assume to be from his world, Dane mutters a sentence that sounds like it could hurt my tongue. His eyes flicker to a soft silver, not the bright version I've seen a few times. With the wound beginning to heal itself, he says the five words again. Are they even words?

"You sound a little Russian."

He scowls as he repeats the sentence again, and the sliced flesh begins to knit together, little thin black tendrils crisscrossing, closing the wound.

The creature can heal himself. I have no chance of ever winning against him.

His eyes don't leave mine, and an odd sensation has me swallowing melting ice. Is it hot in here? Did I drop the candles and they're currently spreading fire through the castle? That would make sense, unlike this nonsense about me opening a diamond for a scroll.

Dane stands, stretches his side to test the skin, and then reaches down for his shirt. When he notices the blood on it, he crushes the fabric with his fist and tosses it aside.

Realization dawns on me. "Why didn't you heal yourself before coming for me?"

Looking from me to the ground, he shakes his head. "I don't know."

"You don't know..."

"Grab the diamond and read this out loud," he says, handing me a piece of paper with the most illegible handwriting. "Say it clearly, and when your mind opens up to its power, you follow the humming noise and grab the scroll. As soon as you do, shut your mind off again, got it?"

No. "How do I say that?" I stare at the squiggly lines. "How is that pronounced in English?"

Dane looks like he wants to kill me. He's impatient, yet patient. "Do as two, do as one."

I curl my lip. "Sounds stupid."

"Just fucking say it."

I do, and the instant the last word drops from my mouth, so does everything around me. I'm falling, flying through colors, my stomach close to emptying with how fast I'm falling. I try to scream, but no sound comes out. Like a never-ending well I've toppled into, down and down I go.

My feet hit the bottom. I'm weightless in a sea of glitter, with tiny black dots—ash— floating around me. The oxygen is weird —it feels like water in my lungs, yet I can breathe.

The silhouettes in my bedroom walls are here, or maybe I just think they are. The dog is barking, frantically running from left to right down one wall, the other has a couple pointing to the right, and the little girl walks with me until we reach a wooden door full of fragments of glass.

I can see my reflection. And it stops me. I'm me but older, and my eyes are silver. She's saying something I can't hear, and she has a terrified expression. I blink, and a younger, more present version of myself stares back.

I can see the scroll. It's near a window, one that I walk towards and peek out to see a humongous castle. Instead of white bricks and looking like something inviting from a kid's movie, it seems to be more of a horror style. Everything is shrouded in blacks and grays and... death.

So much death.

That explains why it's so cold here.

I look up, and above the tallest tower is a spiral vortex, angry and fast, taking up the entire sky. The other night, while Dane and I did task two, that was above us. Maybe not this specific one, but one of them.

Where am I?

The world around me stills—even the vortex halts its spinning—and I frown. Ice trickles against my neck and spine, sending shivers all over, and I have the feeling I'm no longer alone, as if I've been seen. Caught. Close to being a captive within this world.

I rush to the scroll, and as soon as my fingers touch it, everything around me warps into one color, but not before I turn to see a figure with horns charging at me with fire blazing from its body.

I scream, loud enough to hurt my own ears. I drop the scroll, bring my hands to my ears, and let out every bit of breath until the fear unravels and someone's fingers are grabbing my chin.

"Breathe." He shakes me. I know it's Dane, but I'm slipping from this reality again, and I think something from that other world is trying to drag me back. "Breathe, you imbecile."

Everything halts, and my eyes ping open. "Don't you dare call me an imbecile after what you just made me do!"

He lets out a breath, drops his hands from my face, and settles his back against the desk in front of me. Both of us are on the ground. Both exhausted. "Fuck. You were in there for hours."

Shaking my head, I stay as far away from the diamond as I can. "I was there barely minutes."

"That's how it works there. Time is different. The sun is already rising, mortal."

He's right. The moonlight creeping through the windows is gone, replaced by orange and yellow hues filling the sky.

He's still shirtless. I try not to look again. But this time, I'm catching a glimpse of more symbols beneath the dried blood, inked words that make no sense. I want to trace each piece of ink. A forbidden image infiltrates my head and has me gaping at myself, of me dragging my tongue up each ab before dropping to my knees. I... I wasn't thinking about that.

I glance up at Dane, and he averts his gaze.

"You need to stop," he says.

I raise a brow. "Stop what?"

"Everything. Stop trying to figure out my history. You will find nothing. You can stop spending hours in the library with my father's book."

Of course he knows about that.

"What is your reason for looking into my past?"

I shrug, picking invisible lint from my skirt. "I wanted to make sure you're not going to morph into a dragon while you're inside me."

He visibly pales, and I chuckle at his horrifying expression.

Dane gets to his feet, not offering a hand to help me up. "Making jokes about our future unfortunate events is immature."

"If you want to survive in my world, grow a sense of humor."

"No."

His war cry.

I peek up, finding him already watching me. Dane chews his lip, his eyes following my movements as I try to fix my hair and straighten my clothes. "Thank you, mortal. I've been trying to obtain that scroll for weeks."

"Sera," I correct, trying not to blush from the intensity of his gaze. "And you didn't give me much of a choice now, did you?"

"No." He smirks as I shake my head, and I'm definitely going to get flashes of that while pleasuring myself later. "Accept gratitude when offered it and drop it."

"Fine. You're welcome. If you ever ask me to do something like that again, I'll make task five hell for you. Can I go now?"

He stares at me, calculating which task that is, and then nods once.

But as I shoulder past him, skin blistering from the touch, Dane clears his throat and speaks when I reach for the door handle. "You didn't respond to me earlier. Are you even taking these tasks seriously?"

I spin on my heels, my skirt swishing in the air from the momentum. "You better be kidding me right now."

Dane takes a step. "Task three's deadline is in forty hours."

I cross my arms and lean against the door. "Shame. I wanted a few more days to practice with my pillow." He doesn't get it, so I huff. "You can come to my room tomorrow. The rules are for it to be done five times, and for all five to be more than a minute long. Think you can handle that?"

"Can you?" he counters.

We stare at each other, and I'm so sure he's taken another step, I'm almost compelled to do the same, but I keep my back firmly pressed to the door. "Have you ever kissed someone before?"

His jaw tenses. "Yes. I have."

"Because you sleep around in the academy?"

Annoyingly, he smirks again, taking one more step. "I definitely don't *sleep* around, mortal."

"Sera."

"No."

I tilt my head to give him some smart retort, but I fail as his shoe lifts across the ground and he moves even closer.

"Fine," I say. "Prove it."

My heart rate accelerates to a dangerous pace as he rests both of his hands on the door at each side of my head. "Prove what?"

"That you can handle it," I reply, tipping my chin up so I can hold eye contact.

He laughs. "I mean every offense when I say this, but I'd rather rip out my own heart and feed it to the wolves."

"You're such a dick."

I knock his arm away, but he captures me by the shirt to stop me from walking through the door.

"Wait."

One word. One demand. Firmly said through his teeth.

I slap his hand away. "You're the demon version of whiplash. What do you want?"

He waves a finger, and balls of shadows fly to the windows, shrouding us in darkness. "I just remembered I'm busy tomorrow, and I can't risk failing."

He walks into the middle of the room and sits, elbows on his knees, waiting. "Can you risk failing, mortal?"

I gulp, bite my lip, then rub my arm. "No. I guess not."

He hums, a deep sound from his chest. It travels across the room and settles right between my legs. "Then..." He wets his lips. "Come here."

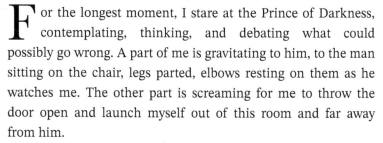

12

For the longest moment, I stare at the Prince of Darkness, contemplating, thinking, and debating what could possibly go wrong. A part of me is gravitating to him, to the man sitting on the chair, legs parted, elbows resting on them as he watches me. The other part is screaming for me to throw the door open and launch myself out of this room and far away from him.

He doesn't actually want to do this.

But as the thought comes over me, I stop fiddling my fingers behind my back and push a step forward. "I have a few things to cover first."

Dane hums so deep I feel it between my legs. "Go on."

"Do you still want to kill me?"

He thinks for a second, pushing his tongue against his inner cheek. "Yes. If anything, I want to kill you more."

I huff. "I'm being serious, Dane. I won't kiss someone who plans to put a stake through my heart."

He tilts his head. "You are a mortal, not a vampire. Or did that somehow slip your mind? I could kill you without lifting a finger."

Glaring at him does absolutely nothing. He doesn't falter. I'm about as scary as a puppy.

"You're all talk," I say boldly. Stupidly. Just to add to the growing frustration in his deep eyes, I keep going. "If you were going to end my life, you would have done it already." I tip my chin. "You're bluffing."

His eyes darken a fraction. "What makes you think I'm bluffing?"

"Actions speak louder than words," I respond, crossing my arms. He's still on the chair, looking handsome and laid-back and annoying. "You aren't going to kill me."

"We shall see, mortal." His brows raise as he says *mortal*, and I want to slap his face. "What else?"

I gulp, unsure if the feeling washing over me is the intensity of his hooded gaze or the image of him being the last person I see before meeting my end. Maybe both. "This is for an assignment."

"Obviously."

"We do this once, for the assignment."

"Five times," he replies, a slight smirk touching his lips. "You said we need to do it five times, a minute each time. For the *assignment* of course, as you keep mentioning."

Instead of humoring him, I tense my jaw, flip my hair behind me, and look out the window above his head. "I don't know how it works in your realm, but in mine, consent is important. I won't kiss you without you being okay with it. For this entire assignment, consent will be discussed. If you don't want to do something, I'll refuse to go ahead with each task. If I'm not comfortable, you will stop. Failure or not."

I zone my gaze to him as Dane leans back in the chair, the wood creaking. "Do actions not speak louder than words?"

Is he talking about the time we shared a bed and he dry-fucked me? Held me until we fell asleep? The image of him sliding his cock against my panties has me flushing bright red.

He clears his throat, and the internal clip of him grabbing my thigh, lifting it to get a better angle, vanishes.

"No. Words, Dane. Verbal consent or nothing. A person's body can betray them in the worst of ways, so we'll use words."

I can't believe I'm even talking about this with him. The first time he ever looked at me, I thought I'd die on the spot. Now, here I am talking to him about consenting to a kiss.

If I'm dreaming, or stuck in a nightmare, I'd like to wake up now. I nip my hand, and I don't wake up in my bedroom. I'm still here.

Dane looks at me like I'm a lunatic. "Very well. If it makes it easier for you to sleep at night, I consent to you walking over here and leaning down to kiss me for this assignment. Good enough?"

"Is there a reason why you're sitting?"

"I'm considerably taller," he replies. "You would struggle to reach me if I was standing."

I roll my eyes, dropping my hands to my sides. "Fine."

But neither of us moves, and after a few seconds, Dane braces his hands on his knees, as if he's getting ready for a fight. The ink mocks me—the symbols I've been studying, the writing I have no idea how to translate.

"I have another question."

He sighs. "Of course you do."

"How did you get your tattoos? I highly doubt there was an artist in your realm, considering you have no idea what anything normal is."

"I do know normal things. I don't know what half of human inventions are. That's all. And as for the tattoos, when one comes into great power, they are branded by that power."

I look at him, confused. "So, no one actually tattooed you? They just... appeared?"

"Technically, no. I was born with mine. I have always been

branded. Any other questions?" His tone is snappy, as if he's getting fed up with being asked about himself.

I try to imagine a baby version of Dane with tattoos and fail. "No."

"Very well." He gestures to the floor in front of him. "Any day now. I may not be growing old, but you definitely are."

How dare he? "You know, being rude isn't helping."

He inhales, holds it, and lets it out through his nose. "Will you please hurry the fuck up and come here? You're overcomplicating it."

For a beat, I debate in my mind if this is even happening. Since day one, this idiot has repeatedly called me names, messed with me, and threatened to kill me. Yet here I am, taking one step after the other, the distance between us eliminated with each step. "I still don't like you."

"The feeling is mutual, little mortal."

"I loathe you," I counter. "Detest. I wouldn't hesitate to step on your foot with my sharpest stiletto. In fact, we need to dance together at the ball—I'll do it then."

"Cute. I look forward to watching you embarrass yourself. Can you even dance?"

No.

Dane chuckles.

He's sitting as calm as a cucumber, his sleepy gaze following my slow footsteps towards him. Gravitating. A pull so strong, I can barely breathe. With my shoes nearly touching his, I watch his Adam's apple move in his throat as he looks up at me. Cocky, yet under the voided shell he's trying so hard to hold up, I can tell he has some nerves.

His eyes shift at my proximity—once green, now the brightest silver, almost as if he has the full moon in them. With him not bothering to stand, I forcibly kick his legs open wider, making sure it hurts.

Well, it might have hurt a human, but all he does is smirk at me as I lean down and rest my hands on his knees. He's making no effort at all, and for that, I dig my nails into his legs. But all he does is raise a brow. "This is all a little over the top for one kiss, do you not think?"

No, I'm nervous as hell, and you're acting far too calm.

The corner of his mouth curls into a half-smile, and I shake my head. "Shut up. Can you make your eyes green again? So it feels like I'm kissing an ordinary person."

I lower to my knees between his legs, but annoyingly, he still towers over me. With lazy eyes on my face, he eliminates some of the distance by leaning his elbows on his knees. "I can't control them."

I sigh. But deep inside, butterflies are going wild as his scent reaches me. No, not butterflies. Dragons are having a battle, with flames and wings and roars. "What does?"

He drops his silver eyes to my mouth and then back to my eyes. A flicker, but I see it. "My mood."

"Why am I not surprised? I swear you are the most depressing person I've ever had the displeasure of spending time with."

He fights a grin, and his eyes shift back to green, and he at least looks human now. "I don't usually know when it happens."

"They're silver a lot around me, so I guess being pissed off brings them out."

"Something like that." He huffs. "Are you done? We have wasted nearly twenty minutes on you being a drama queen over nothing."

"This isn't nothing. We need to kiss, Dane."

Hands grip my hips and pull me closer, but Dane's haven't moved. I look down, my pulse instantly spiking. With his shadow hands holding me in place, Dane slants his head, so I lift my gaze to clash with his. "It's nothing. Stop talking and close your eyes."

I go to speak again but shut my mouth. My eyelids fall, and everything around me turns to darkness. He's looking at me, and I can feel his breath against my face, as if he's leaning down.

"Do you consent to me doing this?" he asks in a whisper, shadow fingers digging into my hips. Not painfully but enough to make my body hum in response. "Do I have your permission to do..." He dips his head fully, and my heart hammers in my chest. His lips are a breath away, and when his nose nudges mine, he takes my bottom lip between his teeth, pulling back until it snaps into place. "This?"

I swallow, nodding slowly, both in sync with each inhale and exhale.

"Words, mortal," he hisses. "Follow your own rules and give me fucking words."

"Yes," I breathe. "Do you?" I tilt my head back, and our lips touch softly for a split second before I ease back to look at him. A low vibration floats between us.

"I do," he replies, and without hesitation, he snatches my nape and smashes his lips to mine.

It's like a bomb goes off around us. A halogenic reaction as our combined forces desperately grab for anything to be completed, intensifying with the low groan Dane lets out.

Something tugs inside me as I break the connection, a rope to my chest, yanking me closer to Dane as I press my mouth to his to feel the detonation once more.

It's a rush between us, and it's addictive. He must feel it too because his heart is racing as I lift my hand to his chest, pushing him against the back of the chair.

Fuck.

The word echoes between us, and it's his low voice, his muttered four letters. It repeats as I pull back ever so slightly, looking into his silver eyes, at his dark lashes, smooth skin, and razor-sharp jawline, before kissing him again. Harder. Crushing my mouth to his.

He tastes exactly as I expected.

"Is this okay?" I ask him because I can feel his discomfort building. It's like a sixth sense between us now. "We can stop."

"Quit cutting us off before one minute," he says against my mouth. "It's fine."

Liar, I think. *He is hating this.*

Dane's lips are softly caressing mine as his ghost hands trail up my sides, settling at my ribs. I gasp into his mouth as, with one swift move, he tugs me to my feet and into his lap, my legs to each side. "When I say it's fine, I mean it's fucking fine."

With his grip on my nape still, he snakes his arm around the small of my back, drawing my mouth to his once again. Our lips part as I settle in his lap, Dane running the tip of his tongue against mine.

I never thought I'd say this, but I'm kissing my worst enemy. The guy who wants me dead. I'm sitting on him, kissing him, with his tongue moving against mine like a starved animal.

His fingers slide into my hair, the other hand coming to replace the shadow on my hip. I try not to gyrate my lower half, even though bolts of electricity are ricocheting through my body, screaming for me to feel him between my legs.

Dane's grip tightens, pushing me back on his legs to keep me from feeling his obvious erection.

I'm not sure, but I think the minute necessary for this first kiss of the task is up.

Reluctantly, I say, "That's probably enough for the assignment."

"Yeah," he replies, our noses nudging, both breathless, swollen lips magnetized together once more.

We aren't stopping. If anything, it gets deeper as his tongue slips into my mouth with more hunger before he traps my bottom lip between his teeth and then kisses it.

I reciprocate by sucking on his tongue, tasting him, devouring him.

A deep groan pulls between us, and Dane caresses his mouth to mine again. I'm warm, as if the room is heating up. I want to remove our clothes and feel skin on skin, bare, naked, sweating and writhing in pleasure.

His hands explore everywhere they can in my uniform.

Still straddling him, I squeeze my thighs to his sides to cause some sort of friction, and he hisses but doesn't stop me. If anything, he's encouraging me by pulling away from my mouth and kissing along my jawline.

My head tilts to the side to give him better access, and a moan slips from me as he nips the sensitive skin beneath my ear and sucks on the flesh.

I bury both hands into his hair and draw his mouth back to mine, and when he growls into my mouth, my pussy clenches, and heat builds at the base of my spine.

Our souls beg to intertwine—a desire, a need so strong I think I might pass out. Each time we connect, more shadows appear in the room—the ground, the ceiling, the walls full of them. I can hear some of them, repeatedly saying words I can't decipher. They aren't the same as the ones that keep me company in my room. These ones seem... hungry and desperate, with an insatiable thirst for something.

We keep pulling away before the one minute mark. I don't think either of us is focusing too much on the time.

All I can focus on is the way his body fits so well with mine, the way his lips feel against my own, and the darkness surrounding us.

"Ignore them," he orders in a low tone, noticing me slowing down and staring at the masses of black. He grabs my shirt and tugs at it to bring me back to his face. "They can't see us, mortal. They can only feel us."

His mouth is like a dark sin. Each lick and slide and bite bounces off every nerve ending. Twisted thoughts rush through me of how his mouth would feel between my legs, and how his hair would feel between my fingers as I rode his face in only my skirt.

I want to hear his language fall from his lips while he's screwing me. To feel all of him as we complete each task, each assignment, each dance at the ball, each time our eyes clash and the atmosphere changes. The shattering energy alone could destroy the entire universe.

God, I want to fuck this man. I hate him. I truly do, but sitting in his lap and tasting him, it's like something is overriding that hatred. Nothing makes sense about how I'm feeling about this – I should hate it. I should be grimacing at the thought of Dane Dalton touching me, kissing me, whispering against my skin in a language I don't recognize.

I gasp loudly as a flash of images slam into me, but they're all too fast, too much to concentrate on. The moment lasts merely a second, but as I freeze in his hold, he watches me, searching my face.

"What is it?" he asks breathlessly. "What did you see?"

I can hear a hint of hopefulness in his tone, but when I shake my head and try to close the distance between us once more, he stops me.

He rips himself away to stand, setting me on my feet.

I instantly feel cold.

His jaw is tensing, his pants tented with his own arousal as he backs away from me, like he's afraid of me. "That's enough." His voice is shaky, and he runs both hands through his hair and down his face. "We're done here."

I nod. Trying to catch my breath, I suck my bottom lip into my mouth, still tasting him. "That was weird."

He drops his hands to his sides, eyes narrowing. The tall, muscular man who swallows all the air in the room couldn't look more offended as he shakes his head.

Flustered, Dane asks with a clenched jaw, "Weird? Explain."

How do I explain the past few minutes? "Just... weird."

"Great." He grimaces. "Fucking weird," he mutters to himself, and I frown as he glances up at me. "I can read your thoughts, or did you forget the other ten times I've had to remind you? You didn't find it weird. And I wasn't going to fuck you. This is an assignment, and that's all it is."

I raise a brow, flicking my eyes down to the tenting of his pants. I walk behind the chair he sat in, gripping the wood, ignoring the ache between my legs. "The assignment is done. You can leave now."

"You think you can dismiss me? This isn't even your room. It's a classroom."

"Yes." I walk to the door and throw it open because I don't have powers like him to blow it off its hinges or teleport into different parts of the castle. "Leave, before I make you."

"And how do you suppose you'd make me?"

I cross my arms. "I have a loud scream."

Blankly, he stares at me and studies me. "I see." He glances up to the ceiling, frowns, and glares back down at me. "Four more. Don't make it as awkward next time."

I scoff and look up, my eyes widening at the lick of flames spreading across the ceiling. Like they're dancing, shrinking back until they're nothing but black tendrils burned into the paint. There's no heat, no smoke, no smell of something burning.

"What was that?"

He doesn't give me an answer.

Sunlight floods the room then, blinding me as the air shifts, and his entire form warps in front of me until he's gone. The classroom grows ice-cold, so cold I can see my breath in puffs. I rub my arms, look around, and swear to myself.

Task three has started, but I still need to kiss him four more times before the timer runs out.

Something awakens in me when I'm around him, and I'm not sure how it makes me feel.

Alive, yet dead.

Free, yet trapped.

It's the biggest confusion, like there are so many questions I need to ask, but I don't know the words.

13

By the time I reach my dorm, students are crowding the halls to go down for breakfast. No one looks at me, or the mess of my hair from Dane running his hands through it, or my swollen lips from being kissed by one of the most powerful creatures on the island.

The twins spot me rushing into my room, and I already know what they're going to ask me. If my disheveled appearance doesn't tell them, my eyes will. Poppy seems to think she can always read someone through their eyes, and so far, she's been right.

"Where were you last night? I came to your room, and you weren't there."

Poppy smiles at me as her sister waits for a reply she isn't going to get. "Did you find more information on Dane Dalton?" She looks at Mel. "I was helping her last night. I suggested she get to know the person she's partnered with, so she'll be more comfortable. Right, Sera?"

I don't deserve her as a friend. "Right."

"Orsen said he couldn't find Dane either." Mel pops out her

hip, eyes dancing with judgment and a little bit of excitement. "Any idea where he could've been?"

We all agreed to no secrets, yet the last thing I want to do is tell them where I've been—or that I had to go inside a diamond to another world to collect a scroll. I also don't want to tell them that I was straddling Dane Dalton on a chair in a cult studies classroom and fantasizing about having him inside me.

Instead, I shrug, ushering them into my room and closing the door.

"No more talk about Dane," I say, pulling off my academy blazer and loosening my tie. It's already a mess from Dane yanking on it, but neither of them notices. I'm usually well put together with my appearance, even down to my socks staying above my knees at the same height. "He was likely screwing someone."

Poppy's nose scrunches. "It's forbidden to have any intimacy outside of your human relations assignment."

I sit down on my bed, exhaustion setting in. "Said who?"

"Did you not read the back of the list of tasks?"

I shake my head, get to my feet, and look for the scroll. Once I find it, I see the small printed words at the bottom of the back of the list. "So we can't kiss or sleep with anyone else?"

Valin nearly messed up my entire year. What is his problem?

"Nope," Mel says, lying back on my bed. Her brows narrow as I unbutton my shirt and toss it into the pile of dirty washing in the corner of my room, fully intent on showering. "What happened to your neck?"

"What do you mean?"

Poppy comes over to me and turns my body so my back is to them. Sliding my hair away from my neck, she gasps. "When did you get a tattoo?"

"What? Never. I don't have any tattoos," I reply, trying to look over my shoulder. "I'd know if I had one."

The twins drag me into the bathroom and turn on the light, facing me away from the mirror. "Look."

I glance over my shoulder, seeing my reflection. It's a struggle to focus from my angle, but from what I can see, it's a black circle with a design inside, sitting at the nape of my neck. The skin around it is swollen and raw, as if I just got it done.

I frown. "What the hell?"

"I've seen this before," Poppy says, following the ink with her eyes. "I looked through the book you had in the library this morning."

Mel comes closer to get a better view. "It's a symbol, isn't it? What does it mean?"

Poppy looks worried as her eyes collide with mine in the mirror. "It means revenge." She bites her lip, peeking at her sister. "But I don't understand the two smaller symbols inside the circle. I'm not sure. To be honest, it looks like the marking of a ritual or a prophecy. It's far too small and compact to really know."

I stay silent, although I'm trying not to panic because why the hell do I have a tattoo?

Mel pulls out her phone and snaps a picture. I'm momentarily surprised that she knows how to do that, then remember she and Orsen send disturbing images regularly.

When my friends eventually leave, I sit on the side of my bathtub, towel tight around my naked body. I can feel it, now that I know it's there. It doesn't hurt or feel uncomfortable, but that doesn't mean I'm happy about it or that I'm not overthinking. The only explanation is that it has something to do with Dane.

> Me: Can you come over? I need to ask you something.

I hit send, hoping he has some answers.

Before I can even stand up straight, the oxygen is ripped from my lungs as Dane appears in front of me. The closeness of him materializing in front of me nearly knocks me off my feet.

He doesn't speak or ask me anything; he doesn't even give me a chance to jump in fright. I'm lifted from the ground by the waist, back smacking into the bathroom door as his lips crush into mine.

Without hesitation, a whimper slips from my mouth and into his, and I part my lips to feel the softness of his tongue on mine.

My towel is dangerously close to opening completely and dropping to the ground, but Dane doesn't pay any attention to it as he kisses me for a full minute. The sixty seconds come and go, yet we keep kissing.

His hands are firmly on the backs of my thighs as he wraps my legs around his waist.

With my pussy bare and Dane's pants rubbing against me, I fight not to roll my hips on him. He's hard and big enough that no matter what I do, I'm pressing against the length of him. This might just be his way of eliminating another part of the task, but me complicating it by dry-humping him is not going to work.

Then again, he did do the same to me while we were lying in bed, so it's fair, right?

I grasp at the material at my breasts, the other hand gripping his shoulder as I kiss him back. His tongue runs against mine, both of us groaning deeply and in unison as the candles flicker and the energy alters to something dark and satanic.

Fucking perfect.

His voice is in my head as he swallows a moan from me, breaking the kiss to trail his lips down my throat and nipping at my collarbone.

Letting go of my thigh, Dane snatches my jaw, pushing my face to the side.

Then he presses a word in a different language against my ear. Deep, low, and husky. It sends bursts of flames and pleasure all over—which only amplify as he sucks on my neck and captures my lips again. Absently, I rock my hips, grinding once and having to fist his hair from the rush of pure adrenaline injected into my veins.

The candles flicker again, and the shadows start to gather around the ceiling, slowly twisting, flashing, and growing more excited as I rock into him once more.

Fuck.

Fucking fuck.

She's perfect.

I try not to blush from the words I can hear in his mind. To refrain from mentioning I heard him, I keep a grip on my towel and bury my fingers into the hair at the back of his head.

I gasp as he grinds into me.

This is not what I had planned when I sent him that message, but as his hands find my bare hips, holding me against the door, I forget about the ink and the possible meaning behind it.

Dane draws my bottom lip into his mouth, sucks it, and then does the same with the top. "What did you want to talk to me about, mortal?" he asks breathlessly before his tongue slips into my mouth again. Easing back, he keeps his face close to mine, waiting for a response.

I tighten my grip on his hair, one white lock hanging over his forehead. With dilated pupils surrounded by bright lights, Dane pants, holding me.

"I forgot."

His gaze drops to the material I'm gripping solidly in my fist, and he swallows. "You forgot..." He releases one of my thighs, rubbing his hand down his mouth when he realizes I'm not dressed. "Fuck. You're naked?"

"I'm in a towel, asshole. Do you have any idea what privacy is?"

Dane looks at me. "We were just..." He flattens his lips.

"What's going on? You sent me a message to come and see you about something."

"And you distracted me," I say, pushing against his chest until he sets me on my feet. "I asked you to come here, not to burst in while I'm just out of a shower and maul me against the door."

"Maul? I was merely covering part of task three."

"I think you're looking for extra credit then," I counter, and he smirks, wiping the taste of me from his lips with his thumb.

I watch his mouth, warmth still at the base of my spine.

I have the sudden urge to drop my towel and order him to kneel, press my pussy to his mouth, and suck on my clit. I'd fist his hair and rock my hips against his tongue. But I shake the thought away and throw the bathroom door open.

I feel his gaze on the back of my neck.

"Where did you get that?" he asks me before I can bring it up. He captures my wrist to stop me from going through one of my drawers for clothes, placing both my hands on the dresser as he moves strands of brown hair from the back of my neck.

Dane is standing behind me, so close I can feel his presence everywhere. I shiver involuntarily, his touch and breath on the nape of my neck, on the tattoo that's staining my skin.

"The twins noticed it earlier," I say. "It wasn't there yesterday."

He steps back, and I turn to face him. I'm a little dumb-founded as to why he's unfastening his shirt buttons, but I watch anyway.

I've witnessed a few emotions from him, but concern isn't one of them. He furrows his brows as he throws his tie across my room.

I hold my towel to my chest. It barely reaches mid-thigh, but it's fine—he's more interested in taking his clothes off with no explanation.

It's a fascinating sight, and a tingling sensation reminds me that we have three more kisses and seven assignments left before this is over. I don't mind that it'll be done, but having a hot guy stripping in my room has been the highlight of my stay here on the island, despite it being Dane.

I mean, we have our other classes and assignments, but most involve classroom-only work, so any time we spend together outside those hours would be voluntary, and I highly doubt that will happen. He's here because he wants to pass. He's as desperate to get off this island as I am, but I think it's for entirely different reasons.

I want to get back to my life. But I think he wants to burn my world to the ground.

The reason is still unknown.

He'll be in jail before the end of his first day.

Muscles upon muscles bunch as he throws his shirt on my bed, but it isn't his impressive physique that's caught my attention.

I step forward, and Dane flinches as my fingertip traces thick black lines on his tanned skin. On the large symbol that starts from his neck and shoulder blades and travels all the way down the expanse of his powerful back. Snakes weave around the outline, writing I can't understand, with a set of piercing dark eyes staring back at me directly in the middle.

It's a lot larger than mine.

And it clicks. My chest caves as I stare. I want to panic. I can feel it building within me, but I swallow down the anxiety and use my words.

"Why do we have the same tattoo?"

Dane turns, eyes blazing. "Who the fuck are you?"

I step back, my heart accelerating at what this could possibly mean at the same time as understanding nothing. "What? Why do I have the same tattoo as you, Dane?"

He grabs his clothes, cornering me with rage. "Are you trying to fuck with me and everyone in the academy? Are you even a human?"

Speechless, I struggle for words, unsure of the absurdity he's speaking. "Yes. You know I am. What's going on?"

"Think, mortal. Why would you have that tattoo?"

"I... I don't know."

And just like that, he shakes his head and disappears.

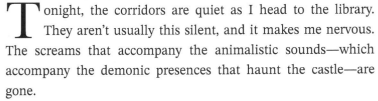

14

Tonight, the corridors are quiet as I head to the library. They aren't usually this silent, and it makes me nervous. The screams that accompany the animalistic sounds—which accompany the demonic presences that haunt the castle—are gone.

I follow the flames from candelabras as I make my way down the spiral steps to the third floor. This is where all the professors sleep, and to the far right, there's a tower that looks over the entire island from its terrifying height.

Someone threw themselves from it not long ago.

I've contemplated doing the same a few times, but I usually snap out of it within a few minutes.

Dane's hasty exit from the room yesterday still lingers in my mind. His words. The look of betrayal on his face. The permanent ink on my skin is identical to his, yet we aren't the same species.

I need answers, and I need them fast.

I've always been human. I have been for the last twenty years. I was born during fall, and my parents used to walk me in my stroller around the lake near our home. There are pictures of me as a child. I have many images of me growing up and legal documentation stating where I was born to prove my nationality.

When my parents died, I went to a foster family, and for some reason, I lasted all but two weeks before they handed me back to the system. The second family were heavy handed. The third had a son who didn't know how to keep his hands to himself. The fourth preferred the star pupil in school, and the fifth left me at home for days before they were reported.

The sixth just didn't like me.

My last family died, and that's when my life had to start. Get a job. Find somewhere to stay. A tiny apartment that I could afford to rent with my low income. Learn to drive. Buy a car. Rescue a dog. Purchase a better mattress. Another car because the first one broke. Credit cards that accumulated debts. More debts. Then, one day, everything just... changed.

I ended up here.

And I don't even know if my dog is okay. Granted, Grayson was there when I was taken and probably has a search party out hunting for me.

What if he doesn't give me my dog back? What if they all think I'm dead and rehome Toodles?

Instead of being there, looking after my furball, I'm trapped here, so Dane's accusations are ridiculous. I have a full memory of growing up as a human. If I was an immortal creature, I'd know. I'd summon whatever power I had and smack him in the face with it.

I'm powerless. That's why I was able to go into the diamond, into the other world with the giant vortex in the sky where the scary beast with horns was. That's why I was able to collect the scroll Dane wanted. He said himself that only someone without any powers could enter.

Is that not proof enough?

But the tattoo...

We have the exact same tattoo. Albeit mine is tiny compared

to the one stretching across his entire back. But still. They're the same.

When I reach the library, I'm relieved to see it's unlocked. Usually, the librarian tends to lock it, to keep people like me out, but recently, she's been leaving it open. Accidentally or intentionally, I have no idea.

I use the glow from the moonlight shining through the windows to walk through the rows of overstuffed bookshelves. My fingers glide over each spine, collecting dust and God knows what else. This is the same route I've been taking since I started coming here. And because of that, the same books have multiple track lines from me touching them as I walk.

I wipe my hands together and reach up to where I've been hiding Dane's father's book, but when I push aside the textbooks, it's gone.

My brows furrow, and I chew my lip nervously. I left multiple notes in it. A list of facts about Dane, what I know of his realm and his powers.

Did I put it somewhere else? Poppy did say she had a look but promised she put it right back where she got it. My gaze trails over the entire shelf, and all the ones next to it, but I give up.

Whoever has it better not show him my list of reasons why I can't be attracted to him. The most important one: Dane is cruel. I also don't think I can stomach him approaching me with it clenched in his hand, questioning why I drew him with a huge forehead, a small dick, and warts all over his face.

I huff and walk to the back of the library to see if the librarian put it in the returns box, freezing when I see Valin. My eyes widen. He's not alone, and this is definitely not a scene I need to witness.

The professor has one of the students by the hair, bent over a desk, skirt up to her waist, heels on, her shirt and blazer on the ground. He's fully clothed, with only his pants unbuttoned.

The book of the Shadow Realm sits on the table, open, and Valin reads the pages at the same time as thrusting into her.

He pounds into her relentlessly, and in my statue-like state, I struggle to move my feet in the opposite direction. She whimpers, and he goes faster, closing the book and throwing his head back on a strangled groan.

It's not until he pulls the person up by the hair that I eventually take a step back, seeing his canines lengthen into fangs. And when he sinks them into her throat, and she moans in pleasure, I spin on my heels and run from the library.

I don't stop until I reach my room, locking the door and hiding under my duvet until I somehow fall asleep.

The same dream comes to me. Fire. Screams. Begging. A flash, and I'm in a diner with a handsome man asking me for waffles.

I wake up in a puddle of sweat and confusion an hour before my class starts.

Within that hour, Dane disregards me four times. I try to approach him in the corridor, but he shrinks into the air and vanishes. I call him, and there's no answer. I'm not sure if he does it intentionally or he just has no idea how to pick up a call.

He straight up ignores me at breakfast when I tell him he's acting like a child, and when I attempt to stop him before he escapes into his changing room, he shrugs out of my grip and slams the door in my face.

And now I need to sit through combat training with Valin telling me to square my stance and to not leave myself open. Dane's attempt at making me his partner—despite everything he's done to avoid me today—went out the window the second Valin grabbed my arm and stared him down, as if to remind him he was a professor and wouldn't be overpowered by a student.

Dane had just laughed, so now I'm stuck between Dane scowling at me every few minutes and flinching as Valin comes up behind me and hisses a "good girl" in my ear while turning my hips to the side.

Dane nearly snaps Orsen in half with a blow to the chest, the sound ricocheting off the cave walls. Even without using his powers, Dane's tight fist is enough to knock Orsen across the arena.

"What the fuck?" he grits, holding his midsection as he tries to get to his feet. "Motherfucker."

"Pay attention," is Dane's response as he walks to him, offering his hand to his friend and yanking him to his feet.

Valin tells everyone to take five minutes since Orsen can barely stand, and I sit down with the twins, a layer of sweat on my skin.

Poppy scowls at her sister. "I told you not to hit my face," she says, crossing her arms. The red mark under her eye is swelling from Mel's right hook. "Careful—I might accidentally sleep with Orsen."

"Go for it. You'll be greatly disappointed."

Orsen throws his hands up. "The fuck is everyone's problem with me?"

Today's lesson is fist fighting, so bare-knuckle boxing essentially. Honestly, every time I punch Valin, my wrists feel close to snapping. My knuckles are red, the skin close to splitting.

I might as well be smashing my fist into a wall.

Once I drink some water, class resumes. I can feel Dane's eyes on me, but I ignore him, like he's been doing to me all day, giving Valin all my attention as he yells at me to guard myself.

I try to go for him, but he slaps me. Actually slaps my cheek. I grit my teeth, glaring. Remembering the way he touched me in my bedroom and nearly made me fail the entire academy, I throw my fist and catch him square in the jaw as hard as I can.

The searing burn across my knuckles comes first, and I silently scream as I cup my hand to my chest. He chuckles, pats my shoulder, and tells the class to get back into their stances.

Valin stands in front of me, looking from me to Dane then back to me. "I would like to warn you about Dane again, but I don't think you'll listen."

I scoff. "After the way you nearly ruined my chance of leaving here? Keep your advice to yourself."

His jaw hardens. "I'm a professor here."

"Congratulations."

My back hits the ground with force as Valin flips me, and all the air whooshes out of my lungs, my vision blurring. I gasp, gripping his wrist as he holds me in place by the throat.

He stares down at me. "Your tongue will get you into bad situations, Miss Winters. I highly recommend you use it wisely."

The insinuation isn't lost on me. Neither is the way his eyes dart down to my mouth, to my heaving chest and parted legs beneath him.

An immense wave of rage washes over me, so much anger that I'm not sure how to contain it. Fire. Rage. Pain. I picture Valin in flames and screaming, but in reality, he's looking down on me like everyone else in this school.

Orsen yells, telling Dane to stop being so brutal.

Valin's eyes are red, like the blood he drank from that student last night, trying to break me. If I was an immortal with powers, I'd snap him in half.

The hold on my throat goes from tight and gripping to gentle, and he caresses my pulse with a look of desire in his eyes. It feels wrong, so I shove his chest. "Get off me."

He lets me up, chuckling to himself and giving Dane a raised brow.

"Now, everyone. We shall begin weaponry. Who here knows how to wield a sword?"

Orsen shakily lifts his hand, wincing still. "Question."

"What?" Valin snaps.

"Do humans use swords?"

A few students look at me, and I cross my arms. "Not really. They did hundreds of years ago before guns were a thing."

"Can you wield a sword, little Seraphine?"

I shake my head at Valin. "No."

"Great. Everyone get back into your pairs."

As I fix myself, the twins giving me a concerned look, I glance over to Dane. He's glaring at Valin. The professor shows a student from a different class how to hold a sword properly before he comes over to me.

The hatred there, in his eyes, isn't about Valin being in my room or the way he shows me how to hold the handle of the small sword. Something happened between them, and Dane despises Valin for it. My nosey self wants to know what that is.

An hour later, Orsen can barely hold himself up without begging for mercy, and Dane is standing unbothered and unscathed with the blade of his sword resting on his shoulder. The twins are limping, but surprisingly, I feel fine. Looking around, I see some students are bleeding.

I grimace at the slash down Orsen's arm as he holds it to his chest.

Despite this being about human combat, no one understands that we don't have powers, or run around our realm with swords longer than our limbs.

"May I speak with you after class?" Valin says to me, taking my arm so he can pull me aside. "In private?"

"You may not."

"You might not think so, but I'm trying to help you." His eyes flicker to Dane. "There are some people in this academy who cannot be trusted. People who keep secrets and lie."

I look at the way he's gripping my arm. "Remove your hold on me, Professor, before I report you."

I feel penetrating eyes on me as I shrug out of Valin's grip and catch up to my friends, all three of us stepping over Orsen.

Dane just surrounded him with what I can only assume are bats and dropped him on his head.

For no reason.

Orsen is strong—he has his own shelf in the history section and apparently battled regularly in his realm. But up against Dane? He's as good as dust.

That shouldn't make me feel things.

I watch as Dane gathers a black mass in his hand and grabs a fistful of Orsen's hair.

"Fine! I give up! Fucking stop," Orsen yells. He lifts a hand to try to block whatever his friend throws at him, desperate for it to end. "If you hit me again, I'll never show you how to send a message again."

I try not to laugh, but my body shakes, and the sound escapes from my lips. It catches Dane's attention, and his head snaps up so he can glare at me. Anytime he's actually deigned to reply to my messages, it's taken hours, and his response is usually one word and pointless. He still struggles on how the keyboard works, has no idea how to take a picture, and keeps failing the mortal quizzes in class.

"As much as Orsen knows how to fuck, seeing him begging for mercy is a little nauseating," Mel says.

"Um, hi? I can hear you?" Orsen shakes his head. "This entire day is a nightmare."

His tall friend doesn't even help him up. Dane throws his arm out to the side, and the mass that was building in his palm fires into the arena wall. He turns his back to me and the twins, and cracks his neck to each side as he whips his top off and wipes his face with it.

I gulp, gawking at his impressive back muscles covered in ink. Openly watching him as he tosses his top and says something to one of the girls, and she blushes.

Blushes.

What did he say?

My hands fist at my sides.

Naturally everyone will find him hot. With the muscles and sweat and wet hair, it's hard not to find him immensely attractive. I glance around the arena, and, of course, everyone's looking at him.

But Valin is watching me, a warning in his eyes about the dark prince. I give him my own look that says to stay out of my way, then I glance over to see Dane heading to destroy Orsen again. He swears to himself and braces for impact.

His silence is annoying me.

Our deadline is tomorrow, and I need to somehow kiss him three more times. But he can't even look at me.

What's the deal if I'm not a human though? Why does it annoy him so much to think I'm not? It changes nothing. We still need to do these assignments, and when we both get off this island, we'll be going our separate ways.

We'll never see each other again.

Although I do think they'll make a documentary about him. He's going to try for world domination, and someone's going to wrap him up and label him as a crazy person. For either trying to summon shadows when his card is declined, or for seeing a cat for the first time and attempting to strangle it.

Knowing Dane, neither are unlikely.

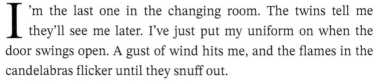

15

I'm the last one in the changing room. The twins tell me they'll see me later. I've just put my uniform on when the door swings open. A gust of wind hits me, and the flames in the candelabras flicker until they snuff out.

I sigh as I'm drenched in darkness.

If I had power, and said power was fire, I'd burn him to a crisp. Instead, I huff and say, "I already said I don't want to speak with you, Valin."

"And it'll stay that way, mortal."

I freeze. Heavy steps echo, and a wave of excitement comes over me at the sound of his deep, threatening voice.

My skin tingles at the tone. The possessiveness of it. I swallow the tension down and pull my bag up my shoulder. "What's with the dramatic entrance?"

Footsteps, and the air around me chills. I should shiver or rub my arms, but I stare blankly at the outline of Dane in the void of the room.

His head tilts. "I want to know who you are."

I groan. "Someone who wants off this island. Are you going to stop acting like an idiot now?"

"Stop trying to insult me with your immature vocabulary."

Dane comes into view in the form of a black mass. A true shadow in the darkness. Where he belongs. Where he thrives and rules and is the most powerful. He reaches out to touch my cheek, but something changes in the atmosphere—the excitement drains, replaced with an unsure, violent feeling.

He grabs my throat, pushing me into the wall instead. "Who are you?"

My satchel falls to the ground. Stuck between two immovable objects, I'm not sure which one I want to press myself into. Away from Dane and into the brick wall, or into Dane, somewhere I feel drawn to, like we're two magnets fighting an unbearable force, and the only way I'll ever feel happy again is to be joined to him.

I dismiss that thought. It must be the assignments. The professor must've put some sort of magic in them to make it easier for us to stomach each other's presence.

I'll tell myself that, because there is no chance in hell Dane is holding me by the throat and I'm liking it. It's a firm hold, but not anywhere near enough to cut off the air supply to my lungs or to mark me. He's keeping me in place.

For what reason, I don't know.

I never know with him.

"Tell me the fucking truth," he says lowly when I don't respond. "Who are you?"

The need to rub my thighs together is sudden, and I almost do. A heat claws at me, building at the base of my spine. It's as if my soul is getting excited by his closeness.

Stupid soul.

"Speak," he orders, his eyes flashing silver. "Think. Think about who and what you are."

"I'm Seraphine," I say, breathing the two words out. I pull my bottom lip between my teeth, and his gaze drops to my mouth before moving slowly back up to my eyes. "Regardless of who I am, it makes no difference to you. We're paired up for classes. That's all."

He ignores everything I just said. "You're branded." His fingers curl around my nape, where the tattoo sits. "You shouldn't have this. Tell me, or I'll force the answer out of you."

My clit pulses. "You can try, but you'll get nothing out of me." The tone I normally use with him is gone. Breathlessly, I manage, "Relax. I'll get laser removal treatment."

His hand slides to the front of my neck, and his thumb presses into my pounding pulse. "My father was the fucking king of our world before he died and knew everything. So why is it, mortal, that he has no answers about you? Why is it that a human walks into our academy and ends up branded by a realm that no longer exists?"

Don't kiss her. She's not real.

His voice is in my head, and I play dumb.

I shrug. "Let me know when you find out."

His jaw tenses as he glares. The harsh lines of his facial structure are sharp and symmetrical, and I want to feel the arch of his cheekbone under my fingertips. But, instead, I glare back at him. "Or go ask your mother. I'm sure she'll have more than enough answers. She is, after all, the one responsible for me being here."

"I'm not speaking to anyone about this until I find out the truth." He slides his hand up and captures my jaw. "We have sixteen hours left before our assignment is due and class is done for the day."

"I told you the truth, now are you going to let me go? You're boring me."

His eye twitches. "I do not bore you."

I raise a brow in response. This shadow prince is holding me by the jaw and against a wall, in a room on our own, and I'm giving him an attitude. I must have a death wish.

"Do you forget I can read you so easily? I can hear your pulse racing. It's like a fucking drum in my ears." Dane steps into me, chest to chest, and I have to crane my neck back to look at him. "I don't bore you. I awaken something in you that you can't control. I can see your eyes dilating." He inhales deeply, and his eyes close momentarily. "Fuck, the smell of your arousal drives me insane." He brings my mouth to his and slips his tongue past my lips as I gasp. Something explodes in my head, and he pulls his face away. "I can taste it too."

I swallow, my toes curling into the soles of my heels. "You're just rhyming off the senses."

He hums, placing his free hand on the wall beside my head, still keeping my jaw in his grip. "Then there's just one more."

A presence appears behind my knees, and I flinch at the contact of his power wrapping around my legs. I don't want to look down because breaking eye contact with him seems to be the last thing I want to do. What I can only assume are his shadows slowly crawl up my legs, stopping at the apex of my thighs. They coil tight, and I bite my bottom lip at the sensation.

"So warm and soft, little mortal. If I touch you here..." I let out a whimper as something strokes between my legs, and everything throbs. "Will you be wet?"

"No," I lie, desperate for him to do it again, but instead, the shadows disappear from around my thighs, wrapping around my wrists and pinning me to the wall.

Dane crashes his mouth down on mine in a punishing kiss, slipping his hand into my hair and tugging. His tongue pushes through my lips, and I'm crushed against the wall by his body. His fingers dig into my scalp, his teeth grazing my bottom lip before sucking on it.

It lasts forty-five seconds before he pulls his mouth away and starts kissing my neck. He nips the area beneath my ear, and I hiss, needing more. He licks and sucks, branding me like the tattoo etched into my skin.

"Dane..." I gasp as his hand leaves the wall beside my face

and pulls my shirt open in one movement, the buttons flying across the floor.

My head drops back as he keeps trailing his lips down to my collarbone, stopping just above my bra.

The shadows unravel from my wrists. My hands find their place in his unruly hair, and I'm unsure if I want to drag his mouth back to mine or tighten my grip and wait for him to pull my bra down. My nipples harden, and I want his tongue to swirl around them, to suck each one into his mouth.

"This doesn't count," I manage to say. "The kisses need to be sixty seconds each for the—"

His tongue glides over the top of my breast, and my thighs slam together, a moan on my lips.

Dane comes back up and kisses me again, and I melt into it. A rush of desire so thick I can't breathe infiltrates every part of me. I want him. I want him to lift me up and press every inch of himself against me.

As if hearing my inner thoughts—which he probably has— he captures the back of my thighs and lifts me into him, giving me enough stability to wrap my arms around his neck and kiss him harder. Another kiss done. Two left.

My back presses to the wall, and Dane rips his mouth away. "Tell me who you are."

"I'm Seraph—"

His mouth shuts me up. His tongue slips into my mouth once more, both of our heads tilting to deepen the kiss.

I can feel his heart racing against my chest, and as his hands roam my body, I arch into him, needing so much more.

A minute passes, and he pulls away again. "That's four. One more, mortal."

I gasp as he thrusts forward, his solid cock rubbing against my wet pussy. He bites my jaw, nipping down the side and sucking my throat so hard, I pulse between my legs and tighten them around him.

"Come to my room tonight," he says as he lets me go, and I nearly tumble to the floor. I catch myself, breathless, my lips raw. "We'll get it over with."

I lean against the wall and close my shirt, my obvious arousal vanishing like his shadows. "We aren't allowed on your side of the castle, dickhead. It's prohibited."

Dane steps into me again, and I've never suffered so much whiplash in my life. He digs his thumb under my chin and tilts my head back. "Come to my fucking room. Understand?"

I smack his hand away. "Just kiss me one last time now."

There's a challenge in my tone, annoyance, and for some reason, I hate how much a part of me wants him to kiss me again. It's like a visceral need to feel his lips on mine, to suck on his tongue and have his hands roam my body.

Dane's eyes darken. "You have to try to control your thoughts around me. I might get the wrong idea. Desperate for task four? Desperate to have my fingers inside you?"

I stare at him, unable to look away. My skirt is bunched up at my hips, my underwear on display. I'm panting, and all I can think about is having him all over me.

"I might think you actually want me to finger-fuck you."

I attempt to keep every image in my mind at bay.

Without waiting for me to say anything, he leans forward. His harsh breaths are on my lips, his pupils dilated so much I can barely see the silver wanting to light up the entire changing room.

"Tell me I'm wrong, human."

I shake my head. "This will be done if you just kiss me again. It's not a big deal. People kiss all the time. You're honestly so dramatic."

Apparently, Dane doesn't like what I just said. His jaw strains, and his eyes flash with annoyance.

I stay silent. Waiting. Needy and wet and unable to concentrate on anything but his mouth, his cock straining in his pants, his hands. I want his hands on my naked body.

If I kiss her again, it will be done, I hear his thoughts, but I don't make it obvious. *I'm not ready for this to be done.*

He keeps staring at my mouth. "I can feel how much you want me." As he runs his thumb across my swollen lips, bringing the bottom one down until it snaps back into place, he smirks. "My room at midnight."

Stepping away from me, he waves his hand, and my shirt repairs, my skirt lowering to its proper position on my thighs. "And stay away from Valin. He's looking to claim you, and I don't share."

16

The twins thankfully join me on a late-night walk, since the rain is off and the wind is calm, giving the surroundings a dark aesthetic and ethereal feeling. It takes us just under half an hour to walk from the castle to the stone beach, before stopping to appreciate the way the still waters reflect the moonlight.

There's a forcefield stopping us from going further, a magical block to keep everyone on the island, but it's invisible. I place my hand close to the perimeter, and a buzz shoots through my palm, like little electric shocks. The scenery ripples before us and only goes back to normal when I pull my hand away.

It's just after nine, and I only know that because the twins tell me. I seem to be the only person who doesn't know how to tell the time without having a watch or a clock.

A light breeze whooshes my hair into my face, and I tuck it behind my ears. "Not gonna lie, as much as I enjoy spending time with you two, I can't wait to get home and lie in my own bed for hours while reading a book."

"Was that your life before?" Mel asks, all three of us looking out into the vast ocean. "Laying in bed and reading?"

"No," I reply. "It was a little more exciting than that. I had a job, people I got drunk with, and someone who was a friend, yet we slept together. No emotions involved. Just fun. A quickie."

Poppy looks at me then her sister. "A quickie? Is that not what Orsen asked you for last night, Mel? What does that mean?"

"Fast and extremely unreliable sex," she replies while I giggle. "If you haven't noticed, Orsen is very outspoken."

"I didn't notice at all," I say as Poppy adds, "Nope. He's very guarded. You never know what he's thinking."

Mel narrows her eyes at our sarcasm. "Fuck you both. I like that he's forward."

"Well I'm just glad he's not chasing after you with crude sexual remarks anymore, and you're finally giving him the time of day." Poppy takes a deep breath. "Me, on the other hand, I'm a little afraid."

I throw a rock through the barrier and into the water. "Of what?"

"I think Brandt might stop seeing me after all of the assignments are completed. I like having him around just now. He makes me feel happy."

Her sister huffs. "He hasn't given you any indication that he's going to drop you. You're being paranoid."

Poppy stamps her foot. "But he also hasn't given me any reassurance! What if he's just acting like Dane?"

I manage to skip a flat stone three times, but instead of celebrating like I usually would, I turn to Poppy. "What do you mean by that?"

"Well..." She rubs her arm and looks down at her sister. "I heard him talking to Orsen after class today, and he said you disgusted him, and he couldn't wait for the assignments to be over, so he'd be done with you."

Mel sighs. "That isn't how he worded it."

"Yes it was!" Poppy retorts. "Orsen saw him going into the changing rooms after everyone except Sera left. He teased him when he came out, but Dane made it clear where he stood with it all. He hates Sera and her entire species, which is fine, because she hates him too." She looks at me. "Right?"

"Right," I force out. "He said he was disgusted by me?"

I shouldn't care, but a pang of hurt stabs me in the chest. He's always been this way with me, but to know he's still saying these things while trying to order me not to speak with Valin, approaching me and kissing me in ways that don't count towards the assignment... He really can't wait to be done with me?

"Yep," the twins say in unison. But Poppy obliviously continues to add to the burn. "He said he can't wait to get off the island so he can kill you and pretend you never existed."

Mel slaps Poppy's arm hard enough to make her porcelain skin welt. "You're going too far. Can't you see you're upsetting the human?"

I'm not upset, I don't think. The lone tear rolling down my cheek is from the chill—and how tired I am. I wipe it away with my sleeve. "I'm not upset about what he said. He's just brutal sometimes. Ever since I got here, he's done everything to make me feel uncomfortable."

And I've been fighting to prove myself my entire life. As a foster kid, as a new sister and daughter, as a young adult in a homeless shelter trying to find work. I mean, I had to go to extreme lengths of overpaying to get my dog Toodles. Everything has been an endless battle, and I just feel like I need a break.

Living is so tiring sometimes.

"He's a real dick. I know, Sera," Mel says. "I've already offered to kick his ass. Are you finally going to let me?"

I laugh, smiling. The thought of her attacking him makes me giggle. She'd slash his handsome face with her blade-like nails and rip his heart out. "Thanks, but no. I don't think that will stop him. I'll just... endure his moodswings until I can get away from him, I guess."

"Have you started task three yet?" Poppy asks me.

I give a slight nod. "He wants me to go to his room at midnight to finish it."

"Make him come to you," Mel says, getting to her feet. "Dane doesn't call the shots, so don't give in to him. If he's serious about completing each task after what he said about you, then don't put in any effort. Go to your room, lock the door, run a bath, and screw his fucking demands."

"You're sounding very human, Princess Melina."

She rolls her eyes and turns around. "I don't have that title anymore. Mel is my name now."

"Because she killed our father," Poppy reminds me.

"You played a huge part in his demise too, sister."

Poppy giggles, and I grin as we all start walking back to the castle. The two of them put their arms around my shoulders in a supportive hug.

I've never had this before. Always moving around to live in different towns made it hard to have friends. I used to get drunk with my coworkers, but none of them I'd consider my friend. However, as I gossip with the twins and listen to them bicker and threaten to kill each other, I'm glad to have them.

When we graduate and get off this island, I want to keep them in my life. I want them to sleep over at my apartment and binge movies while eating junk food. I want Poppy to read all of my romance books while Mel tries to communicate with my dog by staring at him for hours.

After we return to our rooms, I get ready for bed and pace. Overthink. Listening to Poppy's words but in Dane's voice. The more I think of what he said, the angrier I get. I want to punch something, to shove my fist into a wall so hard the plaster breaks and cracks the skin on my knuckles.

I scream into my pillow, punching it repeatedly with both fists while the shadows on my walls watch. The little girl with a balloon is tugging on a lady's skirt and pointing before the large silhouette ushers them away. The dog is barking, and an old man has his head slanted while he peels what I assume is a piece of fruit.

Everything about today has annoyed me. From me being disgusting, to him cornering me in the changing room and asking me who I really am.

Then his demand to come to his room at midnight.

I don't share.

What a ridiculous thing to say.

First of all, I'm not his. He's also made that abundantly clear to his friends.

Secondly, I don't want to be his. He's Dane Dalton. His mere presence infuriates me. And don't even get me started on the way he speaks to me when his tongue isn't down my throat. God, can he be any more of an ass? *I don't share.*

On top of all that, my tattoo has started burning, and nothing, not even pressing a cold, wet cloth to it, has made any difference.

I pull off my nightdress and throw it at the dresser before marching over and shoving it into a drawer, opening the second one, and pulling out a wool sweater and a pair of shorts.

Finding someone to knit me clothing was a struggle, but one of the professors already had a boxful of items she'd made, and all of them fit me like a glove.

Waving to the shadows, I leave my room and head down to the food court. It's late, but supper is still on until lights out.

> Me: I'm going down for something to eat, if either of you want to join.

I know for a fact the twins will be otherwise occupied, but the offer is there.

After I grab a tray and fill it, I sit down at the furthest away table from everyone else, especially the person who won't stop running around in my mind. I can feel his eyes on me, see him muttering under his breath.

The lonely, disgusting human. The outcast. The odd one out.

Talk about feeling unwanted. Dane sure knows how to make someone feel good. I didn't even expect him to be here, given the late hour.

Despite my aggravation towards him, I can't seem to take my eyes off him while I eat my supper. The piece of toast feels like cardboard—and tastes like it too. But I keep crunching it between my teeth and forcing myself to swallow while I give him the death stare.

He's speaking with Orsen, who holds an ice pack to his face. I'm not an expert lip-reader, but he's complaining about Mel, and how Dane's made him look weak in front of her. Dane, being the supportive friend and good person he is, tells him to get a grip and to stop bleeding on his shoes.

I look away when his eyes find mine.

I sip on my glass of water, sighing as one of the professors announces that all students should be back at their dorm rooms in ten minutes. Lights will be out, and all the teachers will be off duty until the morning. If anyone is caught sneaking out, then they'll be punished and potentially sent to the dungeons.

I've not had a bedtime since I was twelve.

To make my night that little bit more unbearable, Valin sits down in front of me with a tray of food, blocking my view. "Good evening."

I drop my toast onto my tray. "Goodbye."

He chuckles, leaning his elbows on the table. "You have quite the attitude on you for being powerless. Brave, but also stupid."

"What would you prefer I do? Hide from you all and drop to my knees when told to?"

His eyes glint with excitement, and the taste of toast turns sour in my mouth. "Don't put images in my head, little girl."

I screw my face up at his attempt at a pet name, then shove my tray forward and wipe my hands together. "I think I'll be leaving now. I hope you choke on your food."

He blanks out my comment. "I know you saw me in the library. Did you enjoy the view?"

"No. And it's unprofessional to sleep with your students."

"I have no idea what you're talking about," he replies, popping a grape into his mouth. "I'm off duty in..." He thinks for a second. "Four minutes. You evidently have no plans, so why don't you hear me out?"

"See, this is where you're the worst professor ever. You know if I go anywhere near someone I'm not paired up with, I'll fail, yet you still approach me. What's your deal?"

"You're branded," is his reply. "You should know exactly what that means. I just want to explain the consequences—that's all."

I turn away, but his voice stops me. "Is it burning yet?"

My hair flips over my shoulder as my head snaps in his direction. "What?"

He pops another grape into his mouth. "Come see me if you want answers," Valin says, winking. "I'll give you the truth, unlike Dane."

I stare at him in silence then glance up at Dane, who's already giving us all of his attention. His arms are crossed, and he's leaning against the table with his hip. He's trying to listen, his jaw set, his gaze lingering on my face before dropping to Valin, who's still sitting at the table.

I've seen Dane looking angry on numerous occasions, but the way his eyes turn to voids of black, a flash of possession in them, I know this is a side I've never witnessed.

Get the fuck away from him.

Despite him looking like a terrifying demon, I pull my bag up to my shoulder and down my glass of water. *Fuck you, asshole.*

17

At midnight on the dot, I'm doing as Mel said and lounging in the bathtub, soaking in the lavender-scented bubbles with the window open. There's a breeze that has goosebumps on my skin, but despite the slight tingling coldness, it's relaxing. The mix of the rain and wind, the heat from the water, has me in a comfortable daze.

As soon as I got back from the food hall, I found an acceptable outfit that wasn't my uniform. To be fair, the dress is Poppy's, but it's better than a short pleated skirt and a shirt Dane can rip apart without even looking at me. But as soon as I put it on, I decided against going to his room.

A part of me had wanted to, that insidious side of me that wanted his mouth and hands on my body. But the semi-sane part of me had overridden that urge and given me a kick up the ass.

So now, I lie amongst strongly fragranced bubbles and wait. Because Dane, in all his controlling and demanding ways, will be banging on my door by ten minutes past midnight at the latest. He's going to warp his way into my room and speak to me like shit. Then he'll make me feel infinitesimally smaller than everyone else in the academy and call me a weak human, in the same breath as accusing me of being someone else and kissing me.

Makes sense.

I check my phone beside the bathtub. It's four minutes to midnight. I have a message from Mel, a picture of all the cuts covering Orsen's body while she sits on his back. They're both naked. I have no idea if she's aware, but this is not the way humans act. Well, not most humans. They've just had sex, she's torn his back apart, and is sending me the evidence? On a normal person, the gashes from her nails would be life threatening. He should be rushing to the medical wing for stitches.

But he's grinning, puncture holes in his ass cheeks, with his thumb up.

I grimace and shut off my screen, then toss my phone onto the ground. Usually in this situation, I'd be scrolling through social media, watching a few funny cat videos, and talking to my dog, who'd be curled up in a ball on the bathmat. Now all I can do is lie here and listen to the haunted castle walls creak and the drip of each drop of water from the tap.

I sink into the tub until only my face is above the surface. My ears fill with water, and I'm met with silence, the dull thump of my heartbeat, and the warmth cocooning me.

I pretend I'm lying in my bed back home, listening to music, drawing on my sketchpad. I'd be doodling myself, dramatizing my cheekbones and lips like a caricature before drifting off to sleep. Then I'd be getting up to start the day and head to work. I'd serve my usual customers, clean up after them, then come back to the apartment to take Toodles for a walk.

I wouldn't be in any sort of trouble, except financially.

I wonder why everything in my life keeps going wrong. I've always felt out of place, trying to fit in and be the same as everyone around me, yet as soon as I got here, something in me awoke, and the Seraphine who badly wanted to be seen died an instant, painless death.

You're late. The voice is so clear, so deep, I almost gasp. *I don't like to be kept waiting, mortal.*

The water turns cold, and I sit up in a panic, instantly chittering. I go to pull myself out of the tub when a wind gathers around me, the air shifting, and a firm, invisible hand forces me back into the water. Its grip on my shoulder reminds me of the hold Dane's shadow hands had on my thighs after our mortal studies class, when he pinned me to the chair and demanded I leave the island.

The other hand wraps around my ankle, and before I can scream or fight my way out of the restraints of his power, I'm yanked beneath the surface. Ice cold encases me, and I'm dragged further. I go down, down, down into the darkness, until I realize I'm no longer in the bathtub, weeds and aquatic animals rubbing on my skin as I try to swim back up.

I desperately swim to try to break the surface, to reach the canopy of trees in sight.

But something tugs inside me, dizziness strikes, and the world shifts around me. The glow from the moon swirls, the coldness close to giving me hypothermia warms, and I silently scream in the water until I'm back in the bathtub and Dane is yanking me up by the chin and slamming his lips down on mine.

He pulls away just as fast, stepping back as I lie breathlessly confused in the water.

I splash his perfectly pressed suit. "What the hell, Dane?"

"You were late."

I narrow my eyes, keeping my breasts covered in bubbles as Dane stares at me. "So you try to drown me?"

"No. I simply materialized you into the castle's lake, left you for a minute to think about your actions, then brought you back." He leans against the sink, crossing his arms. "I said midnight."

I purse my lips. "I'm trying to take a bath. Get out."

"No." He glances at the discarded dress on the floor, the boots and tights. "We had an arrangement, which you failed to show up for."

"You arranged it in your warped little mind," I reply, swooping more bubbles to my chest to hide my nakedness. "I don't remember agreeing."

"Were you just going to fail task three?"

I shrug one shoulder, and his eye twitches in annoyance. I love pushing his buttons. Not only does it bring me joy to see him pissed off, admittedly, but he's hot when he's mad.

"Stand up and kiss me. We need to finish this before morning."

"I'm in the bath, Dane," I say, pointing out the obvious.

"And?"

"I'm naked!"

"I still don't see the issue. I'm not going to look at you, mortal." He straightens the cuffs of his crisp white shirt. "A body is a body. I already had my arms wrapped around yours to throw you into the lake."

I sigh, slouching into the bath and making the water surge over the lip of the tub and splash his shoes. His eyes lower, and I hope his socks are wet.

"You're doing the whiplash thing again. Are you going to go back to calling me a slut and making my life hell once this task is done?"

"Do you want me to?"

I frown. "Why would I want that?"

"I think you enjoy it." He pushes from the sink, hands fisting in his pockets. "In fact, I know you do. The day we were in mortal studies and I had you pinned to the chair, you were soaked. I could smell it, could fucking feel it on my fingers even though I hadn't touched you."

"If you're only going to state the obvious, you can leave." I roll my eyes. "I'm trying to relax, and you're ruining my mood."

A large hand shoves my head underwater, holding me there

by the hair. *I know you can hear me. Drop the fucking attitude, stand the fuck up, and kiss me like a good little human.*

I struggle against the burn in my lungs. My own worst enemy as I say in my head, *Bite me.*

Dane pulls me up, and as I gasp for air, he shoves his mouth against mine and claims all the oxygen from my lungs in a punishing kiss, sinking his teeth into my bottom lip.

I accidentally moan as he sucks where he just bit me.

Call me masochistic, but my pussy throbs from his rough touch, the way his mouth devours me, how he's holding me up by fisting my hair.

He doesn't kiss me for the full minute—he pulls away, yanks my head back, and sinks his teeth into my throat, then sucks the reddening skin, reaching down to grab me by the waist.

I yelp as he lifts me out of the bathtub and flips me so my legs bracket his sides. Both hands on my hips, he turns us and slams my back into the door just as his mouth crashes down on mine again.

"When I tell you to do something, I expect you to do it," he says, hissing as my nails drag up his nape to his hair. "So when I say to be in my room by midnight..."

I scream as the room warps into a smash of colors swirling around us, until they turn black and my back is pressed to a hard surface in a bedroom I don't recognize.

"You'll be in my room at fucking midnight."

18

When the dizziness from him materializing us into his room subsides, I contemplate real-life murder for the first time ever. There have been multiple moments where I've wanted to hurt Dane, but right now, as he holds me up against his door completely naked, I think I might end his life.

Yet my body sings with the proximity—the closeness, and the way my legs are wrapped around his waist and his hands grip my thighs. My skin tingles with his breath on my neck, and I can't pull my gaze away from his silver eyes as he lifts them to look down at me.

Would it be acceptable for him to be inside me while I slap him?

Among the confusion of building heat and my tightening nipples rubbing against his shirt—as well as wishing I could hex him—I listen to him give a deep chuckle, and then my inner dirty thoughts are incinerated to dust as his lips come down on mine.

The kiss is sudden and catches me off guard, yet I respond the only way I feel is right and melt into it. Dane feasts on my mouth like he hasn't eaten for days, a starved animal ravaging its prey with brutality. He's sucking on my bottom lip and biting while his hands keep me against him. I can hear his thoughts—they run wild between us—and I can barely latch on to one as I kiss him harder.

My fingers capture the curls at his nape in a fierce grip as I yank his head to slant to the side, our tongues moving together for this fifth and last kiss. Tasting and teasing. I can feel him between my legs, my bare and open thighs, and I rub against his very clothed, very muscular body.

I sink my teeth into his bottom lip and tug, making sure it hurts.

He hisses and presses into me harder, the ridges of his cock to my core, and I battle the urge to slip my hand down his chest and rip his pants open, to stroke him until he swells in my hold, to grind against just the head and smear him with my arousal.

Dane groans into my mouth, most likely seeing the image I've made, what a very dark, very irresponsible version of me wants from my enemy.

This is all for the assignment of course.

Then I remember how nasty he is, the way he spoke about me to his friends, how he wants to kill me when we get off the island, and I drag my mouth away from him. He attempts to bury his face against my collarbone, assuming that's what I want, but as he sucks on the flesh there, I pull his hair hard and tug his mouth away from my skin.

"That's... that's enough," I say, panting, still keeping a fist of his hair in my grip. "That's enough."

His eyebrows furrow. "That was only fifty-one seconds."

I gape at him, silent as I inhale through my nose, keeping my lips parted. They're swollen from his mouth on mine. Our gazes are locked, neither of us breaking it.

"Nine seconds more and this could've been done with," he says finally searching my face, my forced blank expression. "Was that intentional?"

"You can read my mind. You tell me."

"That's not how it works," he replies, the silver in his eyes flickering back to his ordinary green.

I flatten my lips and glance away from him, studying our surroundings, pressing my chest into his to hide my breasts. He watches me as my eyes travel around us, to the four-poster bed with red sheets, the perfectly stacked books—probably in a certain order—and a rack of weapons. Some I've never seen before in my life. He has a walk-in closet, most likely full of three-piece suits and shiny shoes, and a cage for all his victims.

My eyes lift back to Dane, and I cover my chest with one arm. "I have no clothes on."

My treacherous pussy pulses as he flexes his fingers. They're still holding me up by my naked thighs, my legs still wrapped around him. He crushes into me, and my core vibrates, throbs, and begs for more. "I know."

I let go of my breasts and grab his chin before he can dip down and look at my body. My other hand grips his shoulder for dear life. "Don't you dare."

"I've kissed you, and I had my arms wrapped around you in the lake while you were in this exact state, remember?"

"This is different." I keep my hold on him. "I don't give you permission to look at me."

Shit. I've read all of this—and her—completely wrong.

The intrusive voice in my head is from Dane, and I frown.

His cocky expression falls, and he lowers me to my feet, setting me safely on the ground. "Very well. I apologize."

Huh? "You... apologize?"

Dane ignores me and keeps his eyes above my head as he waves his hand. One of his white shirts appears, and he slides it up my arms to hide my nakedness. He doesn't glance down as he fastens each button, although my heart accelerates unhealthily when his fingers graze my heated skin. It's long enough to nearly reach my knees, the sleeves like parachutes on me. He rolls up each sleeve to my wrist before finally lowering his gaze to me.

"I would never force myself upon you."

I gulp. "You tried to drown me."

"I wouldn't have let you actually drown. I was teaching you a lesson."

If that's Dane's way of teaching someone a lesson, I fear what would happen when someone actually annoys him. I was late for a kiss and gave him a little attitude for talking crap about me, and he dragged me through a dirty lake and teleported me to the other side of the castle... naked.

He won't last an hour in my world.

"I don't plan on lasting an hour, mortal. It will take me seconds to obliterate your precious world, including you."

I glare at him and slap his arm, but I might as well have slapped a wall. "You're an asshole, do you know that? Take me back to my room."

He laughs with no expression as he backs away from me, loosening his tie, pulling it from his neck, and dropping it on his desk. "Not yet. We have a task to finish. Unless you want to keep stopping it before the minute is up." He pokes the inside of his cheek with his tongue to stifle whatever hilarious point he's trying to make. "Be my guest. I have nowhere to be."

"For someone who can't stand me and finds me disgusting, you have no issues jamming your tongue down my throat."

He falters in his cocky charade for a second but then shrugs. "What can I say? I want to pass the assignment."

I shake my head and walk into the middle of the room, trying not to make it obvious I'm enchanted by it. One may say that he sleeps like royalty, but then again, he is the Prince of Darkness and the heir to the Shadow Realm. It's no wonder the place is perfect.

Dane watches me as I explore, running my fingers over the dark oak of the footboard of his bed, the candle holder made of pure gold, and the book spines, their titles in an unknown language. "Can I ask you something?"

He leans back on the desk, crossing his ankles and arms. "If I say no, will you still ask me?"

"Yes."

He fights a smirk, eyes glued to me. "Go on."

"And I want the truth." He raises a brow in response, so I keep going. "Why am I here?"

Silence—deafening silence as Dane finally breaks eye contact and looks to the floor. "I have no idea. That's why I asked you before."

"Your mother hasn't once mentioned why?"

He turns away from me, hands in his pockets as he pretends to look at the art on his wall. It's a portrait of an angel surrounded by black mist, with flames and lightning and blood. "She went to extreme lengths to find you. That's all I know."

"Did she say why it was important for us to stay paired?"

He shakes his head, but his shoulder tense a little. "No."

Too soon. It's too soon.

"What's too soon?"

He spins to scowl at me. "What?"

"You said it's too soon. What is? And why can I hear your thoughts when I'm human? Does it have something to do with the tattoos?"

"Let's just get this final kiss out of the way," he says, changing the subject. "Then we never have to do it again. Don't stop us before one minute or I'll get the wrong idea."

I scoff. If he thinks this conversation is done, he's greatly mistaken.

He quirks a brow, as if to challenge me on what he said.

"It's ridiculous that you brought me all the way over here when you could have ended it when you bombarded me in my bathroom. You kissed me then, and in the changing rooms after class. We could have finished up this task on several occasions.

Instead, you dunked my head into my bath, kissed me, and then kidnapped me."

"You were being annoying."

"Do you usually kiss people who annoy and disgust you?"

He fists both hands. "It might come as a shock to you, but kissing isn't something I do. In my realm, it was viewed as an act of pure romance and love, so forgive me if the thought of pressing my mouth to yours violates everything I believe in."

"That explains the hard-ons you keep getting then. You've never been in that position, so you have no idea how to control yourself."

His jaw strains as he clenches his teeth. "I've been in that position plenty of times."

"You've been in love?"

His eyes light up with something unforgivable. "Yes. Countless times."

I look intently at him, unsure how to approach the next question but asking it anyway in a whispered-out voice. "How many times have you fallen in love?"

"Fifty-seven. Are you done with your questions? Or do you plan on telling me about your love life too?"

Fifty-seven times? He must be as old as Hell itself. Why does he look my age?

"Do you have children then?"

Dane's eyes grow dark, and I feel like I hit a no-go zone. "Don't ask me things like that unless you're willing to tell me your history."

"I have no history. I've never been in love. And you're a lot older than me if you've been in love fifty-seven times. I kind of feel weird kissing you now. I'm not into age gaps."

"You say you've never been in love, yet you have a boyfriend. You said so yourself a few weeks ago. Is he aware of your infidelity?"

I tip my chin. "He's not my boyfriend. I was messing around with him. His name is Grayson, and he's nice, unlike you."

The corners of his eyes crease. "Messing around?"

"Sleeping with him," I clarify. "Anything else you need to know about my private life?"

Dane stiffens, his hands fisting. "Do you care for him?"

"As a friend."

I feel the slight relief coming from him. It confuses me enough to relax my shoulders, until he speaks again.

He snorts at himself. "I expect nothing less from you. Commitment issues. Shock."

Maybe I can run to the bench full of weapons and cut his head off with an ax. Would it grow back, or would he just be headless and still an asshole?

Dane's sour mood shifts as quickly as it appeared, and he tries not to laugh. "Sometimes hearing your thoughts can be entertaining. You're strange, mortal. Very strange."

"Stay out of my head."

"Stop letting me in then," he says, crossing his ankles as he leans against his desk again. "Most of the time, it just happens, but then when you're mad, your thoughts run wild. I find it amusing, listening to all the ways you'd like to hurt me." He rubs the back of his head, and my eyes are drawn to the stretching of his large bicep. "Then there are the dirty thoughts."

"Stop it."

He doesn't stop. "I'm a little surprised how many times an image of me bending you over has flashed across my mind while doing schoolwork. Tell me, human, is that what you want? For me to rip that shirt off your dying body, bend you over this desk, and fuck you until your pussy is raw?"

"Funny. But if I'm not mistaken, those images are coming from you. I prefer to be on top."

Dane falls into silence, staring at me with his jaw tensing once more. It's so easy to get under his skin. He looks like he wants to maul me again, not breaking his glare while I wait for him to fight back. He doesn't, and it's like the atmosphere is slowly altering, as if the room is shrinking to push us together. I don't move, but my body begs my feet to go forward, to press my half-naked body to his and order him to slide his hand up my thigh and thrust his fingers deep within me.

Instead of pleading with him to do just that, I scoff. "I wouldn't allow that to happen anyway. I have self-respect, and when someone calls me disgusting, the last thing I'm going to do is bend over a desk for them."

I sit down on the edge of his bed, keeping my legs closed tightly, not only to create an ounce of friction, and to hide me, but to make sure he can't see how slick my thighs are with my own arousal at the thought of having him touch me so intimately.

Dane gives me a death stare before he straightens, pulls off his belt with terrifying slowness, and tosses it. The strap of leather floats into his walk-in closet. He begins unfastening his shirt buttons, starting from the top. "You talk too much."

"If you're not going to get this over with, I'm leaving," I say, hurrying to my feet and reaching for the door handle.

Dane uses his power to appear beside me, his towering height throwing a shadow of black over me, his chest and the ink littering his skin on show. He covers my hand, dwarfing it, and I throw my own death stare at him. "Let go."

"You aren't going out there dressed like that. You'll be eaten alive."

I try to pull the handle, but he's too strong. "I'll take my chances."

"Why are you being so difficult?"

I laugh. Really laugh. "Are you joking?"

"Do I appear to be amused by any of this?"

"No. All you seem to be doing is getting undressed."

He blinks. I don't—I keep staring at him, waiting for a reply.

"Nothing to say?" I push.

"We need to finish task three," is all he says, his hand still over mine.

"And you need to take me back to my room," I retort. "I'm done with this stupid assignment."

His eyes narrow a fraction as he steps forward, and we're back at square one, with him pressing me to the door. When my heart rate spikes, he notices and quickly backs away. "You're not done with the tasks."

The door is locked when I try again. I try more than once then give up and beat the wood with my fists, turning to lean my back to it, catching my breath. "I hate you."

"Is that why you're wet?"

My heart stops. My eyes widen, and my cheeks are probably a bright shade of red. "Excuse me?"

"I'm an immortal with heightened senses, plus I can feel everything you're feeling right now. Lust and desire are practically radiating from you."

"Go fuck yourself, Dane."

He studies his cufflinks with fascination as he unhooks them. "No. That doesn't seem enjoyable at all."

"Unlock the door."

"No. You have no idea what lurks out there."

I groan and turn to him, barging my shoulder into his chest as I make my way to the other side of his gigantic room. "Then I'll jump out of the window."

"We're at the top of a tower."

I throw my arms up. "Great! Maybe the fall will put all of this to an end."

He stops me, grabbing my wrist before I can even get close. "Stop acting like a brat."

"Stop acting like you own me," I snap, snatching myself away from his grip and putting distance between us. "Whether you like it or not, I'm leaving this room."

He pinches the bridge of his nose. "You're intolerable."

"And you're annoying!" My insults need a boost. "I wish I was partnered up with someone else."

"The feeling is fucking mutual." He's eliminating the distance between us. "If you can't handle this, how are you going to handle the rest of the tasks?"

"I can handle them just fine. What I don't appreciate is you not even giving me a chance to get dressed! You're bossy and rude and controlling!"

"I gave you my shirt."

I sneer. "How caring of you."

"Are you done?"

"Are you?" I retort.

He grabs the collar of the shirt I'm wearing and yanks me to him. My perfidious hormones light up like sparklers. "With you?" Dane's eyes burn into my soul. "No. Not even close."

"Because of the assignments."

Without responding, he turns us, pressing the bottom of my back to his desk. I grip the edge, white-knuckled, waiting for his next move. What will it be? Another dip in the lake? A head dunk in the bathtub? Calling me names, or maybe he'll go one step further and actually cause me some sort of pain?

He can see it in my eyes—my unsureness of his movements, of the way he holds the material of the collar in his fist, of the rigidity of his jaw and every muscle while he lifts me onto the hard surface.

Dane confuses me. How he blows hot and cold, the soft way he caressed my skin as he tasted my mouth and then claimed me as his own—by saying he doesn't share—yet proclaiming behind my back that I'm disgusting.

A body is a body, he said earlier.

Fine. Then that's all he is to me. He's nothing but an assignment.

Before he can take control of our last kiss, I snatch his jaw and pull his mouth to mine. He doesn't stop me or do anything but kiss me back with equal measure. My legs fall open on instinct, and as Dane settles between them, I use my free hand to tug down the shirt to cover myself while I part my lips and let his tongue slip against my own.

Something snaps between us, like the first time we kissed, and the world blew up around us. A crack in the island. A wave high enough to swallow the entire castle in seconds. It's like a stress ball exploding, a group of fireworks lighting up the dark sky while a crowd cheers, and a rush of adrenaline spikes in my veins.

I can sense it all through him too, amplifying the exhilarated, powerful feeling. It bounces from me, to him, then back to me, again and again and again. I almost moan from the intensity. My hand slips into his hair, bringing him even closer to me, and the deep groan he releases vibrates through my entire being.

All previous thoughts of protecting my self-respect are slowly simmering away, but I clutch at them fiercely, the same way my other hand shoots up and tangles in his hair, pulling his mouth from mine.

I whisper against his lips, "I don't like you. In fact, I hate you the most out of all the immortal creatures in this school."

"Is that why you're enjoying kissing me so much? You intentionally stopped us again before the full minute again, didn't you?" he asks, snatching my bottom lip between his teeth. "My shadows are hiding from you." His palms slide under the shirt concealing my body, stopping at my hips. "They quiver when you're around, and nothing scares them. They think you're sadistic and evil, and that you're going to be my end. If that's the case, and you're really here to kill me, then you might as well get full use of me, am I right?"

I swallow, the coiling sensation at the base of my spine like an enraged snake, trying to slither into my veins with a hiss of its tongue. A veil of darkness creeps under his door, through his windows, gathering around his shoes. "I'm not here to kill you."

"But you would like to kill me..."

"Sometimes."

He smirks. "Do I have permission to do this...?" He lifts his hand from my hip, taking the side of my face in his palm. He strokes my cheek with his thumb, a lot more intimate than he probably planned. Slowly, so slowly that goosebumps take over, Dane curls his fingers at the nape of my neck. The other hand squeezes my hip, caressing the naked skin there. "To hold you like this?"

Somehow, through the nerve endings exploding, I manage, "Do you want permission?"

"Yes." *Fuck, yes, I need your permission. I'll always need your permission.* "But only if you want to give it."

I let go of his shoulders and press my hands to his chest, where his shirt has unfastened, so his naked skin is on display. His heart rattles against my hand, and a wave of nerves smashes into me. His nerves. "One last kiss?"

Dane doesn't blink as he searches my face. "If that's what you want."

My palms slide down to unbutton the rest of his shirt, his pupils dilating in the middle of the sharp silver. His breaths are labored as I untuck his shirt from his pants to get the last two buttons, and he adjusts his grip on me so I can slide his sleeves off before placing his hands back on my body.

"Once this task is done, I want to know more about the Shadow Realm."

He licks his lips, pulling me to the edge of the desk, his hardening cock pressing against my inner thigh. His shirt bunches at my hips, and I'm fully aware that if he looks down past my face, there's a chance he might see me. It scares me more that I don't care. "Fine."

"Fine."

Dane, using his grip on my nape, pulls my mouth to his once more and doesn't wait around to slip his tongue past my lips. I don't pay attention to the shadows appearing, though I'm fully aware they've returned, maybe to see if I'm going to slay their master. To see if my sadistic and evil ways will result in me slitting open Dane's throat and watching him bleed over my naked body.

Instead, I kiss him with a hit of desire, tilting my head for better access and to feel the softness of his lips more. He tastes like the dark he weeps in, frantic as he sucks on my tongue and takes my bottom lip between his, then the top one, pulling back to look at me when we pass the sixty-second mark. Only we go in for another kiss as I let out a pleading moan.

My lips move with his as he slowly unbuttons the shirt with one hand, keeping the other firmly on my neck to control each thrust of my tongue and the angle he kisses me. I whimper as he abandons the buttons halfway and palms my breast, pushing me back on the desk as he rolls my tightening nipple between his thumb and finger.

He tries to remove his hold on my nape, but I scream.

Something violent and painful ricochets all over me as the room flashes with light, and it feels like my brain is on fire, like my skin is splitting as I gasp into Dane's mouth. He hisses and manages to yank himself away completely.

"Fuck!" he yells, gritting his teeth and clutching his wrist "What the fuck?"

Speechless, I grab the back of my neck and grit my teeth through the pain, unsure why it's burning and throbbing—far more intensely than before. I look down to see his palm is completely skinned, the flesh bubbling as if he dipped it in acid. I wince and lean forward when another unbearable wave hits me, my spine twisting in agony.

Dane catches me before I hit the ground, and as he moves my

hair from my neck, his eyes go wider than I've ever seen them. "Shit."

"What is it?" I ask, breathless, wincing again as another shock rushes through me like haunting wildfire. He looks genuinely concerned. "Dane? Oh God. Please. Make it stop—it hurts."

Our surroundings grow extremely cold, and I can see my breath in puffs, all the candles snuffing out. A low hum reverberates around us as Dane looks up before swearing to himself.

"Your tattoo. It has tendrils coming from it, like black ink in your veins." He lifts me into his arms, waving his damaged hand, and a pair of extremely human shorts appear on me. "I need to get you back to your room."

His room warps into nothing then as Dane's shadows rally around us, and I hear whispers that make no sense, about kings and queens and wars and revenge.

Before my mind closes off and the burning at my nape stops, the last thing I hear is Dane muttering in a different language.

But for some reason, my mind translates each word.

Why the fuck is this happening so soon? We should have more time.

19

I t burns.

    My skin hardens before cracking and bleeding, peeling away with the blazing heat, the inferno lashing angrily around me. Flesh slides from my bones as I push through the flames, trying to see, trying to find him. My bare feet stick to the rug, melting from the fire spreading all over my house. A window downstairs smashes. Something pops. An alarm bellows. I try to scream, to yell out his name, but my lips are sealed.

    As I reach up to try to pry them apart, I stare at my hands, the knuckles and veins and nerves bubbling like acid. My clothes are nonexistent, like the family I once knew, all dead as their lives are dragged from their bodies.

    A door is thrown open, and I plummet into a world I shouldn't know. A darkness so deep I can neither see nor focus on it as vines encase me in a tomb.

    Death to her.

    Death to all.

    Death to her.

    Death to all.

    "Death to her! Death to all!" The echoing voices ricochet

around in the shadows. Howls and laughter. Screams and cheers as blue flames erupt around me once more. "Death. To. Her!"

No. Please stop, *I say in my head, begging the lost souls to stop this, to release their curse and take me back to my family.*

The astral projection keeps forcing me from the tomb to a cliff to a tower, stopping on a platform surrounded by crowds with their hoods up and faces blurred out.

My lungs are filling with smoke, my vision slowly going. A faint light shines before me, but as I try to reach for it, excruciating pain blasts through my withering body, and I scream as loud as humanly possible, ripping my lips apart.

"Look at me," a familiar voice says from behind me as no more sound emanates from my throat. I try to turn, to look at the person over my shoulder, but I'm frozen in place as flames climb up my legs. "Look at me."

The person's tone changes to anger, and frustration, as if I'm a pesky child behaving badly. As if there isn't a full riot trying to kill me.

I turn and run—or think I do. The world morphs into a new one, and I'm standing by a lake, a kingdom full of love and laughter behind me, and a tall, strong presence to my right.

Then my throat closes up, and my skin splits, blood draining out of my neck as if I've been stabbed.

A little girl appears before me, holding her hand out for me to take. She has silver eyes, a sweet smile, and the whitest of white hair that reaches her waist.

Large, firm hands snatch my shoulders from behind and shake me hard. Hard enough that my spine nearly snaps. Yet no pain follows, even with the rising panic of dying. I'm a vessel with no nerve endings, no hope or life or future as my lungs no longer burn, and the blood no longer puddles at my feet.

The little girl vanishes with a puff of black smoke, and the sky lights up red, an inferno blazing through it.

The person shakes me again, again, and finally manages to

turn me to look at them just as a blinding light flashes, an explosion so extreme my heart restarts, and I'm pulled from my nightmare.

I gasp and throw myself into a sitting position, sweat dripping down my face and back, my lungs heaving in as much air as possible. My chest is tight, my hair sticking to my neck.

These dreams are becoming more insane.

My hands are fine. They look fine, and I have clothes on.

I stare at the shirt I'm still wearing, the top two buttons unfastened. The cotton shorts on my bottom half are far too big, sliding down my hips. Strange. Everyone in the castle dresses like they should be in a castle, even the ones trying out a new style for fitting in with humans.

Why am I wearing gray cotton shorts I'd usually see in my world and a white dress shirt far too big for me?

My lips feel swollen as I touch them with my fingertips, and everything from last night comes back to me. Hands all over my body, his mouth on mine, sucking his tongue and tasting every drop of sin, feeling him between my legs as he palms my breast on his oak desk.

A desirable sensation passes through me, my cheeks heating. I need more. Want more. The feeling is intense, as if my body can sense him close to me and is seeking him out. Hunting. Obsessing over his touch.

With the lingering scent of fire and death is a mix of everything Dane Dalton.

And I need to snap the hell out of it before I actually throw myself from the tallest tower. Knowing my luck, that's where Dane's room is.

The shadows in my walls watch me as I toss my covers off and head to the bathroom, the tattoo still burning at the nape of my neck. It sizzles when I press a cold compress to it, and I hiss, screwing my eyes shut with the sting. Touching it, I feel the deep ridges of the ink, the swollen skin around it.

My hair keeps sticking to it, so I pull it into a ponytail then wrap it into a bun at the top of my head. I press the cold cloth to the tattoo again and try to see it in the mirror. Only having one makes it impossible, so I sigh and hunt for an antiseptic cream in the bag of toiletries Poppy gave me.

I find a white tub of soothing balm, so I gather a generous amount on my fingers and reach up to smooth it over the burning ink.

"It'll only get worse if you try to heal it."

I freeze, glancing through the mirror at Dane behind me. His sleeves are uncuffed, the top four buttons unfastened on his shirt, and his hair is a mess, as if he's just woken up. I drop my head. A migraine is building, and I can't be bothered with his snarky comments or bossy attitude. "Go away."

"It doesn't want to be healed, so stop what you're doing before it gets worse."

"I think I'll take my chances," I reply bluntly, hissing again as I cover the area with the balm. "Why are you here?"

He leans his shoulder against the doorframe and shrugs. "It's not by choice. I had to babysit you because you kept screaming in your sleep. Do you know how unattractive that is?"

I glare at his tired eyes. "Go away, Dane."

The idiot laughs. "Always trying to push me away, mortal. Do you forget we're basically tethered to one another?"

I throw down the cloth. "For the insufferable assignments and security measures, yes." Although he's barely adhered to those. "After that's all done, stay the hell away from me."

"We are partnered up for every class until the end of the year. What makes you think after task ten you'll be free of me?" He doesn't give me a chance to respond as he pushes off the door-frame, shoves his hands in his pockets, and closes the distance between us. He whispers against my ear as our eyes clash in the mirror. "You'll never be free of me. That's a promise. After we're done with the academy, I will follow you to the ends of your world and make your meaningless life hell."

"Such a big mouth for someone who never follows through with his threats. It's embarrassing how much you try to scare me, try to dominate me with your words and presence." Against my better judgment, I keep going. "You don't scare me, and you never will."

A cold gust of air brushes against my ear as Dane backs away, not once breaking eye contact. "You should be scared of me. I don't think you understand the power I wield."

I snort. "I couldn't care less, if I'm honest."

He opens his palm, finally looking away to stare at it intently. I almost scoff at his ridiculousness but hold my breath as tendrils of smoke twirl around each finger and his wrist until a ball of black forms. Electric forks snap from it, the miniature storm in his hand filled with anger and the need to destroy, and as he flexes his fingers, it grows in size.

"Every magical creature has a limit on its power." It grows larger, until I need to step back. "An endpoint that will either kill them if they don't stop or cause them to lose their powers altogether. Some are born with that power, and some earn it through years and years of intense training, depending on their bloodline. Most of us have eternity to learn how to use it, but some perish before they see how deep the well goes."

The candles blow out, and the flashes from the ball full of dark energy in his palm are the bathroom's only light. His eyes usually change to silver when we have moments between us, but right now, all I can see is black. There's no color to be seen, as if the giant orb is sucking all the happiness from the room.

I want to touch it. It's impulsive and stupid of me, but I want to eliminate our distance and feel it in my own hand, to feel the power of Dane Dalton. I blink away the building ache to do so and cross my arms.

"Is that your power?"

"Not exactly. This is a fraction of what I have. I've mastered all the elements and combined them into one expression of power. I also have the shadows, and even death. I could shove this down your throat and watch it carve my name all over your body while you suffocate, then bring you back from the brink of your end."

I gulp. "I'm unimpressed."

"I could make you see things."

He stays where he stands, but hands grab at the back of my knees, parting them. My eyes clash with silver ones as another version of Dane appears on his knees before me.

His lips don't move as the real Dane says, "I could make you feel things. Say and do things. Do you want to know how far I can push my power, mortal? Because I. Have. No. Limit."

I stare into his eyes—they burn into mine as his carbon copy circles his thumbs up my inner thighs, and my core pulses so hard I think I might hit the floor with a cry of pleasure. I grit my teeth. "You sure make it your mission to make me hate you."

He narrows his eyes, his mirror image vanishing as he fists both his palms to snuff out the ball in his hand. The candles light, giving his furious face a beautiful golden glow he definitely doesn't deserve. "Your smart mouth will only get you so far."

"As long as it keeps you away, then I'm fine with it."

Dane's jaw tenses, and I try not to laugh at how angry he's getting. He thinks I'm going to be terrified of him, but he's greatly mistaken. Yeah, he's immortal and really could kill me in half a heartbeat, but I didn't survive multiple abusive homes without building thick armor around me.

He can do whatever he wants, but I will never, ever roll onto my back and submit.

"Did the fact that task four is imminent not cross your mind? I can't stay away from you."

"That doesn't need to be covered until next week." I turn and wash my hands in the sink, ignoring him, even when my arm grazes him as I reach for a dry towel. "In the meantime, go hang around with your little group of friends and give me peace."

Dane chuckles lowly. He also ignores everything else I said. I toss the towel aside, fold my arms again, and say, "I'm going for a bath, one I'd like to enjoy uninterrupted, if you wouldn't mind getting the hell out of my dorm room."

"You're saying things to make you seem angry, but you're not. I don't understand." He tilts his head, snow-like strands flopping forward, a few of which slide into his line of vision. The silver glint in his eyes dances with the flames of the candelabra. "You don't want me to leave, do you?"

No. "Yes."

He smirks. "Very well, mortal. I'll see you in class."

"Great. Don't let the door hit you on the way out—unless you're going to Houdini instead."

"What does that mean?"

"Even in your world, you don't know Harry Houdini? The magician who did famous stunts? You know what, never mind."

"The only person I know in your realm is you."

I raise a brow. "You don't know me."

Dane doesn't respond, so I walk by him, pausing in my steps at the sudden spinning in my head and the flash of a swing with a little girl grinning. The moment is half a second, a beat of an image, but it's undeniable.

"What was that?" I ask, turning to face him. "I know you saw that too."

He rubs a hand down his face. "I think having us partnered up has caused some sort of connection. I got a similar image when I tucked you into your bed last night."

"What does it mean?"

He doesn't give me his attention as he shrugs. "I'll ask my mother."

Then my eyes go wide. "Wait. You tucked me into bed?"

"I had to—you were cold." He glances at the shadows gathering in my walls, the ones that keep me company. They don't cower the way they did with Valin. His stare stays on the little girl, and she doesn't hide. If anything, she tries to step towards him. He looks away quickly. "And your tattoo was bleeding. I had to... contain it."

"Meaning?"

"It was trying to spread, and I stopped it. Are you done asking questions?"

My bare foot slips on something wet on the floor, and I grab the side unit to stop myself from falling. Dane doesn't flinch, doesn't do a thing to try to help me. Not that I needed it. I scowl at him anyway then glance down at the floor.

I pale. "Why is there a puddle of blood on my floor?"

I look up at Dane, and he just stares at me, his calm and controlled expression unchanged. "I forgot to clean it." He removes his hand from his pocket, flicks a finger, and the mess is gone. "I told you—your tattoo was bleeding."

I touch the sensitive skin at the back of my neck, the swollen ink burning still.

The shadow prince walks over and sits on my bed, leaning back on his elbows. "We have mortal studies today, something about music and television. But then we have practice. Please tell me you know how to dance?"

"What? Practice for what?"

He smirks like the devil himself. "The ball at the end of term. Didn't you hear? You're my date, little mortal."

Without letting me throw him a retort or argue, he vanishes, taking the electrical charge of the room with him, along with the shirt I'm wearing and the shorts hanging from my hips.

20

On my first day here in the academy, a tall guy with wavy white hair told me I didn't belong here, that I'd be ripped apart by the end of that week. He told everyone that I was a whore and human filth, that I carried a highly contagious sickness. If they knew what was good for them, they'd steer clear of me. He even went as far as burning my books, locking me in my room so I'd be late for class, and volunteering me to help him show the class how to defeat an enemy with one hand.

Me being the enemy. Also the one who lay on the ground and wished death upon him.

The twins were the only ones who saw through his lies.

Now he's walking into my mortal studies class ten minutes late, and I'm trying to pretend I'm not gravitating towards him. It's like our souls are trying to intertwine and rule the world, magnetic and charged and desperate to look at each other, to touch and taste and be close.

It's been four hours, and as pathetic as it is, I have to admit that as soon as he left my room and I bathed, I relived every moment of last night in my head while I slipped my hand between my legs.

I swallow and look down at my notes—a bulleted list of my favorite musical artists.

The back of my neck itches as I bring my attention to the twins' third fight of the morning.

Despite being princesses, they argue like any other siblings when it comes to fashion and makeup and style. Mel finds it ridiculous that humans find release and calmness from music, and Poppy looks like she wants to hex her into next week when Mel says the music playing on the professor's magical box is giving her a headache.

We haven't even gotten to the bands.

They've been at it for hours. Poppy was, and still is, wearing Mel's top, which Mel thinks is a heinous crime. I witnessed them rolling across the corridor with fists flying as soon as I met them in our dorm hall, and no matter what I did, I couldn't split them up.

I ended up sitting on the stone stairs until they gave up trying to kill each other. I even looked at messages between me and Dane to pass the time and contemplated talking to him. But either he'd have taken a week to reply, or he'd ignore me and tell the school I'm a whore again.

My heart rate picks up as Dane sits right next to me, intentionally pressing his thigh against mine.

"What are you doing?" I ask through gritted teeth, whispering so no one can hear me. "Sit elsewhere."

"Nope."

And he doesn't. For the next three hours, the professor talks about different genres of music in the mortal world, how musicians make their money, and the fame behind them. She even mentions YouTube, and how the website launched multiple worldwide artists.

Dane doesn't seem even slightly impressed by the fact humans work hard for their earnings. He's naturally rich. Born into a family who probably bathes in gold. From Poppy's calculations, and conversion rates that shouldn't exist, Dane is worth hundreds of billions.

Yes, billions.

Maybe he'll pay his way out of prison.

He kicks my foot. *I can hear you.*

I don't care. Stay out of my head.

Are you ready for practice?

I sigh and continue writing notes from the board, and he kicks me again, hitting his thigh against mine. When I ignore him again, my pencil flies out of my grip and hits Orsen on the back of the head.

"Hey! The fuck? Who did that?"

"Language, Mr. Zeller. Pick up your pencil and copy what I'm writing on the board!"

You're evil, I say in my head.

But not scary, right?

Weirdly, I can hear the tone he's using in my mind. I nearly blush and dig my fingernails into my palm instead. *You're about as scary as a butterfly.*

The teacher drones on about homework and upcoming tests, but I cancel out everything around me as Dane's deep, cold, yet enchanting voice flows through my head. *I can assure you, mortal, that after task four, you won't be comparing me to a fucking butterfly.*

Task four: Both students will take part in the fourth stage of human contact. Intimate touch until completion.

An explicit scene unfolds before me, and I know it's from him.

Firm shadow hands part my thighs as he stands behind me with a grip of my throat, tilting my head to the side. A moan slips from my mouth as the ghost touch of a fingertip drags down the front of my underwear before the soaked, dripping fabric is moved aside, and I gasp as he pushes two fingers inside me.

The hold on my throat gets tighter.

His mouth presses against my ear with a deep, thick growl, followed by words in a different language. But the translation is there.

Scream for me, little mortal.

I gulp, audibly, and lick my lips as I cross my legs. *That's quite an imaginative scenario. Too bad it's fake.* I try to make the last part sound as false as possible, but with the building warmth at the base of my spine, I might as well beg him to make it happen.

Do you want me to complete task four right now?

I snap my head to him with a confused look.

He doesn't move his eyes from the board as he writes each word down, the multitasker that he is. He speaks in my head again. *You can say no, and that's fine, I'll stop. But I can feel you. Stop denying it. It is unbecoming of a mortal who depends so much on trust and has such complex needs.*

I level my gaze on the professor again, my body jolting in my seat as something warm wraps around my ankle. A few students gape at me, but I clear my throat and pretend I'm listening, looking down to see a black shadow circling my ankle, crawling, climbing up my right leg to my knee. It tightens as Dane knocks my thigh with his again.

My shadows will do anything I ask. If I want them to kill, they'll kill. If I want them to protect, they'll protect. If I want them to please someone, then you better fucking believe it when I say they'll do that too.

I think that goes against the rules for task four. I have no idea how I manage to give him a response, but I do. My hands grip the edge of the table as the mass circles higher, like a snake trying to capture and strangle its next meal.

Something else glides up my inner thigh, and when I glance down, Dane's hand is on my left thigh, holding me under my skirt, his fingers a nanometer away from my drenched panties.

I clench my thighs, and a groan vibrates between us. It's loud, but only to us. The classroom focuses on the work while Dane shifts in his chair, not moving his hold, fixing himself. There's a tingling sensation between my legs, different from my own arousal.

Whatever the connection is between us, it's getting stronger. I don't need to look down to know that his cock is solid. He probably doesn't need to touch me to know my underwear is soaked through, that my core throbs with desperation for his next move.

Absentmindedly, I press myself forward, biting my lip as his fingers slide ever so gently against me. All my nerve endings are on fire, screaming for more. I try to grind against his fingers again, but he lightly slaps my pussy, and I stifle a moan.

He tuts, voice as deep as the ocean. I swallow another moan, flinching as he taps my sensitive area again. *How much do you want me to touch you?*

I respond by dropping my hand under the desk and sinking my nails into his wrist, gripping him, keeping him there. *How much do you want to touch me, Dane?*

Fuck.

Being at the back of the room, no one knows what we're doing—no one knows that I'm trying to grind my pussy against Dane's hand in a class full of immortal creatures.

I give you permission to touch me.

But as I whimper from the firm press of his thumb against my clit, the professor slams down her large book and tells everyone the class is over.

We mentally and physically break away from each other, temporarily severing the connection, and I try to regulate each breath as he collects his bag. "See you at practice, mortal."

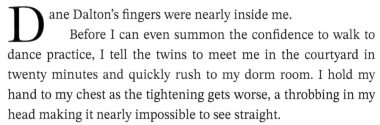

21

D ane Dalton's fingers were nearly inside me.

Before I can even summon the confidence to walk to dance practice, I tell the twins to meet me in the courtyard in twenty minutes and quickly rush to my dorm room. I hold my hand to my chest as the tightening gets worse, a throbbing in my head making it nearly impossible to see straight.

Somehow, I make it without passing out.

I slam the door shut, press my back to it, and breathe.

In. Out. In. Out.

Thighs clenching together, I try to ease the tension between them, only adding to the frustration of my brain on fire. My knuckles turn white with the death grip I have on my pleated skirt, my eyes closed, images of him all over me running wild in my mind.

They feel like memories of a life I haven't lived. They completely overwhelm me.

A young boy with white hair sitting across from me at the extremely large and golden dining table.

The wink he sends me as he and his parents leave our castle.

A kiss on the cheek that has me blushing all over.

Me smiling at the young boy, both of us teenagers. Him gathering the confidence to speak with me despite his nerves. I press my palms to my eyes and beg them to stop, the unknown scenes unfolding in my mind at rapid speed. *His soft, tattooed hand taking mine as he helps me onto a tree swing; me letting out a giggle when I fall off and drag him down with me.*

The design inked onto my hand transferring to his as fire engulfs us.

My back slides down the door as a wave of grief hits me. Undeniable loss, unexplainable despair that has my heart accelerating. Death. Fire. More death. Screams fill my ears, and no matter how loud I let my own out, they're louder.

Breathe.

Breathe, Seraphine.

Don't let it win, my love. Fight. You need to fight.

Stay with me.

Please—stay with me.

A large mass appears in my mind, battling an unknown presence with swords and immense power with a deafening roar of victory, and then everything is quiet.

And I'm in my room.

Confused, I keep inhaling and exhaling, wondering why I was just panicking over nothing. My head, eyes, and ears ache, but I don't know why. Or why I'm sitting on the floor with my back against the door with a blank mind.

What just happened? Did I pass out?

I stand with furrowed brows and fix my hair, straightening my skirt and shirt, still reeling from what nearly happened with Dane. The feeling is dominating how lost I am, wanting to know why I was on the ground yet thinking of him everywhere.

He was so close to touching me in a class full of students. And I was going to let him. I wanted him to move aside my panties and sink two fingers inside me. I wanted it so much, and he knew it. He could feel the wetness on my thighs, the ache in my core that vibrated between us. He would have smelled my arousal, the neediness, my desire to have the shadow prince bring me to orgasm while surrounded by immortal creatures.

I glance at the black silhouettes occupying my walls. They are calm, collected, and watch me as I begin to pace the full length of my bedroom with my hands in my hair.

If I go to practice, Dane will no doubt tease me, or worse, I'll start to feel that tempting sexual attraction. It's suffocating. It's confusing. But most of all, admittedly, it's exhilarating. I hate him, yet the thought of continuing these tasks makes me warm, makes me want to march down to that ballroom, drag Dane into the nearest broom closet, and demand he lower himself to his knees and fuck me with his mouth.

Three knocks on the door yank me from debating lying on my bed and ridding myself of this hunger. I stop dead, staring at the door. "Who is it?"

No one speaks. If it were that idiot, he'd use his magic to break in, probably pin me to a wall, and throw dirty words and insults my way. I think I might actually want that.

God, I need to get off this island.

"Go away," I say, annoyed as I rummage through my makeup bag for wipes and fresh lipstick.

I grab a spare pair of panties and quickly change.

The door knocks again, and I huff, close my bathroom door, and throw open my main one. "What?"

I stare at nothing.

No one is there. The hallway is clear, and there are no students around. "If you've gained the power of being invisible and you're messing with me, I will slap you, Dane."

Nothing.

I close my door and lock it, then head for the courtyard to meet the twins.

———

They're sitting on the edge of the fountain bickering about nail polish when I find them. I sit between them, leaning down to rummage through my bag to find my phone.

I know I have it here somewhere.

"Oh," Poppy blurts out. "Sera, do not freak out."

I stop and straighten. "What?"

"Your tattoo is... bigger."

I touch the ink at the back of my neck, but the raised skin feels the same. "What do you mean?"

"I just caught a glimpse. Pull your shirt down at the back so we can get a proper look."

I do as she says, and the twins study the tattoo. "You have another one now. Just below the first one. It's linked by... is that writing? What does it say?" Mel asks her sister, who must answer with a gesture because I hear no response. "Yeah, I think so too."

My heart skips a beat at their long silence that follows. "Hello? What's going on?"

I move to stand, facing them. Poppy chews her lip. "It's like it's starting a chain of symbols down your spine."

I should be freaking out, but I just cross my arms in annoyance. Given how my life has been going, this is miniscule. I'm sure it's just from the tasks I'm doing with Dane. "What's the other one?"

In unison, they both say, "It's the symbol of a realm."

"What one?"

Mel gives Poppy a look—she shrugs and smiles sadly at me. "The Mortal Realm."

My brow furrows as I stare at the twins.

The overhead noise reminds us to go to practice, so the conversation ends. I trace the ink with my fingers as we walk, but Mel slaps my hand away. "No, don't make it obvious. You having those markings is not a good sign. You are human. Act like one, Sera."

Well, that's... comforting.

"You're worried," Mel says to me, pointing out the obvious. "We'll find out what's happening to you, okay? Let's get this dreadful class out the way and we can have a night of the girly things you humans do."

Poppy grins at me. "I'll paint your nails and braid your hair."

"Sounds great," I mutter as we walk through the large double doors into the ballroom.

All three of us stop walking and take in our surroundings. The hall is large with a high ceiling, excessively decorated with black and white roses, thousands of candles to light the place up, and the middle of the room has been completely cleared of anything—our dance space. It's gothic, dark, yet beautiful.

Soft music is playing from nowhere, and the cult studies professor and Dane's mother are dancing, showing another class a routine everyone has to do during the ball.

I can feel eyes on us from every angle as we make our way to our gathering class. Orsen winks at Mel, who rolls her eyes, and Poppy gives Brandt a smile, which he returns. Dane is staring at his shoes with a scowl, probably thinking I'm going to step all over them and ruin their shine.

If I hadn't realized how different the twins were the moment I met them, the way they're looking at this room would tell me exactly that. Poppy's eyes have lit up, her smile growing as she twirls in circles and claps in excitement. Mel grimaces at her sister, regarding the decorations and the music with distaste.

Maybe if bodies were hanging from the ceiling in shackles, butchered and skinned alive, and blood smeared on the wall, with the added extra of Orsen in chains and naked, she would be as excited as Poppy. I should be scared of Mel. She's evil. She even looks evil. But for some reason, we're good friends.

I trust her, even though she could kill me without even blinking.

"You're coming to my room tonight," Orsen tells Mel, taking her waist and pulling her to him.

She grabs his throat and shoves him back. "No thanks."

But the way they're regarding each other, there's no doubt she'll be in his bed by midnight. I hope I don't receive any nudes or video clips of them fucking.

She did say she wanted to show me how big he gets while she's sucking him off, but I kindly declined. I might actually block her and not tell her.

Dane—his back to me—is talking to a student with long blonde hair. I know she's attracted to him, her red eyes matching her latex outfit. She giggles at whatever he says, and I imagine her body in pieces, drained of blood, and set on fire.

Maybe I'll carve out her eyeballs and shove them up her—

Calm down.

I grit my teeth. *I am calm.*

Dane turns, dismissing the girl, and quickly gives me a strange look I haven't seen before, almost as if he's concerned. As if he wants to come over here and ask if I'm okay. I can feel it somehow. I can feel his anxiousness—that he wants to walk over here and sweep me away from everyone. It's quite a strong need too. I tilt my head at him, but he turns to his friend instead.

Dane's hands are fisting as Orsen speaks to him.

I can feel him looking over at me again as the twins discuss their dresses for the hundredth time. His eyes stay on me while I walk to the bench, where we take our seats. When I lean down to fix the laces of my boots, his burning gaze follows.

Stop looking at me, creep.

I was merely glancing, mortal. And stop fucking speaking to me like that.

The corner of my mouth curls, but I wipe it away with my hand and pretend to fix my hair. I've made sure I keep it down, if only to hide the growing tattoos. There's an itch at the top of my spine, and I know it's the ink embedding further into my skin.

A hint of amusement flows through me, and I send it his way.

Or what, Dane? Are you going to punish me in front of everyone?

He gulps—I can hear him gulping from away over here. The strain of his muscles as he shifts in his seat. The soft, wet glide of his tongue across his bottom lip.

The headmistress claps once, grabbing our attention. "Okay, class! We have already allocated you a partner for the ball, and I want to cover a few rules. I will not tolerate violence or any sexual contact during dances. You come up here, do your routine with your partner, thank them with a kiss, then get off the floor."

I need to kiss him again?

Dane's mother crosses her arms. "Dance, kiss, then go away. Will that be a problem for anyone?"

When no one replies, she nods. "Let's all gather round."

She shows us all the routine, and for some reason, I know exactly what steps she's going to take before she takes them. The confusion has me dumbfounded, so much so that I touch the back of my neck, feeling the heat and symbols at my nape.

Maybe someone is playing a prank on me. Or maybe someone has hexed me with a spell that covers mortals with tattoos, to show that I'm beneath them—branded with the symbol of the Mortal Realm as a sign of where I should be.

Valin walks into the ballroom, sans his usual three-piece suit. His white shirt flows around his body, his sleeves rolled up and the top three buttons unfastened. The suspenders clipped to his pants hang on each side, and his hair is disheveled.

Dane clears his throat and leans his elbows on his knees.

"Have I missed it already?" Valin's deep voice asks.

"Of course not. Are you wanting to learn the routine?"

He nods, his eyes finding mine, staying on me for a beat too long before walking towards Dane and sitting beside him.

The headmistress watches them then instructs the first pair to the middle of the floor.

22

By the time the twins are up and down, Poppy is crying, Mel is comforting her, and Orsen is apologizing for stepping on Mel's toes. It's my turn, and Dane doesn't offer me his hand like the other partners did—just walks right into the middle of the room with his hands in his pockets.

He doesn't look at me when I join him, or when he takes my side and pulls me closer to him. The touch burns, but when my hand slips into his free one, a blazing inferno blasts through me. Fire and electricity and a forbidden urge to melt into him.

My core pulses, my clit throbbing against the material of my panties.

Concentrate.

I'm trying, I admit.

The academy is trying to do things the way mortals do and has found some songs to use for the dance. But for me and Dane, the headmistress doesn't play the same song the rest danced to.

A piano rendition of the song begins, the faint melody filling the ballroom.

"Follow Dane's lead," his mother says. "This is not your

typical slow dance, Miss Winters. I will excuse myself. I don't think I have the stomach to witness my son kissing a human."

Before I can offer a retort, reminding her she's the one who refused to let us switch partners, Dane spins me so my back is to the door, where his mother exits.

The students had chatted while previous partners danced, but now, everyone is silent and still. They're watching us, not making a sound as their gazes follow us around the dancefloor. My feet do exactly what Dane's do, and each time he twirls me and snatches my waist again at each crescendo, he keeps his eyes everywhere but on me.

Why isn't he looking at me?

He abruptly dips me, my hair touching the floor, and our eyes crash together like thunder in the middle of a stormy sea, the waves of recognition and regret between us making everyone around us disappear. He keeps me in this position, his hand on my thigh, gripping, tightening, his throat moving as he swallows.

Suddenly, I feel overwhelmed again. I've felt like this before, like I was suffocating on my own thoughts, but now it's an emotion that's flooding me. One I can't pinpoint.

He pulls me to my full height that's barely to his chest, and takes my hand to the right, his other on my waist again as I follow his steps. Him being around eight feet, I struggle, but with the grip I have on his shoulder, I somehow don't let go.

"Please pay attention. Your feet are not moving correctly," he says quietly, spinning me away and then back to him, and I slam into his chest. "You said you weren't a virgin."

He gives me whiplash with how abrupt his conversation is. "Why are you bringing up my virginity?"

He swallows, and a wave of nerves hits me. "Tell me what happened."

I laugh, but he glares down at me, so I ask, "What, the first time? Why?"

He stops moving, and I trip over his feet. "There have been other times?"

This guy is unbelievable. "Obviously, Dane. I'm not talking about this, okay? Pay attention."

"Who?"

"Not telling you," I reply, refusing to tell him about mine and Grayson's friends-with-benefits set-up. He'll call me a whore like he always does, and I can't be bothered with his mood swings. "Poppy looks like she might throw a hex at us if we keep missing steps. She's very serious about this dance."

"Valin?"

I sigh and drop my head back. "Just shut up."

"Yes or no. Have you fucked Valin?"

"What is your deal with him?" He's silent, so I raise a brow. "Did he steal your girlfriend or something?"

"He stole something," he says. "Stay away from him."

"Don't tell me what to do."

The cult studies professor tuts. "You have stopped moving!"

We both huff, and Dane pulls us into the routine again.

I know the routine for some reason. I move before he does, and he needs to follow my lead. I slide my leg up to his side and throw myself back in another dip.

His hand is warm at the small of my back, holding me in place. I let go of him, running my fingers through my hair as he lifts me into the air by the hips, my navel in line with his mouth. He looks up at me, eyes dancing, shining, a flicker of silver sinking in as I slide down his body to my feet.

He watches me the entire time now, and without meaning to, or knowing that I can, I dive into his mind and the wave of loneliness and grief I find there nearly chokes me. I gasp as he holds me in his mind, traps me, and I see a river of blood flowing, rapid, full of the faces of everyone I love.

He releases me from his mind, and before I can push away or react, the song ends, and Dane dips me one last time. His mouth lands on mine, and I shove my hands into his hair to hold him to me as I kiss him back. I'm not sure what kind of kiss we're supposed to be ending this with, but Dane's fingers wrap around my thigh, my back sliding onto the ground as he settles on top of me.

Our bodies become one as our lips part in unison, tongues moving together, tasting each other's sins as we ignore all the students and keep going. His hand inches higher on my leg, a shadow of a touch on my throat as his other hand presses to the ground to keep his full weight off me.

I sink my teeth into his bottom lip, and he growls, a low growl that makes me want to kill everyone in the room so I can have all of him.

He tilts his head to deepen the kiss, devouring me with an audience. He laces one of our hands together, and my palm stings. I ignore it, ignoring the people around us, ignoring my own thoughts telling me to get a grip as I hook my ankle behind his leg and slide my tongue against his.

"No one can see us," he says against my mouth. "They think we are still dancing, mortal."

I pull back and glance around—a dome of black is over us, an image of us reflecting off it, Dane spinning me around and me following his lead.

Something wraps around my throat, holding me to the ground. Dane sits up, looking down at me. "I could kill you right here, and no one will know."

"Are you going to kill me?"

The Prince of Darkness cracks his neck to the side, eyes burning silver. "I'm undecided."

For some reason, I smile. "Shame. This—"

I halt my words as Dane forces open my thighs with his shadow hands, pinning them to the floor as he hovers over me. "Shut up. I'm undecided if I should kill you or..." He trails his middle finger up my inner thigh, and my core pulses. "If I should finish all the tasks right now."

"Both sound terrible."

He smirks down at me. "You think so?"

"I know so."

He drags his bottom lip between his teeth as he grabs the waistband of my skirt and drags it up, until the only barrier is my panties covering my pussy.

"You're wet. Your scent is so strong, I can practically taste you. Is that because the idea of me fucking you with my fingers sounds terrible?"

I swallow, my lips parting as he runs his finger up the seam of my panties, teasing me, gathering wetness on his fingertip and rubbing it between his finger and thumb.

"You're a little liar, aren't you, mortal? Do you want me to drop the spell, so everyone can see how desperately you want me? Do you want me to do this?" My back arches as he pushes against the material with the tip of his finger, right against my entrance. "And they can watch?"

Sliding two fingers against my core, he pinches my clit between them, cupping my pussy in a firm hold.

"So wet for me, human," he says with a groan, caressing me as he rubs against my core, his eyes lighting up as I moan. "So much hate, yet you want me to keep going, don't you?"

I nod, and the invisible vine tightens around my throat, forcing me to stare at the ceiling of the black dome, stopping me from seeing what he's doing.

"Words."

"Yes," I breathe, trying to slam my thighs together to ease the tension as he moves his hand away. My clit throbs to be touched, to be kissed and licked and stimulated.

My heart pounds with exhilaration and something far more terrifying as Dane appears above me, resting his elbow beside my head, the shadow hands still keeping my thighs open for him.

His gaze stays on me as he shifts aside my underwear then smirks as he sinks a finger into me, making my entire body tense. His ring is cold against my heat, pressure I can barely handle as he sucks on his lip again. He eases his finger into the knuckle, pressing his thumb to my clit and circling. I try not to moan, but I can't stop the sound from leaving my throat.

I've been fingered before, and it's never felt like this. I'm not sure if it's a magical thing, or if his powers make the tingling sensation more intense, but as he pushes a second finger in, my toes curl, my hands shooting up and fisting at his shirt.

I want to grind against his hand, but the hold the shadow hands have on me keeps me completely still.

They caress my thighs as Dane fucks me with his fingers, watching me, not breaking eye contact as he thrusts in and out, his thumb pressing harder to my clit and making my back arch off the ballroom floor.

My breath catches, and I screw my eyes shut as another wave of pleasure smacks into me. I'm tipping over the edge as he snatches my jaw.

"Look at me," he grits, the shadow hands opening me wider. "Fucking look at me."

I do, and as soon as I see the hunger in his eyes, a coiling heat starts at the base of my spine, swiftly wrapping around it to the tattoos on my neck. They tingle, sending similar waves ricocheting around my body, my nerves on fire as I let out a strangled moan.

His strong shoulder rises and falls in my vision as he drives into me.

Whatever pleasure I'm feeling, it's vibrating across a bridge between us. And I can feel him harden, swelling against my outer thigh, his own pleasure tightening at his balls.

His jaw tenses, my walls clutching at his fingers as my pleasure builds to blinding heights.

We don't break eye contact as he sinks deeper, as my arousal soaks my thighs and puddles on the floor beneath me. The thumbs of the shadow hands rub at the sides of my pussy, parting me wider as Dane adds another finger, sending me crashing into a world of no return.

My vision blurs, and my muscles spasm as my walls clench over his fingers repeatedly. I shake under him, the orgasm rippling through me as Dane curls his fingers deep inside me and fucks me harder, faster, deeper, licking his lips as he watches me unravel.

No one around us knows that I'm screaming. That my mouth drops open, that I grip his clothes with desperation as my orgasm hits its pinnacle, and the white flashes before my eyes slow down.

For a split second, I recognize the man above me. *Really* recognize him. The man who fastened my corset after a night of making love then escaped the room before my father caught us.

A kiss to my hand.

The deafening scream of his mother when a knife lodges in his chest.

I gasp and stare at him in disbelief. "Dane?"

A tear slips down my cheek, and the recognition comes over to Dane. He nods once, pulling his fingers from my core and wiping away the tears. "If you're ready—stay. Stay with me."

My lips part with words I need to say. They're on the tip of my tongue, but dizziness has my eyes rolling to the back of my head.

The darkness drops over me like a veil, a whisper against my ear of a voice I don't recognize. It tells me to let go.

An explosion in my mind has me wincing, and he takes my cheek in a soft hold, swiping another tear. "Seraphine, focus."

"I can't." The vine around my neck and the shadow hands at my thighs vanish, and I sit up, wrapping my arms around him and holding on for dear life. "I can't, Dane. I c-c-can't."

I have so much to say to him, but as all the thoughts start to fade, I struggle to contain the crying, the sobs into his chest, the thick presence of loss and guilt and rage.

Then everything goes silent, and my body goes ramrod straight in his hold.

Dane is cradling me against him, and I frown, pulling away, unsure why I'm so upset or why he looks so worried. He lets go of my cheek, and the expression drops.

"What's going on?" I blurt out, confused.

His eyes darken, his jaw clenching. "Hello, mortal."

But one second he's on me, and the next he's tackled off me and thrown to the side.

I sit up and pull my skirt down, my chest rising and falling, lips swollen, to see Valin on top of Dane. He punches him across the face twice, and all Dane does is laugh and headbutt him. He tells him to hit him again, and Valin does. Orsen drags him off, Dane wiping blood from his nose.

Valin looks down at me with disgust then at all the students gaping before he straightens his shirt and walks out.

Mel fixes the mascara under my eyes as I sit back down. "As hot as seeing them fight was, I'm going to need to know the details. Why is Valin pissed?"

I shake my head, the after-effects of the orgasm having me speaking quietly. "I have no idea."

"Why was Dane hiding you both?" Poppy asks. "It was so weird. Like we all knew it was fake, but we couldn't see you."

Mel shakes her head. "Are you okay?"

I nod. "I think so."

Dane licks the black blood from his lip, and the split skin heals itself. Orsen offers to kill Valin, but he tells his friend to shut up and that he can handle the professor.

His stare is devastatingly haunting when it lands on me. A silent reminder that task four is only half completed. Even when they aren't silver, Dane's eyes are still mesmerizing to look at, making me feel like his teeth and tongue are dragging all over me.

The class ends, and I make it halfway to my dorm before something wraps around me, my entire body tugging from the inside as I'm materialized into the dark forest. I gasp as I fall against a tree, pressing my back to it, unable to see a thing.

The moon shines above the canopy of trees, but not near enough for me to see what's ahead of me. Something moves in the bushes—footsteps against the snapping branches.

My palm itches, and when I glance down, black tendrils are wrapping around my fingers, climbing up to my wrist. It burns, and the tattoos on my neck burn too.

And when I look back up, Valin is there. He has his hands in his pockets, taking a step forward.

I press into the tree behind me. "What are you doing?"

"Do you recognize me? At all? When you look at me, do you feel nothing?"

My spine crushes against the tree as I try to back away more and fail.

I try to scream, but Valin teleports closer, slamming his palm over my mouth. "You and I are going to have a little talk, and you're not going to remember a thing. If you do, and you tell Dane what we do tonight, I'll kill you."

And then everything goes blank.

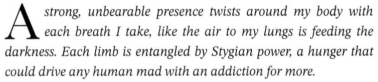

23

A strong, unbearable presence twists around my body with each breath I take, like the air to my lungs is feeding the darkness. Each limb is entangled by Stygian power, a hunger that could drive any human mad with an addiction for more.

My body writhes against the intensity as my wrists and ankles are bound to the sacred slab of stone beneath me. My innermost self laughs at the danger, the potential death sentence as the space above me opens up like a giant eye full of blinding light.

I can't scream—she won't let me. But a huge part of me doesn't want to. It aches for the energy to seek out more of my fractured soul, to devour it from the inside out. The gradual build-up of the swirling vortex calls to me like my master, praising me for all my hard work.

The veil between me and the monster is thrown up, and I gasp for air.

Thunder growls around me, flashes of lightning above my body doing nothing to help me see my surroundings.

The vortex grows in size as the monster within me battles to be freed once more. Only, I don't want it free—I want it gone. I want to push it into an afterlife far from me and the ones I love.

Black tendrils of power burn through my veins, crawling up my arms and legs. The power whispers to me to let go, to allow the force to overwhelm me.

Blood seeps from wounds all over my body as I silently beg for mercy, not daring to say it aloud for the monster to hear. My mind slips, and the mask drops once more as a grin plasters over my face.

"Death to her. Death to all." I utter it like a mantra, a witch's spell, a curse. "Death to her. Death to all."

I will not yield to these pitiful fools. I will slay them without a second thought.

They don't deserve an apology or for me to be merciful. They deserve everything they have coming to them. They deserve the ruin of their damnation. The fall of their worlds.

No, they don't.

I don't want them to die.

"Her eyes are black," a voice says to my left. "Do it now."

The blade cuts through my gut, and I grit my teeth, welcoming the pain. I laugh without wanting to, but it doesn't seem to sound the way it should. The noise coming from my throat is a loud rumble, a haunting echo around the cave as the knife cuts deeper.

The cave walls crack with the power I throw out, but the person wielding the blade doesn't shift. He pushes it deeper, and the thunder gets louder, closer, and needier.

A snap goes off in my mind, and I fall from the cliff that I've been dangling from. I plummet for seconds, minutes, hours, maybe even years. I cry out for more. To end the suffering within me and my realms.

More.

I want more.

I need more.

Deeper.

Deadlier.

I want death. I need it. I need them to kill me before it gets worse—before it spreads to places within me that I can't control. The Blade of the Gods needs to penetrate my cursed heart and destroy my soul.

Only in the living dead of Seraphine Winters can we be damned. All of us, to eternity. The wars are lost, but battles are won. But mine... As I fall into the abyss, I beg the gods above to keep my family safe from the rest of the darkness taking over the realms.

I mutter a mantra in my head and wait for the reaper to appear, to sweep me away from this carnage. I'm shoved aside by the grinning monster again as its claws plunge into my skin.

They don't know what they're doing by stopping me.

Their lives are in my hand, and I will clench my fist and drive it into their worlds. I'll split the universe in two. I'll alter timelines and destroy all the gods who try to stop me.

Realms will be no more.

Life as we know it will cease to exist.

He'll try to stop me, but not even love can pin me down. He's deluded to think the old me will break free. She's trapped, falling into nothing, for as long as I allow.

Within the confines of my poisoned mind, I grab onto the talons of the monster and drive my fist into its face. The force pushes it back, and I take control.

I can't hold on much longer. It's much stronger than before, and soon, I will be gone, and she will take over. Soon, I will be nothing but someone who used to exist.

I grit my teeth and tug at the vines wrapping around each limb, pulling at the restraints with everything I have.

But I don't want to be free. I want to die.

I need to.

I need them to plunge the Blade of the Gods deeper, through my muscle and flesh and drag it down—only then can I let the dark power exit my body. It thrashes within my bones, cracks them, and stretches my senses to a point of near no return.

But I need to finish what I started.

Green eyes appear before me, a soft hand on my cheek. "Fight it, my love. You have to fight it, or it will overcome you."

"I'm trying." The voice sounds like my own, but it seems distant. The monster within me is attempting to take over again. "Please. Kill me."

Green eyes vanish, replaced by someone else.

I can't see his face, but his voice is familiar, almost soothing. "You cannot let it control you, daughter. If you do, it will win. We'll all cease to exist."

Tears pool in my eyes as I fight, and I search for my father's face, to see what he looks like. I forget. After all these years and being without him, I forget what he looks like. He's a ghost, my shadow, my protector in the dark as I run into battle.

Father always came back for me, even in the afterlife. Even after the monster within me burned down our kingdom with everyone still inside.

But my mother remains a lost ghost. She's trapped somewhere, but she doesn't want to be saved. Not by me anyway. She's terrified of the curse that was put upon me.

A blinding light explodes from my body as the blade sinks deeper into my gut—to the hilt—and instead of crying and begging for help, I close my eyes and let the power run away from me. It spills out of my wound and sinks into the stone beneath me. It whispers that it shall return, and when it does, death will greet me.

I open my eyes to see Dane holding the handle of the blade, his face filled with grief as he yanks out the knife and sinks it into my chest, crushing through my bones and flesh until it penetrates my heart.

The last words I hear are from him. They're a sob within the screams gathering around us as the curse spirals from my body in a helix and smashes into the vortex above me.

"Come back to me, Seraphine. You must come back to me."

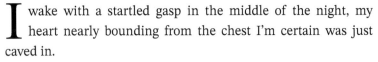

24

I wake with a startled gasp in the middle of the night, my heart nearly bounding from the chest I'm certain was just caved in.

Sitting up, I press my palm to my midsection, pulling it away to see there's no blood or wound. Beads of sweat drip from my forehead, down my cheeks, and coat my chest. My back is soaked, and so is the mattress beneath my trembling form.

There's no thunder. No lightning coming from a vortex on the ceiling above me. There isn't a voice yelling at me to give in or a stranger hovering over me with a worried look on his face.

Who was he?

Was I dreaming?

I rub my hand down my face, wiping some of the perspiration from it.

I'm soaked. Drenched. And not in the way that Dane had me yesterday while everyone watched as our stunt doubles danced around us.

I touch my lips gently; they're still tingling from the kiss. He didn't need to kiss me the way he did—or deepen it so much that I warped from the inside out and begged for more.

His shadows are nearby, and I have no idea why I can sense them. As a human, I shouldn't be able to do a lot of things, especially delving into the mind of the heir of an entire realm and grasping at his grief like a madwoman.

Something bad happened to Dane at one point in his life. I could feel it haunting him when I was in his head.

My skin heats at the memory of the orgasm rippling through me, which is weird, considering I'm in a bed that's not mine, in a room I've only seen once. I should scream or jump out the bed, or at least be a little concerned.

I study the room, letting my eyes fall over the painting on the walls, the gathering of shadows, the rug settled on the floor in front of a fireplace, the calm flames heating the room.

Dane stands at the large window, staring out of his tower at the vast ocean of nothing. His hands are in his pockets, his waistcoat discarded on the seat pulled up beside the bed I was sleeping in.

The muscles upon muscles bundle at his shoulders, pulling taut at his white shirt, his sleeves rolled to his elbows. The ink peeks out at his nape, his forearms full of designs scribed by his realm. I can see from here the veins swelling beneath his skin from how hard he's fisting his hands.

He's silent, even as I pull myself into a seated position and hug my knees. The walls are crowded with silhouettes, all huddling to stare at me, waiting to see what Dane's next move will be.

The little girl who usually appears in my room is here, and I tilt my head at her as she does the same, lifting a flower she must've picked from her shadow garden. The corner of my lip curls into a smile. A tall figure comes up beside her, takes her hand as the flower drops from her fingers, and they vanish.

I lick my dry lips and notice I'm in his clothes again—his shirt to be exact. A gasp falls from my lungs, but not because of what I'm wearing. My hands shake as I lift them in front of me.

My fingertips are stained black, with tendrils snaking around my fingers as if ink has been injected into my veins.

"It will fade soon," Dane's deep voice says, though he doesn't turn around. "I had to put you to sleep to try to extract the curse, but some of it still lingers."

"The curse?"

"That's what I said."

His snappy tone should irk me, but I'm too stunned by my hands to give him some sort of retort or ask what his problem is.

Curse?

My heart beats hard in my chest, my breathing uneven. "I was cursed?"

"Very much so," he says blankly.

"By who?" I ask, confused.

"That seems to have been erased from your memory, mortal. What is the point in you being here if someone can infiltrate your mind so easily?"

Still, he doesn't turn around. He cracks his neck to the side, shoulders tensing even more.

"Weak and useless."

I want to slap him. "That's unnecessary. If I'm so useless and weak, why try to remove the curse? Why not let it do its job?"

A chuckle—a deep, low vibrating laugh that makes me shiver. "I ask myself the same question, and still, I fail to find an answer."

How did I even get here?

I remember going to my dorm last night and... I went to sleep. Right? I got into the bathtub, read a book, and slipped into bed. I remember. I have a full memory of the sequence of last night's events.

Right after he fingered me on the floor of the ballroom.

I close my mind off in a way I didn't know I could. He doesn't need to know that those images keep flying through my mind. That I *want* to see them.

I don't like Dane Dalton, but that doesn't mean I can't want him.

Frustratingly so.

As much as being in his vicinity both annoys me and livens me up, I want to go back to my room and get away from him while I'm like this.

Instead of walking over and turning him around, then sinking to my knees like I want to, I ask, "Did you kidnap me again?"

He ignores me, but his shoulders are still tense as he fists his hands in his pockets.

"You need to stop doing that, if so. As much as I'm flattered you want to spend time with me and see me in your bed, I'm not interested. So if you could rein in the creepiness and go back to pretending I'm shit on the bottom of your shoes, that'd be great."

I kick off the heavy blanket and get to my feet. His shirt reached my knees before, but now it's higher up my thighs.

My brows pull together. "Why am I wearing your clothes?" I don't ask him why I have no underwear on. My pussy is bare beneath the fabric. My breasts are free, my nipples rubbing against the material. "Why am I here?" I ask when he doesn't respond. "Dane?"

"Don't say my name," he says quietly, but I can tell the words are escaping through gritting teeth. "Don't even speak, mortal."

I cross my arms. "What is going on?"

He's always spoken to me like shit, but he's acting like I cut off his balls and locked them in a jar somewhere far from him. Maybe I will, just to teach him a lesson. I'm sure there's a witch in this school with the magic to do so.

His shirt smells of musk and spice, a combination I had no idea I'd crave when not around him, and I fasten the top two buttons to cover my cleavage. The idea that he stripped me shouldn't heat my skin, but it does.

My feet are cold against the dark wooden flooring as I start to close the distance he's put between us. "Hello?"

I walk into an invisible wall. "I said shut up."

"Screw you. You can't kidnap me and take my clothes. There are boundaries, Dane. Learn them."

"Boundaries." He scoffs and shakes his head, still with his back to me. "You know nothing of boundaries."

Don't look at her.

Don't fucking look at her.

Instead of pointing out that his mind is very open to me, and I can hear his desperate thoughts, I sigh and lean against his dresser, dragging my cursed fingers over the surface. I stare at my hands as the black tendrils slowly crawl beneath my skin. It burns. But not as much as the need for him to look at me.

I have no idea why I feel this way, but everything in me begs for Dane to turn around, to tell me why I'm here, to admit to himself that he wants me as I do him.

Where do these thoughts even come from?

The only reason we're tolerating each other is for these assignments. The classes we're forced to be paired up for. If it weren't for them, he'd be knocking me over in the corridor, calling me names like a school bully, and making my stay here absolute hell.

"Can I at least leave? I have class in the morning, and I don't fancy showing up in an heir's clothes."

He removes his hand from his pocket and gathers a cloud of darkness in his palm, turning his head ever so slightly to study it, showing me his perfect side profile. "You're not going anywhere."

I need a mental cold shower because all I can feel is the need for him to be worshiping my body. "Don't tell me what to do."

I should demand answers about the curse staining my skin, but all I care about is having him look at me.

The orb in his palm grows, a spark of lightning and snakes of fire twirling around it. "Sit down or I'll make you."

He's still standing with his back to me, showing off that he's powerful and I'm a mere mortal. I grab one of the pillows and throw it at him, hitting his back—apparently that shield he threw up only keeps me out.

I need this to end. The push and pull are haunting me.

"I want to finish all the tasks, right now." I have no idea why I just said that, but I mean it. As soon as they're done, so are we. "We have the rest of task four, and another six. Do them now."

Dane glances over his shoulder, enough for me to see the shadow the moon drops over his face. "What?"

"Once we finish task ten, I only need to suffer sitting beside you in class."

He chuckles, making me want to sink into the mattress and hold another pillow to my chest, but I stand here, a breeze away from showing off how naked I am underneath his shirt. "You wouldn't be able to handle the rest of the tasks in one night."

"You have no idea what I can handle. You don't know me. You don't have the first clue who the fuck I am."

With that, Dane turns to me with a furious expression, and I nearly faint. "I know more than enough!"

I'm not registering his words; my eyes are on his face and clothes. My hand lifts to my mouth as I gasp, and I straighten from the dresser, stepping back, as if the splattered blood down his front and slashed skin down the side of his face may hurt me. "What happened to you?"

"Don't change the subject," he snaps, aggressively shoving his hands back into his pockets. "You think I don't know you? I'm fucking haunted by you. Do you think I want to be here? That I want to wake up every morning and have to spend time with you in this castle? In these fucking classes? It's childish and beneath us both."

I tip my chin. "Then finish the tasks and be done with it."

"You have no idea what you're asking me, Seraphine."

My cheeks warm at the way my name caresses his tongue, the way it slips off and sounds like music to my ears. "Since when do you call me by my name?"

He freezes, realizing his mistake, then stalks towards me, eating up the space between us. As he draws closer, I not only note that my head now reaches higher up his chest than before, but I also see how deep the wound on his face is.

Blood soaks his collar and down his front, and as he pulls his hands slowly from his pockets with each stride, I see he has blood all over them too. His shoes are an inch from my toes as he looks down at me. I shouldn't pay any attention to the different colors of green flecks surrounded by a deep red, or to how dark and long his eyelashes are against the harshness.

"I know what I'm asking," I say, trying to be confident as I press the palms of my hands to the dresser behind me. "Finish the tasks, Dane."

Blood drips from the open wound on his face. "Don't say my name."

I challenge him as I drag out his name. "*Dane.*"

I'm either going to strangle her or kiss her.

"Don't you dare kiss me," I say, wanting the opposite. "It'll ruin everything. We covered that task, so we don't need to kiss again."

Dane glares down at me, hums, and curls a lock of hair behind my ear with a bloodstained hand. His fingertips glide against my cheek, and the touch sends shocks through my body, but I don't show it. I swallow, gripping the dresser.

Before he can speak or do anything else, his head snaps up and directs his gaze to the door, his jaw ticking as his nostrils flare.

Dane pushes away from me and grabs his jacket. "I have an issue to attend to. Stay here. I won't be long."

"No, you're staying here." I step towards him. "I'm not a dog, Dane. Stop treating me like one. You can't make me stay here."

Something cold and heavy snakes around my arms, and I'm thrown onto the bed with a yelp. I look to see metal cuffs on each wrist with a chain bounding me to the headboard. "Hey! What the hell?"

"You'll stay. If you leave, I cannot protect you."

I tug at them and scowl at him, closing my legs so he can't see my pussy and how annoyingly wet it is for him. "Who protects me from you?"

He rolls his eyes. "Shut up."

"Very mature response," I snap. "When will you return?"

"Soon. And when I do return, I want you to explain to me where you've been with Valin."

I frown and stop pulling at the manacles on my wrists. "Valin? What are you talking about? I was with you yesterday during practice!"

He wets his lips and straightens his suit jacket. "That was three days ago."

What? "I don't understand," I say, confused, my eyes flitting from side to side as I try to remember. "I went to my room once we finished practice and woke up in here."

Right?

I even remember sending Poppy a text saying she'd love the cinema.

Dane tosses the duvet over my bottom half and wordlessly lights a candle. He notes the dumbfounded look on my face and huffs.

"After you failed to show up to class and your insufferable friends couldn't find you, they came to me. I managed to track you and found you in the middle of the forest." He doesn't look at me, but his tone changes as he adds, "You were unconscious and have been for the last three days. I kept you in here until we got answers."

My brows reach my hairline. "What? I've been asleep in your bed for three days?"

He gives me a look. "That's what you pick up from what I said?"

"I went to my room after practice yesterday. I took a bath and read a book. Then I went to bed and texted Poppy before I fell asleep. You're wrong."

"I am *not* wrong. You were blue. Your lips and your skin were blue except for this." He gestures to my hands without touching me. "At the time, I couldn't do much, since your—a very intense power was attacking me for taking you. I tried to extract it, but it fought back and I only broke through it a few hours ago."

That explains the mess of his face and clothes, the gash on his cheek that runs down his neck. I want to touch it, to reach forward and heal it. But I don't have powers.

"I really don't understand." I bite my lip and try to think, but the play-by-play of me spending my night is clear. "I..." My eyes sting, frustration running wild in my head. "I..."

"You're safe now—that's the main thing."

I scoff. "Like you care."

I see the faintest smirk as he straightens away from me and turns towards the door. "You are my partner."

My voice shakes as I speak again, stopping him in his steps. "Is there a possibility that I was... that our partnership for these tasks may be void."

Dane glances over his shoulder at me. "You weren't touched from what I could see or sense."

"Stay. You can't leave me here."

He stares at me. "I'll try to explain later. You're safe here. It's important for you to rest. My shadows will watch over you while I'm gone."

"Wait." I study the blood and gashes on him. "Why haven't you healed yourself?"

"That's none of your concern," he says. "Sleep, mortal. Only then will you be strong enough to go back to your dormitory."

Dane opens the drawer of his dresser and places a pile of clean clothes on the chair at the far end of the room. "Your clothes were covered in blood, so you need to wear mine."

I look down at my body, at the long white shirt already on me, not seeing any wounds.

"It wasn't your blood."

I feel my expression dropping. "Whose blood then?"

He vanishes from the room without answering me, and I lie here in annoyance for the next three hours. The sun is due to come up, my skin itches from the cuffs, and his shirt has ridden up my thighs. My head lolls as I fall asleep, but I jump as the door swings open—then slams shut with an abrupt bang.

Dane stands there, breathing heavily, leaning his back against the wood and dropping his head back as his eyes close. "Fuck," he mutters, green eyes looking at me as he opens them again. "Can you be any more of a fucking headache?"

"What have I apparently done now?"

"Doesn't matter." The cuffs around my wrists vanish, and the clean clothes appear in my lap. "Go bathe, mortal. I need to take you back to your dormitory before you get caught."

"Why would I get caught?"

He pinches the bridge of his nose. "Because by the time the sun appears on the horizon, I'll be apprehended for murder, and I don't want you anywhere near me when I do."

My eyes widen, but something close to excitement shoots through me when it shouldn't. "You killed someone?"

Dane narrows his eyes. Either he felt what I did, or he's annoyed by the question. "Would that really surprise you?" he asks, walking into the middle of the room and removing his suit jacket and tie, then unfastening the buttons of the blood-stained shirt. "I am a monster to you after all."

Monster.

A monster.

Why does that word make me shiver?

"Should I be worried about my own safety?" I ask him, hugging myself.

Dane takes a deep breath and stops undressing, staring at the painting on his wall before he lowers his head and drags his finger back and forth on the dresser, exactly where I had traced earlier. "No."

I hiss as a burning sensation rips at my skin then, and the tendrils start to join together, like they're stitching up my wrists. I stare at them with wide eyes.

Dane appears in front of me, taking both my hands. "This will hurt."

"What will?"

I scream as pain ripples from my elbows to my fingertips, my eyes pinging open wide to stare at Dane, then down at my hands, where the black stains and tendrils slowly crawl onto him, sinking into his skin like they belong there. He closes his eyes, and his entire body tenses, his teeth clenched.

He's taking the pain from me. Releasing my hands, he falls back, trying to catch his breath as tendrils stitch together at his face, the veins in his neck injected with black. He closes his eyes and takes a few deep breaths until they bleed into his body, vanishing into nothing.

I stare at him. "What did you do?"

"Nothing you need to worry about," he says. "How do you feel?"

"Fine. I feel fine." I lower to his level, kneeling as I cup his face. "Did you just take that from me?"

"No, I can only take small amounts, or it will kill us both." He sighs, not pulling my hand away. "As I said, you're a headache, little mortal."

We stare at each other, and my eyes drop to his mouth, the

urge to close the distance almost unbearable, but instead, Dane stands, my hand falling from his face.

I watch him walk into his bathroom then hear him run water into his bathtub.

Walking in with my arms crossed, his shirt riding up my thighs, I stare at the golden tub in awe. His is huge compared to mine. It could fit five of us within it. Maybe it's the magic, but it fills within seconds, and Dane turns the tap off.

He comes towards me, still panting from taking some of the curse. He reaches for the buttons of the shirt on my body and starts to unfasten them from the top.

"What are you doing?" I ask, breathing out the question without stopping him.

Having him so close to me has my nerve ending on fire, my muscles tingling, and my core pulsing. He smells so good, even if he's covered in blood. It doesn't mask his scent at all.

"Did you get shorter?"

"No," he replies.

My brows pinch together as I look down at my body. "Did I get taller? Can the curse do that?"

Dane doesn't answer me as he keeps unbuttoning the shirt. His eyes clash with mine, and I hold his stare, even as the shirt slides from my shoulders and pools at my feet. He doesn't look down and doesn't break eye contact as I take shallow breaths.

"Get in," he orders, his eyes flickering to a bright silver, back to green, then to silver. "I'll make sure no one is in your room."

I glance at the bath and then back to him. "Can you stay?"

"That's not a good idea. Do you forget I'm about to be apprehended?" The silver of his eyes brightens a touch as he tuts and pushes hair behind my ear again, stepping forward until my naked breasts press against his blood-soaked shirt. "There isn't enough time for us to finish the rest of the tasks."

"We could finish task four."

He tilts his head ever so slightly.

I gulp, pushing aside my nerves as I reach for his belt, tugging it free from the loops. Dane watches me carefully as I throw it aside and quickly unbutton his pants, dipping my hand under the waistband and grabbing his hard cock.

Although I already knew it was thick and long from him dry-fucking me in my bed, I gulp harshly at how my fingers barely touch as I wrap them around the thickness of him.

The low, deep groan from his throat has me wanting him even more. His cock is warm, soft, thick and long, and I wonder if I could fit it into my mouth without dying.

My palm traces the veins as I pump him in my hand, watching him slowly lose control as I walk him back until he hits the sink.

I use my free hand to push his pants down while I stroke the length of him, from base to tip, and watch as his lips part.

Fuck.

I twist my wrist when I reach the swollen head, leaking with precum, and he tenses all over as I swipe it with my thumb and smear it over the head of his cock. He drops his head back, dried blood and black veins all over. I want to lick the skin and suck it between my teeth, to mark him for others to see.

His hand flies up to my throat, not cutting my air supply off but showing that even though I'm stroking him with my hand, he's in control. He keeps his fingers around my throat while I pump him harder, tightening my grip, more precum leaking over my fingers.

Dane thrusts into my hand, his grip on my throat loosening as he lets out a *fuck* and a groan.

I want to sink to my knees and suck him into my mouth. I want to drain him of every drop of cum and make him admit that he's mine. I want to dominate him, for him to praise me but also degrade me. I want all of it as I feel something twisting at my core, my spine tingling as warmth gathers between my legs.

A faint echo of an intense high has me moaning as Dane

lowers his forehead to the top of my head and groans so deep, I feel it everywhere. He orgasms from my touch, and his hips freeze, no longer thrusting into my palm as he releases up my arm and down my leg.

Instead of pushing himself away from me, Dane captures the cum trailing down my thigh, his other hand flexing on my throat as he shoves his fingers deep inside me. I gasp, whimpering as he pushes another thick finger inside and fucks me with them until I find my own release.

As mine smashes into me, it bleeds into Dane, and we both let out gasps as we fall against each other. More cum drips from his cock as I pulse around his fingers, throbbing, strangling him as his second orgasm vibrates against me, and I scream as I gush around his fingers.

I want all your firsts, my love. Your firsts and lasts and forever.

You can take it.

Does it hurt?

I'll stop.

You have me until you no longer need me.

Marry me, not him.

I'm not sure how long or how many times, but each time one releases, the other follows—a back and forth that has us dropping to the floor and panting in our mess. He covers my mouth with his palm just as he presses his thumb to my clit and rubs, easing more of his cum inside me with his fingers, stretching me as his length swells in my hand.

"Should we skip straight to our most awaited task? Should I fuck you into oblivion and keep you trapped there?"

I nod and squeeze his cock in my hand. There is so much cum from us both that I have no idea how we have the energy to keep going, but I know we can.

"Open your mouth and stick out your tongue." I wince as he pulls his fingers from me, gathers his cum from my thigh, and drives his fingers between my lips, shoving them into my throat as his knuckles hit my teeth.

Dane hums. "Such a good little human."

I gag around them, tasting the mixture of his cum and mine as he drags them back out against my tongue with dilated pupils.

He rubs his thumb across my bottom lip, a mass of shadows gathering above him as they urge us on.

Dane's voice is deep as he says, "Part your thighs so I can fuck you."

I don't think about protection or birth control, though I really should.

I widen my legs, and he shifts so he's above me, my back to the tiles. He strokes himself once, my eyes zoning into the glowing tattoo on the underside of his cock.

I want to ask him what the tattoo is, but all I can focus on is having it inside me.

"Remember, you asked for this. I warned you before what could happen if I fucked you."

"Don't make me hate you even more," I reply, panting. "Hurry up."

"This changes nothing between us."

"Agreed," I fire back.

A smile breaks out across my face, and his silver eyes flash with his own smile as he lowers his body onto mine.

"Take a deep breath," he whispers, his nose nudging mine as he lines his cock up to my entrance.

Before he can crash his mouth down on mine or thrust his cock inside me, his room door is blasted open, and the castle guards storm in.

25

We are so close. So, so close to having sex. If I had power, I'd snap all their necks and order Dane to screw me already.

Dane growls into my ear in annoyance before throwing a blanket over my naked body as the guards continue filtering into his dorm room. The bathroom door is slightly ajar but open enough that they see us without having to search.

Whatever high we were climbing to is instantly diminished, even though my pulse is still spiking and my body aches for him to kill them all, toss aside the blanket, and sink into me until I'm seeing stars.

Instead, I'm panting and watching Dane pull up his pants, catching a glimpse of the glowing tattoo on the underside of his cock again. He cracks his neck, readying himself.

I cradle the fabric to my sticky skin and press my back to the bathtub, my heart nearly pounding out of my chest as the building high is slowly replaced by terror.

The guards don't hesitate to shackle Dane, and he doesn't fight against them, chuckling at their efforts to drag him away.

My breath hitches as a black mass smashes into one guard's chest as he attempts to cuff me. He lets out a string of swear words, groans, and slides down the wall, holding his fist to his body and wincing as he tries to stand.

Dane glances over his shoulder at me. "If any of you look at or lay a finger on her, your body will be unrecognizable by the time I'm done with it."

That shouldn't set my pulse into a frenzy, but it does. Dane threatening someone on my behalf is almost... *hot.*

None of the guards approach me for a moment, but then one curses under his breath and points a sword in my face. "Stand."

I clutch at the blanket and do as he orders, making sure all of my private areas are hidden.

"Are you armed?"

I raise a brow and look down at myself . "Where am I supposed to keep a weapon?"

Dane tugs at the magical handcuffs he's in as the guard steps towards me with a sneer. "Careful, or I'll have you arrested for aiding a murderer. I could think of a number of ways you'd find yourself useful down in the dungeons."

As soon as the words are out, a snake of a shadow wraps around his throat, and I nearly drop the blanket covering me as he's hauled out of one of the windows with a parting scream.

Another deep chuckle comes from the shadow prince as the remaining guards pull him out of the room.

His voice is in my head a few seconds later. *I'll send the twins for you. Don't you dare leave the room alone.*

Staring at the empty space of the room, I try to fathom the last hour. My heart is beating too fast to be healthy, with a mix of emotions choking me.

I press my palm to my forehead and walk over and sit on top of his bed, trying to breathe, to come to terms with everything that just happened. We were seconds from screwing, and now he's been arrested.

And how exactly will you send the twins when you're being dragged to the dungeons for murder?

Who did he kill?

He must be too far away to hear me or respond, so I toss the blanket aside, quickly wipe myself down with a cloth, and pull on a pair of his briefs and a black shirt that smells exactly like him.

The shadows are all still here, not with Dane. They usually follow him around, but they're gathering on the walls with the ones that usually keep me company in my own room.

A knock sounds twice, and Mel pushes the door open. "Oh, great. I was fully expecting you to be chained to the bed."

I grimace. "Why would I be?"

She hesitates then shrugs. "It's Dane."

A spike of jealousy stabs into my chest at the thought of him with others. I glare at the four-poster bed then back to my friend. "Nice to know."

She inspects me with wide eyes. "Dane said he found you in the forest. Are you injured? We tried to look for you, but it was like you'd vanished off the island."

"I'm unscathed, but I have no memory. We need to go to the headmistress—she must not know Dane has been apprehended."

"She knows. The notice that a student was found in pieces has been all over the school. They've been hunting for the killer, and when they found evidence, Dane admitted to his crime. His mother gave him a few hours to speak with you before they came for him."

That must have been when he came in and said I was a headache. He spent his time left in freedom with me?

Dane hates me. Why the hell would he do that?

And who the hell did he kill and why?

I make his bed, flattening the wrinkles in his blankets. "Speak with me about what?" I ask, fluffing his pillows.

"Did he not mention anything when he came back?"

I shake my head, and she hums, looking me up and down. "You smell like him. Please tell me you didn't fuck Dane while he was covered in someone else's blood?"

"We didn't have sex," I say, popping my hip out as I cross my arms. "Do you know who he killed?"

"A student. He was from the Fire Realm—that's all I know."

I nod. "Should I be freaked out? I mean, I'm not used to any of this, but I feel calm?"

She gestures to my hands. "Could be the curse Dane has been trying to extract. Me and Poppy have been doing our research, and we found that it tries to channel darkness, like it's hunting for evil within one's soul. Your emotions will be partially muted and your inhibitions lowered as a result, and you'll have quite erratic dreams."

I lift my hands, the tendrils barely visible from Dane taking most of it. It'll get worse again, but for now, it's manageable. "It's a good thing I'm human then. The darkest my soul will ever get is from dodging my taxes."

She blinks at me.

"We should go. We aren't allowed on this side of the castle, especially not in the heirs' tower."

I snort. "Can the heirs be any more spoiled?"

"Well, Orsen did get offered a newer uniform, and even added that he could eat with the professors, but he said no because then he won't see me."

I follow her out of the room, closing the door with a click. "That's kind of sweet."

Looking at my friend and how she's not towering over me like before, I frown. "Am I taller?"

My arm bumps hers, and she sniffs her skin, ignoring my question. "Please bathe when you get to your room. I can smell Dane on you. Why is it all over you if you didn't have sex?"

I try to cover the last few hours as inexplicitly as possible as we make our way down the tower. The spiral staircase feels like it goes on forever.

Poppy joins us when we reach the bottom, and we go into the closest empty room so I can change into the clothes that don't scream, *I fucked someone last night!*

I've done the awkward walk home on numerous occasions from Grayson's apartment, but this is nothing like those times. We didn't have sex, but I came with such a force that it's still an echo in my nerves.

It wasn't like any other orgasm. Each time I unraveled, it bounced off Dane, and then his orgasm sent tingles all over my body. It was like we were connected, a bridge of pleasure, a never-ending cycle of my pussy clenching around his fingers while his cock pulsed in my hand.

If our orgasms from foreplay were like a game of ping-pong, then what the hell is it going to be like when it gets more intimate?

The twins take me to the medic, and she checks me over, staring at the curse spreading on my hands, but her main concern is the strong trace of Dane all over my body.

I tell her I consented, especially since everyone currently thinks he's a murderer.

She grows uncomfortable and asks if I'm on birth control when she realizes Dane's cum is inside me, but when I try to explain we didn't have sex, it opens up even more questions I refuse to answer.

After she gives me a contraceptive shot that makes me gag on fresh air at how large the needle is, she gives me more tampons than necessary. Poppy asks for some too so she can study them. Then the medic tells me to leave and rest, sending slips to all my teachers saying I'll be off for a few days.

Poppy asks me again what I remember about Valin, but I come up empty. The same sequence of events he imprinted in my mind comes out instead.

Maybe he accidentally erased what my old foster family looked like too? Come to think of it, I can't even remember their names. I try to picture them all, but it's foggy, like there's a blank canvas staring back at me.

"So you can't remember anything Valin said or did?"

I shake my head. "I don't even remember seeing him."

Mel takes a deep breath. "We go to Valin and ask him straight out what he did. I can't promise not to kill him, but I promise to wait until we have answers."

If I was a powerful immortal with a violent, deadly bone in my body, I would try to kill him too. But if I even attempted to, he'd probably kidnap me again.

I thank my friends for walking me to my dorm then shut the door, rest my back on it and close my eyes. I breathe in the calm air, the smell of my room, the smoke from the candles.

Can you hear me?

It's a long shot, but maybe he can tell me what to do to get rid of this curse on my own.

"Took your time."

His voice makes me open my eyes. Dane is sitting on my bed, ankle crossed at his knee, reading a textbook from the Fire Realm. He throws it down. "You've underlined the wrong letters by the way. You need to emphasize the D in *zedorphia*, not the Z."

"How are you here?"

He shrugs. "One of my powers—"

"No. I mean, why are you here, in my room, when you should be in the dungeons?"

"The only strong connection I have for materializing is to your room. I can't leave through your door; it's like I'm locked in here. I can go back to the dungeon if I travel, but that's all." Then he stands, tilting his head. "It's probably a good thing, since I need to siphon that nasty curse from you every few hours."

I glance down at my hands, which are already staining again. "Will it eventually kill me?"

"Yes," he says, and my eyes go wide. Dane closes the distance between us, and my heart gallops from his proximity and towering height. "But as long as you let me do this, I can slow it down until I find a solution. There is always a loophole."

Electric shocks rush up my arms as he takes my hands. "Why?"

His green eyes are on me, studying my face, and his stare feels like a soft caress on my soul. "Why what?" he asks.

"Why are you helping me?"

He massages my palms with his thumbs then circles his fingers around my wrists. The pulling sensation has me gasping with pain as he grits his teeth, transferring what he can of the curse to himself. He keeps his eyes on my face until the staining fades, his own veins injected with ink as his pupils dilate.

Before, the veins in his neck turned inky; this time, the dark vines crawl up the side of his face and his right eye turns entirely black.

He forces out, "Like I said, you haunt me."

We break away, and as I press my palm to my chest, he slams his against the wall, causing the room to vibrate like we've been struck by an earthquake, focusing on filling his lungs until the burning stops.

"Are you okay?" I ask when he stays silent, his back turned from me.

He straightens. I bite my lip nervously as he turns and looks at me again with a contorted expression. "You should take that bath now, mortal. As much as I enjoy the scent of you covered in my cum, I need to go back and pretend to be the imprisoned heir."

My cheeks heat, and I turn away from him to hide my blush. "Did you do what they say? Did you kill someone?"

"I might as well have."

I slant my head. "Meaning?"

He comes up behind me, shivers wracking my body as he whispers against my ear, "Be a good girl for me, little mortal. I'll return in the evening."

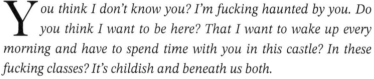

26

You think I don't know you? I'm fucking haunted by you. Do you think I want to be here? That I want to wake up every morning and have to spend time with you in this castle? In these fucking classes? It's childish and beneath us both.

That spiel from Dane replays in my mind like a broken record. The words were spoken so harshly it was as if he was offended that we were both here, like it was all my fault.

I'm fucking haunted by you.

Haunted.

I'm starting to think I'm haunted by him too. Because even though he isn't here, I can feel him nearby, smell the mind-bending scent of him, the spice and musk filling my senses.

He visits twice a day. Once in the morning, then again in the evening. While he's here, he makes my entire body quake as he siphons what he can of the curse. It hurts, but we've grown more comfortable with it. He tells me to take a few breaths before he starts. One of the times it was so bad that we both passed out on top of my window seat, and I woke up with his head in my lap.

Usually, after the torture, he sits around for an hour until his powers regenerate enough for him to travel while either being a dick to me, teasing me about my mortality, or commenting on how fast my heart is racing without him even touching me. He'll do something to piss me off, I'll threaten him with objects around me, then he vanishes until the next day.

No matter how many times I ask, he won't tell me about the person he killed or why he did it. The academy hasn't mentioned anything else regarding the matter, as if nothing happened at all. Valin is still teaching. The twins still want to kill him. I haven't left my room. And Dane is still trapped between here and the dungeons.

Shivering, I lie on my back, staring at the ceiling as the shadows dance around, as if there's a silent chant that has them excited that Dane should be here soon.

The little girl skips while holding a large hand, a dog runs after a ball, and an old man cleans his glasses with a cloth before reading a book.

It's not clear what exactly each silhouette is doing. It's a guessing game if they're even humans or creatures; if they're bad or good. But I just know they're protecting me.

There are more here than usual. Some sit in the corner of my room, watching me like guarding statues, and some follow my bare feet like dogs sniffing on the ground as I walk into the bathroom.

They usually disperse when I use the bathroom, thankfully.

I try to sit up, and dizziness has me falling back down again in a huff. My knotted hair sprawls over my face, sticking to my skin.

To my dismay, I'm sick. It started last night, after Dane left. My skin burns, my tongue is drier than a desert, and I think I've sweated away half my body weight.

I also don't answer the door whenever someone comes knocking, even if it's the twins sliding trays of food under my door—via magic presumably—with a note.

Yesterday it was Poppy. *Eat up, my little dandelion.*

Today is evidently Mel. *If you don't eat, you'll die.*

I sent Mel a message only hours ago, informing her that I wasn't dead or kidnapped again, and that I was perfectly fine and needed as much sleep as possible. I was simply feeling under the weather.

Because humans get sick, projectile vomit while drunk, come down with viruses, and suffer from illnesses that vary from giving us the sniffles to making our organs fail before the light leaves our very mortal eyes.

Unlike these undying creatures who don't even know what goddamn asthma or diabetes are. I once tried to explain to Poppy the applications of injecting insulin into one's body and why, and even described an inhaler and how it opens our airways. She just stared at me as though I'd grown two extra heads. Which isn't exactly uncommon around here.

When I bathed this morning, I waited for Dane to abruptly crack the atmosphere in two, to appear and shove my head underwater. I wanted him to. I crave the feel of his hands on me, even if it's in an act of violence.

So, so badly I wanted him to slide his rough hand between my legs and pleasure me into the abyss while the water splashed across the floor. I wanted my lip between his teeth, wanted him sucking on my throat while he edged me.

When he didn't appear, I tried to do it myself. Sans the throat sucking because I'm not built that way. I gave up, hoping he'd appear and finish me off. He still hasn't come for his morning siphoning session, and I may or may not be wearing the most revealing sleep clothes I own here in the academy.

From being seconds from having sex to him only touching me when he grabs my wrist, I'm close to exploding. I know everything we've done previously has been for the assignments we need to complete, but we've already overstepped on other tasks, so why not now?

I truly hate him, but I would gladly let him dominate me

from every angle. Does that make me sick? Maybe. But that doesn't explain why I feel like I'm physically on the brink of death when I'm not around him.

Since that moment we nearly joined as one, my body has never felt so alive, which is weird, since I feel like I'm dying.

If I had a thermometer, I know it'd be hitting a feverish temp.

Sweat coats my skin, and I slowly blink as the saltiness drips into my eyes. I wipe it away with the back of my hand and freeze, lifting the other to study both as I flex my fingers.

The staining on my hands is getting considerably worse. It usually takes an entire day to spread, but now it's happening faster. Both of my hands are completely black, burning and spasming every so often, with tendrils curling around each wrist, spiraling in vines as they climb up and snake at my elbows.

When Dane left last night, he had to siphon more than usual, and he fell asleep on the chair beside my bed. I woke to the chair being empty and what I could have sworn felt like the linger of a kiss on my forehead.

I attempted to grab my phone from the top of the dresser this morning and it practically flew to my hand.

If it weren't for all my memories of growing up, I'd swear I was a witch in disguise—or something a lot worse.

It's the curse. It has to be. Because not only am I experiencing all of this, but I can also hear and feel Dane when he isn't even near me. I know when he's asleep in his cell, when he wakes, if a sense heightens, or when he feels strongly.

The curse building on my hands is to blame—it has to be. Humans simply cannot do what I'm doing with Dane.

But going by the book on the Shadow Realm that magically appeared in my room days ago, I should be dead. Dane siphoning it is slowing down whatever it's doing, but even extracting an infinitesimal amount of a curse to this degree depletes a creature's powers—which is why he struggled to properly fight against the guards or heal his wounds but was able to toss a blanket over my nakedness, so the guard didn't see my exposed body.

Despite all these thoughts, all I can think about is... If he was as weak as that, how the hell was he going to have sex with me?

So, yeah, all tasks are still on the table. At least we finished task four. Next, we need to pleasure ourselves in front of one another without touching each other. Either at the same time or at separate times.

How do I even bring this up in conversation?

God, I feel terrible.

If you can hear me, I'm close to being a corpse here. I'm either unwell, or this curse is kicking my ass.

Then I say it again, out loud.

Nothing.

I feel like an idiot for talking to myself, but I look over to the shadows in the corner, the ones that belong to Dane. "I think I'm dying."

The silhouettes of the statues don't move an inch.

I sigh and throw the duvet over my head, burying into my pillow. Coughing, I nearly choke up my lungs for a good three minutes before it settles, and then I pee for the hundredth time today.

If I die on this island over the goddamn flu, I will scream.

Forever the dramatic little mortal, aren't you?

I stop in the middle of the room as my heart rate instantly accelerates, my head spinning from the pressure of being out of bed. I need to sit down, but I'm frozen in place as I look around.

You can hear me? I ask.

Unfortunately.

I audibly tut. *Where are you?* I ask, slowly making my way to the bed, trying to ignore the pang of excitement and relief that I'm hearing from him.

Somewhere dark.

I roll my eyes. *How descriptive. I thought you said we were too far apart to speak like this when you're in the dungeons?*

Then his voice is there again. *It seems I've regenerated enough of my powers, no thanks to you, mortal. You seem weaker than usual.*

Will there ever be a day you don't insult me?

No, he replies instantly.

Idiot.

There is an inspection in one hour, then I can come, he says, and, annoyingly, I smile. *Does that excite you?*

My smile drops. *No.*

Liar. You are terrible at hiding your emotions. I can feel everything you feel, remember?

My lungs stop working when something wraps around my thigh, and I shove away the duvet to see the shadow of a hand gripping me. A trace of a snake circles my other thigh, and my breath hitches as they force my legs apart.

What are you doing?

Dane's answer is instant. *Passing time. Should I stop?*

I gulp, the tether between us pulling taut as my body lifts from the bed, floating an inch in the air as my underwear is moved aside.

This isn't a task, Dane.

Yet you haven't told me to stop.

My hair cascades to the pillow as I levitate in mid-air while an invisible force parts my pussy, opening me, and my clit throbs. It drags a groan from Dane through the connection between us, feeling what I feel, the tingling and coiling warmth at the base of my spine.

Don't stop, I practically moan.

My pussy pulses as cold air hits it, and my eyes flutter shut. Nipples tightening, I feel a pressure between my legs as if it belongs to me—something different, something outward, not inward. I want to touch, to stroke, to feel my touch trace the tip.

The bridge between us grows stronger, our synapses inter-linking for a deep connection. I picture nails dragging down his powerful back, and he forces the image of me on my knees for him, my mouth open, tongue out and waiting.

God, I need this man deep inside me.

Do not whimper to your god, little mortal. I'll burn down the remaining realms before I hear you call out to someone else.

My eyes close, and when I try to touch myself, to find a release, vines wrap around my wrists.

Not yet.

His cock is hard. He's gripping it in a fist and gritting his teeth while I suck in a deep breath as my arousal drips onto my bed beneath my floating body.

He's thick. It's growing long and hard and stiff. It's leaking, and the veins bulge with the ghost of a stroke from base to tip.

Focusing on his actions, as if I'm sitting right in front of him, I reach for him, shoving against his chest and controlling his own hand, tighter, faster, twisting his wrist with each up-and-down motion.

His voice is breathy in my head. *Would you look at that? You can feel me too.*

A lick of a low groan presses to my cheek as his shadow of a touch to my thighs slides up, and I can still sense him around me. We're connected, and each time he strokes himself, I feel each ridge and twitch.

We are the epicenter of arousal as we become one entity. Each time he breathes in, I feel his lungs filling with air. I feel the valves in his heart pumping blood through his body and hear the swallow in his throat as his Adam's apple shifts.

My nerves spark along with his, suspended in the air as the snake of his power licks against my inner thigh. The vines slowly slide away from my wrists, a silent order.

My hand slips between my legs almost on instinct, my arousal coating my palm as I grind against it. With strength I never knew existed, I rip my underwear completely off, tossing the soaked fabric aside.

It's like he's here beside me, and I can see him fucking his hand while I press against my own, sinking my middle finger into the first knuckle, teasing myself as I spread my wetness to my clit.

Dane's own heart is racing, his hips moving, his free hand slamming against the bars of his cell. He drops his head as I push two fingers inside me, curling them against my sweet spot.

An image of him sliding down my body and burying his head between my legs spreads wildfire all over, and I moan through the psychological bridge between us.

Practice for task five, I say, my voice breathless, even in my mind.

He doesn't respond, but he doesn't have to. His grip on his cock tightens, the head sensitive as he curls his wrist at the tip, swiping his precum with his thumb and spreading it over himself.

I can feel how soaked you are, he tells me. *You're so warm around your fingers. Are you going to come for me?*

Only if you come for me, I counter.

I always fucking do, he growls, and everything shatters into smithereens with how deep his voice is in my head.

As a multitude of orgasms smack into me like tidal waves crashing, my inner walls crush my fingers with each spasm. Dane tenses on a groan as my release reaches his side of the connection, stilling his movements until the tenderness of his balls eases off.

My body collapses onto the bed, and I'm completely spent.

Dane's forehead is against the cold wall as his heart races, sweat coating the back of his neck like mine.

We stay in silence and lingering euphoria for minutes, possibly hours. When the intensity calms, I can sense him wiping the string of cum from his pants while I pull my fingers away, panting on the mattress.

The urge to be inside you is just getting worse, he says, his voice strained. *But we can't take any shortcuts. No more recklessness. Understand?*

I frown at his change in tone, unable to do anything but catch my breath. *Shortcuts?*

I meant it when I said I'd kill you if I fucked you. You are a human, and I am not. Your body needs to be trained to be able to handle me.

My toes curl from the lingering pleasure vibrating in my bones, sweat coating my skin. *Trained?*

There's a crack in the air, and I yelp as Dane materializes on top of me, pinning me down by the wrists as he starts painfully siphoning the curse from my soul.

My fingers tingle as the tendrils transfer to his own skin, his eyes the brightest silver despite the pain he's currently feeling. Black clouds puff around the silver, and I can't avert my gaze.

"Yes, trained," he rasps as he uses his knee to part my legs, settling between them. I'm bare. He's fully clothed but unzipped. But despite the material, I can feel he's still hard. He presses against me, drawing a breathy moan from my lungs. "What do you think the tasks are for, little mortal?"

27

D ane Dalton can suck my imaginary dick.

I mean it. If I had one, it would be freakishly big, deadly thick, made of sandpaper, with blades poking out from every angle, and I would make him suck it until he begged me with his eyes to stop.

Then I'd watch him bleed to death.

An exaggerated sigh brings me back to the present as Dane pinches the bridge of his nose. "I really hate that I can hear what you're saying in your mind. Sometimes it's funny, but other times I think there is something genuinely wrong with you. Did you hit your head one of the times you tried to escape?"

He dodges a candle I throw at his face.

"And you're violent. I think you forget I could stop your heart without even looking at you."

"Shut up, asshole. If you ever want to pass mortal studies, then stop being a douche and actually pay attention."

"So moody," he muses, narrowing his eyes at me. "Was your first day back at classes not to your liking?"

My eye twitches as I look down at my notes. "I was distracted."

He hums, lifting the textbook on electronics. He really needs to soak up the information like a sponge. The guy knows nothing about humans. I nearly died when he said he had no idea what a TV was—or a gaming console for that matter. So, since he can't attend any classes but is still being forced to take his tests in the dungeons, I've agreed to help him.

But when I made an appearance in class yesterday, I couldn't focus. I had a headache, and all I kept thinking about was the night before.

When he siphoned the curse, it overwhelmed us both and we dropped onto the floor in a heap. A connection formed between us, and Dane reached out to me and pulled me into his mind. Everywhere was blurry, dreamlike, echoes around us, and each breath in and out of my lungs felt fake. I initially panicked, but he kept his hand in mine as he pulled me through the corridor of his tower.

I followed him into his room, all hazy and full of fog. I could hear soft moans coming from the bathroom and gasped when I saw us both, the *real* us, collapsing to the floor with my hand on his cock and his fingers touching me.

There was a burning sensation on my hands, and when I looked down, the black veins were twirling around my fingers and up my wrists.

Dane told me to watch, to focus on us.

I could feel it all, and the intensity of pain mixing with plea-sure had me screwing my eyes shut. My thighs clenched, and my lungs tightened from a wave of euphoria hitting me just as my true self began to writhe beneath the real Dane.

We were ghosts watching ourselves, and I got turned on by it.

I kept my eyes closed, desperate for release, to go back to my real body and feel it in the flesh. To tell Dane to finish the tasks, regardless of how dangerous it would be.

"Open your eyes, human," he ordered me, and when I did, he

came up from behind and held my nape, his other hand a ghost on my hip. "Watch what I do to you."

We were dragged from the dream the moment the guards burst into the room, and a vortex of white pulled me back to my own body, where we lay on my bedroom floor, panting, the curse seeping into Dane's sweating skin.

He lifted me into bed, told me to sleep, and that he'd see me later.

I could still feel it all as if it just happened, as if the back and forth of our orgasms were still vibrating like a wire between us.

The echoes of his orgasm are still zapping through my every nerve ending now, setting them alight whenever the images come to mind. His touch and taste and the way his eyes glazed over when he shoved his cum inside me are permanently etched into my mind.

Since the night I levitated in the air and fucked myself with my own hand, with Dane's voice in my ear, I've been feral.

Earlier, when the world around me went silent, a coiling sensation bloomed down low. My nipples tightened, my thighs clenched uncontrollably with the need for friction, and a building pleasure had me standing from my seat in the class I was in and excusing myself for the rest of the lesson.

I hurried to my room, lay in bed with my hands fisting the sheets, and tried to work out why I was still feeling the after-effects of Dane Dalton. I wanted to slide my fingers between my legs and hear his voice telling me what to do.

Distant. A growled-out whisper. An order. A plea.

But instead of giving myself pleasure, I showered with frigid water, went to my next class, and tried to ignore the ache.

It kept happening randomly throughout the day. The need for touch. Just before he came to see me, I was concentrating in my last class, writing a paper on different animals in the mortal realm, when I felt a wet stroke against my cleavage. My knee smacked my desk as I jolted, and every student stared at me while I tried not to make it obvious that I was instantly aroused.

I glanced down, seeing a shadow wrapping around my thigh, and I just knew what it was and who was doing it. But despite him being locked away in the dungeons and only able to see me twice a day, it's like a part of him is with me all the time, lingering, teasing, doing what he can to drive me insane.

It's been over a week since Dane was arrested, and no one has mentioned it. The twins are the only ones who ask if I know what's happening, but Dane told me not to tell anyone that he can reach me.

If the academy finds out, then there's a chance they might use a barricading spell on him until his trial, and I won't be able to slow down the curse on my own.

Simply, I'll die if Dane gets caught sneaking into my room.

So, yeah, it's been over seven days of everyone pretending life is normal, going to classes and laughing and making sure all their homework is completed on time while I walk around wearing gloves to hide the deadly staining. Not once has anyone spoken about the brutal killing of a student or the fact that Dane, the popular heir who everyone bows down to, has been absent from each lesson. And not once have I been able to sleep without feeling like something is missing, without the urge to leave my room and go to him when he returns to his cell.

I look up from my notes, watching his forest-green eyes flit left to right as he reads. His lashes are so dark and thick, matching his brows. I won't tell him, and I'll shut my mind off while I think about it, but I saw him in my dream last night.

When I closed my eyes, I was smaller, younger, my voice gentle, grinning with excitement when I saw him hiding behind one of the stone pillars. A younger version of the prince of shadows. Around sixteen. A tall, white-haired boy with a smile that could light up the sky.

My family was staying in the kingdom for a few days. We'd snuck around after dark, away from prying eyes.

I remember the softness of his hand as he held mine while we ran through the tunnels beneath his father's castle. I don't know how I knew it was his father's castle—I just did. Everything looked familiar, comfortable, like home.

And I'm surprised at how much those thoughts don't scare me.

We'd giggle, then I screamed and laughed as he picked me up and carried me to our secret spot under the tree. We'd cradle each other among blankets, where I'd trace his growing tattoos and kiss his lips, watching the sunrise, only to separate again when we returned to our kingdoms.

Quite strange that my mind conjures up these crazy scenarios, considering Dane is anything but the cute, charming boy from my dreams. He's rough and ruthless, and doesn't hesitate to scowl at me and snap back at my attitude.

He's aggressive and has a thing for trying to drown people.

Hell, I think if we were in a sword fight, he'd pin me down with the blade to my throat and make me surrender by begging for mercy, then make me crawl back to where I came from.

Not that I ever would.

I don't remember the name of the street I live on.

Strange.

He must be getting beat up or abused in some way because he hasn't been able to heal himself, and he has a gash on his cheek, a cut lip, and bruising around his neck, as if someone tried to strangle him with a large metal chain.

I did try to ask what happened when he materialized in here and fell into my wall, but apparently I've to stay out of his business and focus on my own problems.

"Okay, so. First question. Who invented the television?"

Dane glares at me. "What kind of fucking question is that?"

"A relevant one."

"Disney," he answers, quirking a brow, pleased with himself. "Walter Disney."

I bellow a laugh. "Are you serious?"

He sags on a huff. "Do all mortals know the answer?" he asks, his jaw ticking as his patience wears thin. We have nine questions left, and I have a feeling he's going to get all of them wrong.

"Well, most do. Do you at least know the year it was invented?"

His tone deepens. "Your voice is annoying me."

He ducks when I toss a pen at him.

I shriek as he grabs my ankle and tugs me across the bed. I kick him and move away, and he shakes his head. "Stop throwing shit at me."

I roll my eyes and put distance between us again. "You said my voice was annoying."

His shoulder raises lazily as he lifts his own notebook, probably full of stick men of him killing me. "It *is* annoying."

"Four inventors were involved in creating the first television," I say, reading and making sure I have the correct names because I really don't know the right answer. "It was first demonstrated in 1927."

"Stupid," he says with a scoff. "There isn't a chance that all humans know that. Ask me something else. Something important."

I smile to myself. "Who's the better singer... Billie Eilish or Taylor Swift?"

"Who?"

I toss down my book. "I think it's time for you to leave."

Dane chews on his lip, pressing the tip of his pen to his temple. "Here's a question for you then, mortal. What happened to the Shadow Realm?"

"This is for the mortal studies test."

"Answer the question."

I frown. "How am I supposed to know?"

"You've been studying me and my world enough—surely you have an idea."

I try not to stare at his bottom lip, which he's holding between his teeth, or the lone lock that's fallen in his eyes. "It was destroyed."

"When?"

I shrug. "I assume it was a while ago?"

"Five hundred and seventy years ago," he says, leaning back on his elbows on the bed in front of me. "Give or take a year. I've lost track."

"Why didn't you just teleport to the Mortal Realm instead of doing this school thing?"

He stares at me for a second. "Jumping between realms is an extremely rare occurrence. Only the most powerful are capable. I'd die if I even attempted to do it."

"There are immortals here that are more powerful than you?" I ask, tilting my head.

He scoffs. "Of course not."

"How was I brought here then?"

Dane stares at me for a long moment. "Power linking. If we combine our powers, then it's possible, but again, rare. Whoever took you must've linked. Unless they used a portal, which isn't safe."

I flatten my lips and think back to that day I was taken. "Whoever took me drew runes or something on my wall and a sort of hole opened. Is that not the same as jumping between realms?"

"No. Portals aren't the same, but have the same outcome," he replies, dropping his gaze for a second. "Is there a reason you're asking all these questions?"

"Do you know who kidnapped me?"

"No." Dane tilts his head, gesturing to my book. "Ask me the next question."

"You're just going to change the subject?"

"Yes. This is more important." He sits up and leans forward, placing my book back in my hand. "You don't want me to fail, do you?"

I lower the open pages. "One more off-subject question. What did Valin do to me?" I ask, chewing my lip and looking at the words in my textbook. "You never told me, just that he took me and that's it."

"He didn't hurt you. He removed your memories and planted a new one there in its place. Almost generic."

"But *why*? Why did he take me?" I ask, looking back up at him and curling my legs beneath me.

Dane sighs and drops his book, giving up on the questions. "Valin thinks you belong to him after one taste. He's delusional. I'll deal with him once I get out."

I snort. "Why would I belong to him? I've never been near Valin for him to get a taste."

For a second, Dane seems stuck on words. He clears his throat and gets off the bed. "You don't need to lie to me. There have been multiple occasions where you were alone together."

Fucking multiple, he says in his head as he fixes his tie.

"Although jealousy on you is catching me off guard, I've never as much as kissed Valin."

"Jealousy." He scoffs, cracking his neck to one side then the other. "Kneel," he says, gesturing to me to rise to his height from the bed. "Let's get this over with."

I do as he says with a scowl on my face. He wraps his fingers around my wrists, and I take the opportunity to sink my nails into his skin. "Stop being such a dick to me for no reason."

Dane glares at me. "Do you need to be so fucking violent?" he hisses.

I tip my chin. "Yes."

He clicks his jaw, tightening his hold on my wrists and

tugging me forward on my knees. "I'm starting to think you actually want me to kill you."

I snort. "I'm seeing that word very differently now."

I'd kill you if I fucked you.

A long silence, a slow blink, and then he says, "Meaning?"

"How exactly would you kill me?" I ask, tilting my head, a lock of brown hair falling in my face. "An ax to the gut? A ball of lightning to the chest? Maybe properly drowning me?" My eyes light up, and I see amusement in him.

Dane fights a smirk, leaning closer as he pulls me to the edge of the bed on my knees, until I feel his breath on my face. "I have imagined your death in many ways, mortal. But not quite like that."

"I hate you."

"You really don't," he counters.

"I saw you kill me once," I say, and his hold falters on my wrists as he looks at me with shock. I keep going. "I was on a stone altar-type thing, and you stabbed me with a knife."

"Quite imaginative, mortal."

"The Blade of the Gods."

Dane's body freezes, his eyes widening. "How do you know about that?"

"I told you. I saw it in my dreams. You stabbed me with it."

"What else do you know about the blade?"

"Nothing at all. What does it mean?" I ask. "The dream?"

But then I scream as he abruptly siphons the curse pumping through my veins. I fall into his chest, panting, but neither of us lets go as his entire body goes stiff against me.

My head drops onto his shoulder, and he does everything he can to bear my weight as he takes the burning blood, the dark poison transferring to him.

My eyes close, and my body grows tired and limp.

Wake up. You need to be awake for this to work.

I open my eyes—they're watering and stinging with pressure

behind them. Lifting my head, I look at Dane, who has blood dripping from one of his nostrils, his forehead pressed to mine.

Stay awake.

Keep your eyes on me.

Push through it.

Ten more seconds.

I feel it the moment the last string of the curse is plucked from my soul, and as my body gives in to the exhaustion, Dane manages to catch me and drag me onto the bed, where his own body gives up, and he passes out beside me.

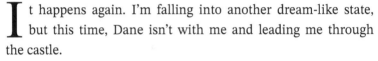

28

It happens again. I'm falling into another dream-like state, but this time, Dane isn't with me and leading me through the castle.

I'm standing in a dark chamber, a cell, that smells like blood and dirty water. The dungeons. I've never been underground, and I have no idea what it looks like, but it seems my mind has built up an entire aesthetic of where creatures go when they're arrested.

My breaths come out in puffs as I look around. Blood stains the walls, where chains dangle, a hand still attached to one of them. I grimace at the smell and press the back of my hand to my nose and mouth.

When I push open a large oak door, I find myself in the main corridor of the dungeons. It's dark, with no candles leading the way like in the rest of the castle. Water drips from the old, broken bricks all around. It smells like sewage, beady eyes peeking from the holes in the walls.

And every now and again, as my feet step in the puddles, my surroundings creak and growl, followed by a psychotic laugh that will forever haunt me.

My footsteps are silent in my dream, but I'm drawn to the last cell on the left. I push it open, seeing a small boy hugging himself and rocking back and forth in the corner, claw marks down his back.

His sobs are like echoes, as if he's trapped at the bottom of an old well.

Hello? Are you okay?

I try to speak, but the words are in my head, a whisper, a thought, nothing more than a breath with no sound as my lips move.

I reach for the boy, who's covered in tattoos, but a black mass launches towards me, wrapping its claws around my throat and shoving me out and away, chasing me back to the place I belong. The chant is repetitive, the haunting words I've heard before.

Death to her, death to all.

I wake with a start, gasping, unable to properly fill my lungs until I drag in a long breath and stop shaking. I wipe sweat from my face, but when I try to move, a heaviness on my side stops me.

I look to see Dane with his head on my shoulder, arm and leg slung over me, caging me against the mattress. His other hand is in my hair, a loose grip.

His snow-like locks are soaked with sweat, droplets sliding down his face and neck and drenching his shirt collar. It's mixing with a trail of blood from his nose.

"Dane," I croak, my throat dry. "Dane."

Nothing.

I blow out a breath and look at my hands, completely free of any of the curse. Usually, when he siphons, he takes as much as he can before it overwhelms him. But it seems he's taken so much it's no longer visible on my skin.

I frown at the thought of him hurting himself more than other days. "Dane," I say again, shaking his shoulder. His body is hotter than a furnace. I shift to free myself a little as I press the back of my hand to his forehead.

It's burning. Dane is burning up badly.

But immortals don't get sick—unless the curse has messed him up?

Dane? I try a different way. *Can you hear me?*

I push him lightly, rolling him onto his back, freeing myself somehow from the heavy bane of my existence. I say his name once more, but there's no response. "If you can hear me, I'm going to take your shirt off, okay? I need to try to cool you down."

I work the buttons of his shirt. It's wet from how much he's sweating, and I gasp when I undo his collar and see the thin black veins on his neck, stretching down his chest and merging with the tattoos there.

The more buttons I unfasten, the more of the curse I can see on his body. I ignore his defined abs as I run my fingers down them, tracing a thick vein injected with black that travels down beneath his waistband.

This can't be good.

He doesn't make a sound as I struggle to get the shirt off him, rushing to my window and opening it wide.

When I press a cloth I've soaked to his face, his eyes flutter beneath his eyelids, erratically pinging from side to side. I drench the cloth in frigid water again and squeeze it over his hair and chest.

I should go find help—ask one of the twins or Orsen to do something, but then he'd be caught and trapped. It'll be a last resort if I have to do that.

The bathwater runs cold, and I keep checking on him as the tub fills. The shadows in the walls are watching, guarding, and seem to be concerned for their prince as I climb back onto the mattress. "Dane, I'm going to pull you off the bed, okay?"

My attempt to drag him off results in me slipping on my ass

too many times, until I finally use my feet to kick him off. He tumbles to the floor, and I gasp when he groans.

"What are you doing to me, mortal?"

"You're burning up! I'm trying to get you into the bathtub."

He tries to lift his head to look at me and drops back. "Fuck."

I somehow get him into the bathroom, where I flick cold water on his face by cupping my hands and throwing it at him. He doesn't open his eyes, but I know he wants to scowl at me.

"Hips up," I order. "I need to take your pants off."

His brow moves, but he does as he's told. "You've said that to me before. Do you remember the night of our fourth ceremony?"

I frown. "I assume you're confusing me with a former flame."

He grunts as he shakily gets to his feet, and I try not to stare at him in his briefs. I can see the outline of his cock, and I really *shouldn't* look. I focus on the black veins pulsing all over his body—that larger one that crawls under his waistband, and I wonder if...

My eyes bulge as he kicks off his briefs and I get a full show of his cursed cock—the black veins are even in his dick. If this was a different moment, my curiosity would win out, and I'd tip it up to see what the tattoo is on the underside. I've had it in my hand while it was hard and terrifying, but even soft, it looks thicker than his wrist. "That thing should be illegal."

Dane lifts his wrist, studying it. "Interesting."

But when he stumbles, and a trickle of blood drips from his nose, I catch him and help him into the tub.

A normal person would gasp or scream at how cold the water is. I should have known Dane is far from normal.

Unbothered by the water, he slouches and rests his head on the lip of the bath. And quickly, I realize he's passing out again.

I slap him. "Wake up."

One eye opens. "Do that again and I'll drag you in here."

I cross my arms. "You wouldn't dare. I—"

I catch a mouthful of ice-cold water as Dane yanks me in

with him, my entire body ramrod straight and shaking as I shriek. "Dane!"

He wraps his arms around me and pulls me on top of him, but I'm far too cold to pay attention to our position.

When I shove against his chest and straddle him in the bath, him naked and me in a pair of short shorts, my eyes go wide. "The curse is spreading to your face. Why are the whites of your eyes turning black?"

"Looks like I might be dying, little mortal. It's your lucky day. It's a shame we never got to do the next task."

When he coughs up black blood, my heart stops.

"Don't worry. A minor setback. I'll catch you in the next life."

Panic takes over, and I have no idea how I know, but I press my hand firmly on his chest, focusing on the curse, on the tendrils knitting together in his soul. I squeeze my eyes shut and call to it.

I call.

And call.

And call some more.

The flames of the candles flicker, a wind gusting around us, whipping my wet hair around my face as sharp, searing pain claws at my fingertips, latching on, drawing closer as it seeps under my nail beds and into the creases of my fingerprints.

My heart accelerates, and I continue to call to the curse, to knock it off course as it aims for the center of Dane's darkening soul.

"Fuck, Seraphine, no."

The black veins on Dane's face start to fade, as well as the ones on his throat and chest. We both writhe in terror and pain, my bones feeling like they're turning to ash as water sloshes around us. Dane tries to pull my hand away, but it's stuck, until something rips me away from him, catapulting me out of the tub and against the bathroom wall.

The gust of wind stops, the candles settle, and I breathe

heavily as I fall to the ground. Dane climbs out of the bath, wraps a towel around himself, and comes to me.

"You idiot. What the fuck were you thinking?" he snaps, pulling me up from the floor and carrying me to bed. "You shouldn't have done that. They'll know you used a power link."

I have no idea what I just did. Or who *they* are. I close my eyes. "I wanted to help."

"How did you know what to do?"

Silence for a long beat because I have no idea. I shrug. "I just did. Are you better?"

I took some of the curse back, but not enough to harm myself. I also shouldn't know that, but I do.

"Just say yes or no—I'm a little dizzy."

"Yes." He nods, sighs, and instead of leaving or even getting clothes on, he tugs the duvet back and pulls me against him, my back to his chest. "You can't be left alone right now. No human should ever power link."

"Are you trying to complete task five?"

He chuckles, and his breath against my cheek makes me comfortable; makes me forget about the fading pain. "I wouldn't be allowed to touch you if that was what I was doing."

"If I ask you something, will you tell me the truth?"

"No," he replies, and I huff.

Dane smiles against my neck, and a flutter of electricity rushes through me. "No more questions. My brain hurts from them. Ask me later."

"You called me Seraphine again," I point out. "Can you call me by my name from now on?"

"No."

I roll my heavy eyes.

We both fall into a calmness, and at some point, his towel falls from around his waist, my wet clothes clinging to my body, and his hand holds my breast.

243

The heat between my legs is making me lose my mind. "Are you awake?"

"Obviously."

"Can we do task five?" I ask bravely.

Dane lets go of me and pushes back, putting distance between us. "Now?"

"Yeah. I need a distraction."

I sense the spike in nerves between us, but also a hint of excitement. There's a long pause, and I'm desperate for him to speak, to tell me that we can. It'll take my mind off my soul rattling. And also because, well... I want him.

"Fine. Can you keep your hands to yourself?"

"Can you?" I retort as I lift my hips and tug down my shorts.

I gulp as Dane digs the towel from beneath the sheets and tosses it on the floor. It's dark out, the glow from the candle's flame highlighting his face and tanned abs. I want to drag my tongue against them.

Dane groans. "Your mind is very open right now, human."

My cheeks heat, but nerves take over as he completely removes the duvet, my bottom half exposed.

"Why are you hiding yourself?" He gestures to my closed legs, my hiked knees, and the way I've covered myself with my hand. "I've seen it all before."

He rests on the pillow beside me, not hesitating to fist his cock and watch me as I slowly part my legs.

"Keep thinking of what you want to do with that tongue."

I go to playfully slap his arm but remember the rules.

We can't touch.

Dane's mind is closed off, which I find extremely selfish as he dives into mine.

The silhouettes are fading into the walls, hiding, giving us space as the flames of the candles grow larger. I should be concerned about the weather randomly changing from calm to an incoming storm, but my eyes are on Dane's hand as he works the length of him.

"What is your tattoo?"

He chuckles, trapping his lip between his teeth before releasing it. "I'll tell you another time."

I stare at the largeness of him. I still can't see the ink there, and I so badly want to know what it is, but I'm too focused on his veiny hand gripping his girth and stroking to push for an answer. "Task six is going to kill me,"

"You'll manage. Now open your legs for me."

I let my legs fall open, my knees to the mattress on each side.

"Show me how you get yourself off."

I swallow, my nipples tightening under my top as my fingertip grazes my clit. I look away from his face, keeping my attention on his hand as I circle, arching my back as I tease my entrance with my middle finger.

Without stopping his up-and-down movement, Dane shifts forward, closer, so he can see and hear the sounds my pussy makes as I sink two fingers deep inside. His jaw clenches, free hand fisting as I thrust my fingers, pleasuring myself while I watch him stroking his cock.

My eyes roll, my toes curling as I arch my back and grip the sheets, feeling my walls closing over my fingers repeatedly. "Keep going," Dane orders as he strokes himself faster, both of us breathing heavily, the room growing hotter as whimpers and moans mix between us.

His foot touches mine, a graze, but it's enough to drag me out of my build-up to frown at him.

We just failed task five.

"Really, Dane?" I blurt, pulling my fingers out and slapping his chest while he keeps stroking himself with his hand. "You just touched me!"

Dane flinches and stares down, his eyes lifting to my hand. "Did you just put your pussy juice all over me?"

My cheeks heat, seeing the wetness on his chest as mortification overwhelms me. "No. And please don't say it like that ever again."

He reaches up, scraping some of it with his thumb and lifting it to his mouth. My eyes widen as he closes his lips around his thumb, sucking the taste of me from it. "Hmm. Not bad for a human."

I can't help it. I shove him back with force and smack his chest again. Despite my horror and anger, he grins.

"Stop with the insults, you asshole!"

Dane chuckles deeply as he dodges my slaps, capturing my wrist and yanking me on top of him. "Weak and powerless. Can you be any more of a disappointment?"

"You're being mean now."

"No. You're just soft," he replies, smirking as he snatches my other hand, the one I used to pleasure myself, and sucks my middle and ring finger into his mouth. "At least you taste good," he mumbles around them.

I pull my fingers from his mouth with a pop. "I want to hurt you."

"And I want to kiss you."

I'm momentarily frozen by his words. Other than the tasks and usually taking them too far, we've not really been intimate or kissing outside of them. "Careful, Dane, I'm starting to think you have a crush on me."

Eyes flickering with silver look between my mouth and my narrowing gaze. "The universe will cease to exist before I ever admit to that, human. Besides, this..." He pinches my cheek. "This probably isn't your real face."

I hit his hand away, pulling up my shorts and getting to my feet, aiming for the bathroom to lock myself in. "You can't call me a human then say that in the same sentence."

He rushes off the bed, wrapping the towel around himself and snatching my wrist. "I just did."

"And what about you?" I yank free. "What is the real face of Dane Dalton? Or is that even your real name?"

He chuckles, perfect teeth flashing white. His canines have always been a little bit longer.

His naked chest is right there, and my eyes keep lowering from his face to gawk at the muscles and ink, and I accidentally drop my eyes to the perfectly sculpted V between his hips.

"I may be able to change my appearance and species, but my name I cannot." He tilts his head. "And what makes you think this isn't my real face?"

"Ugly personality, ugly manners, ugly handwriting." I lift his notebook from the dresser, the one I can barely read given how illegible the words are. "I assume you make yourself look..." I gesture to his face with the small navy book, and he raises a brow. I groan and force myself to say it. "You make yourself appear handsome to hide the rest of your hideousness. You probably made sure you had a big dick in your human form because the real one is small and pointless. Smart move, shadow boy."

I take a breath.

He licks his lips, and I wait. Wait for him to react, to throw abusive words my way, to choke me with a shadow.

"I'm not sorry," I say before he can force an apology out of me. "Sometimes, the truth hurts."

With that, Dane laughs. Not a deep chuckle or a snort. He bellows as if I've just told the best joke in the universe.

Yet again, he dodges an object I throw at him. His jotter flies across the room instead, landing on top of his discarded clothes.

I place a hand on my hip. "You done?"

"Not even close," he says. "From all of that, I picked up that you find me attractive and think I'm well endowed."

"*Think* being the key word. That doesn't mean you are."

He grips the towel in one hand, as if it's about to fall, running the tip of his tongue along his bottom lip. My traitorous eyes follow the movement. "Would it scare you if I said I'm neither human nor creature?" He takes a step towards me, and I retreat to keep our distance. "What if I said I'm worse?"

Another step forward from him, and one back from me.

"Maybe..." Another step and my back hits the wall beside the bathroom door, trapping me between two immovable objects. "Maybe I'm a shadow? *The* shadow to be exact."

His hand comes up, and my breath hitches as he traces my jawline, pupils dilating as the green flickers to a dim silver, not quite as bright as it gets when he's... excited.

He grits his teeth and slants his head to nudge my nose with his. "Would that suit my hideous soul?"

My throat works on a swallow, but a lump gets caught as the closeness of him infiltrates every sense, every shred of common sense.

The strap of my top slides down my shoulder, and Dane's eyes follow it slowly, mesmerized by the piece of fabric against my heated skin. His gaze doesn't falter as I reach up to fix it back into place.

A wildfire spreads all over my body as Dane captures my throat and presses me into the wall. "I asked you a question, mortal."

"Yes," I breathe.

"Yes what?"

I have no idea. All I know is that my mind is going a million miles an hour, and if I'm not careful, Dane will pick up on the one thought that hasn't stopped repeating since we were on the ballroom floor.

I block him out when he tries to infiltrate my mind, and I somehow manage to keep him trapped in the confines of a part of me filled with conversations between me and the twins while I dig deep into his.

But he's doing the same as me.

We're trapping each other, keeping each other from knowing what we're thinking about, the images we're seeing. He forces me to watch his hand slide up my thigh while in class, while I thrash against his mind from frustration.

As if I have a death wish, I want to tell him to fuck me. Death be damned.

I want to peel down my panties, dip my fingers deep inside myself, and let him taste me again. I want him to drive his cock so hard into me that I scream loud enough to shatter every window in the castle, to snuff out candles, to scare the monsters hiding in the walls.

I want this man far too much to be deemed normal. It isn't a case of lusting or catching feelings for him. This feels like an obsession. A dangerous, terrifying obsession. Because when he isn't around, I wait for him. I think of him. I imagine a different life with him that I haven't lived. I even dream about him.

It must be the pairing. And with each task we do, something between us grows stronger. It's like I'm adjusting to him, to his life and his personality. He's still rude, but not in the way that he used to degrade me and actually bully me.

He pinned me down by the thighs with his shadow hands in class once, and thinking back, I want him to do it again.

I want Dane Dalton.

I'm not sure when it happens, but he slides out of my mind, freeing me, and tucks a lock of hair behind my ear, his brows knitting together. "What are you doing to me?"

"I think it's the tasks," I manage to say breathlessly. "We seem to want each other the more time we spend together, and the more... things we do."

Dane pulls away from me completely, tsking. "Of course it's the fucking tasks. Why would I ever want a human? Why would *you* ever want me?"

Fifty-seven fucking times, he says in his head.

The abrupt change in him is like a slap to the face. "Wait, what do you mean by fifty-seven times?"

"You wanted me to be cruel. An enemy. You wanted me to

make you hate me. This big idea that falling in love with me again through these tasks is ridiculous. How can you when you despise me?" Dane shakes his head. "This was your idea. This was all your idea, Seraphine. It isn't working. It never fucking works. And this..." His hand takes mine, lifting it between us to see the faint lines of darkness as the curse starts to reassert itself. "It's strong. It's never this strong and I don't know how to slow it down without killing myself in the process. You've never been human, so we have no idea what happens when you die. I'm fucking stuck and I might lose you forever."

I stare, confused, as I pull my hand free. "I don't understand."

He grips his hair and turns his back to me. "Fuck," he blurts out. "I can't fucking do this anymore."

"I think you need to sleep. I've no idea what you're talking about. What was my idea?"

"You were ninety years late, and then Orsen and I found you as a human. What changed, Seraphine?"

He's delusional from siphoning the curse. "I am human, Dane. I don't know what you're talking about. I was born twenty years ago. I have a full life of memories. I'm Seraphine Winters from Chic—"

"No," he grits, his eyes glazing over. "Your name is Seraphine Dalton, Queen of the realms, and have been for nearly six hundred fucking years."

I blink, holding my breath. None of what he's saying makes sense, and the look in his eyes tells me that he's losing his mind.

"You need to leave," I say, my voice shaking. "You're scaring me."

He rubs both hands down his face. "I'm sorry. It's not your fault. I'm just..." He walks to me, cups my cheeks, and strokes his thumbs under my eyes as if he's done it a thousand times. "I'm tired. I'm so fucking tired, and I miss you and can't stand talking to you this way. I'll keep trying. You gave me orders and told me not to take shortcuts. I won't. I'll make you forget just now—and the power linking. It's too much of a risk for you to remember."

Frowning, I try to find words. "Make me forget what?"

He presses his forehead to mine, then presses his lips softly against it. "I won't fuck up again, my love. I promise."

A wave of guilt hits me. Unexplainable. It nearly suffocates me as the back of my eyes sting. "Dane..."

"I'm sorry," he replies. "So, so sorry."

My lips part as he pulls his face away, but then my gaze follows a lone tear falling from his eye as he mutters something in a different language. My chest tightens, as if something is being pulled out of me. My vision blurs, and a part of me panics and wants to pull away, screaming for him not to do this, but there's a snap in my head, and my mind goes blank.

I blink a few times as Dane moves away from me and wipes his face, rubbing his eyes, waiting for me to speak.

"I think it's the tasks," I manage to say, breathless all of a sudden. "We seem to want each other the more time we spend together, and the more... things we do."

He nods. "It seems so, mortal. Sleep—you will need your strength for tomorrow."

"What happens tomorrow?" I ask as he wordlessly magics himself a fresh pile of clothes and starts pulling them on.

"You'll see."

And then he winks at me as he disappears into nothing.

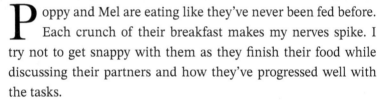

29

P oppy and Mel are eating like they've never been fed before. Each crunch of their breakfast makes my nerves spike. I try not to get snappy with them as they finish their food while discussing their partners and how they've progressed well with the tasks.

Meanwhile, I have managed to skip the deadlines until Dane returns to class. If he returns. From what I've gathered from reading too many books in the library, it's unlikely.

But I can't help but feel uneasy about the possibility of him suffering. He *is* suffering. Going on the bruises and marks over his body last night, he's being beaten down there.

He might be getting beaten right now.

I worry my lip as I look around us, everyone eating their breakfast and chatting among themselves. Orsen keeps glancing over, probably trying to get Mel's attention. The moody princess is mad at him for some reason, giving him the finger when he asks to speak with her. He's been quite lost since Dane was arrested. He has other friends, but Dane was his best friend. Orsen was his right-hand man, stuck to his hip unless Mel clicked her fingers and wanted attention.

I'm surprised he hasn't asked me where Dane is. Maybe he knows and doesn't want to make it obvious to others. Or maybe I'm trying to pass the time by thinking of anything but Dane and what he could be going through right now.

Worried about me, little mortal?

I lift my gaze to the bickering twins and shove a spoonful of porridge into my mouth, suppressing my shift in mood. I refuse to show that his voice uplifts me.

Never.

Liar. I can feel how anxious you are about my current living situation. Would it make you feel better if I said the other person looks a lot worse?

Get out of my head. I gather more porridge on the spoon and put it in my mouth, a bid to hide the annoying smile trying to break free from hearing his voice.

A few minutes pass, and some students leave the food hall. Dane's mother watches me as she walks in, grabs Orsen, and leaves again without sparing me another scowl.

I want to roll my eyes at her, remembering the way she excused herself because she didn't want to witness her son kissing a human.

Well, said son did kiss me. Multiple times in fact. Maybe I should tell her that he spends hours a day with me, that when he was arrested, her son was close to fucking me on his bathroom floor. That he actually tolerates my company, considering he used to hate touching me and claimed I was dirty.

Weak.

Dying.

Oh, and just a warm body, if I remember rightly. He was mortified that he had to be paired with me, so much so that he cornered me on several occasions and demanded I either leave the academy or refuse the pairing.

I squeeze my spoon in my hand, growing unsettled.

"You're very quiet today, Sera. Everything okay?"

Poppy is smiling at me—a small, gentle, friendly smile.

There's a fire in me that ignites anger, and I snap my next two words without intending to. "I'm fine."

How can they sit here and act like everything is okay? Their realm is in ruins, they killed their father, and they've been sent here. Poppy is beyond excited about being around humans, and Mel couldn't be any more disapproving of it. They sit here and eat their breakfast, laugh between them, discuss lessons and what to do on our days off as if we can go to the movies or have sleepovers.

We can't. Because we're trapped on this stupid, godforsaken island, with rules that stop us from doing anything but being good little students.

Dane is in the dungeons, I have gloves on to hide the curse slowly killing me, my memories were messed with by Valin, and all they want to do is talk about the stupid ball and what we're wearing.

I clench my teeth, the twins staring at me, waiting for me to say something else. "What?"

Mel narrows her brows at me. "She was only asking if you were okay."

My shoulders sag. I don't know what's gotten into me recently. I'm losing my patience with everyone.

"I guess I'm not as good as you both at pretending everything is okay. I'm sorry. I'm tired, and this entire experience is exhausting." I swallow but then hold my breath as Valin pushes open the main doors to the hall, marching in with his assistant behind him.

Although I was just a bitch to her sister, Mel gets to her feet. "I'm going to kick his ass."

Poppy grabs her arm. "Please don't."

Mel listens, and I offer her a half-smile when she gives up glaring at the professor. "I'm going to speak with him after class tomorrow. Alone," I add when she goes to speak.

Well, Dane will be in my head, but yeah. I imagine Valin will refuse to talk to me if I have the twins with me, so I need to go myself.

"I don't think that's a good idea, Sera. He's a lunatic!"

My shoulder raises in a shrug. "I need to know what his deal is. Surely I deserve to know? I can't wait for Dane to be released and deal with him. I'm not a feeble human who needs backup."

"Human, yes. Feeble, no." Poppy leans forward. "And who said Dane was being released? He's being charged with murder, remember?"

Then Mel adds, "He'll be lucky if he gets to see you again in your lifetime. Not that either of you wants to see each other anyway."

"Right." The word feels like poison on my tongue, but I refuse to admit that my hatred for Dane is starting to be dominated by something else, something strong and... undeniable.

I like when he magically blows into my room and insults me. I also like it when he gives me a certain look that sets all my nerve endings on fire and warms my cheeks.

I mean, he held my breast last night when we lay in bed, and I enjoyed it.

What is happening to me?

Valin sits at the furthest-away table from us, and I'm thankful. He does, however, keep looking over, trying to catch my eye. Mel gives him one of her deadly stares, and he quickly retreats to his food while chatting with his assistant.

"Who are you going to the ball with then, Sera?" Poppy asks, leaning her chin on her hands, elbows on the table.

I hum then shrug. "I don't have a date. The professor hasn't mentioned a replacement."

"Do you want me to ask Brandt if any of his friends need a date?"

Answer that and I'll set your bed on fire.

In my head, I'm tutting and saying, *Shut up.* "Only if they want to."

Human.

Poppy pulls out her phone while Mel gulps down her water. "I'll message him and find out."

"Thanks."

Are you trying to anger me? Because it's working.

I don't have a date. If this bothers you, which it shouldn't, then maybe you should have thought about the consequences of your actions before deciding to kill someone.

Funny. His voice holds no amusement, yet it has me fighting another smile I conceal with a bite of my lip.

———

When we finish up and head to a lesson in socialization with mortals, I drown out the voices around me and focus on doodling stick men in my jotter.

"Miss Winters," the professor says. "Can you explain to the class what your life expectancy as a mortal is?"

My eyes go wide as everyone turns to face me. "Oh, uh…" I fidget with the gloves concealing my fingers, gripping the hem of my skirt. "It depends on one's health, I guess, but a lot of people live to their eighties, some even a few years over a hundred."

"That's all?" someone asks with disgust on his face. "That's sad."

Someone else giggles and says I'll be dead before they've even lived, and another student comments on my skin and how awful my hair is—that it's no wonder I cake myself with makeup.

For the first time in forever, I feel like crying. Not from their words, not really. I'm just drained. So drained.

I wet my lips and look down.

This class sucks.

I want to ask Dane to blow into here and take me away, to

stab them in the heart and crack their skulls. Rage rushes through me like an inferno, and I have to hold my breath to stop myself from exploding. Pressure builds behind my eyes, but I can't stop it.

I gasp as a blistering sensation comes from my fingers under the gloves, like a bolt of raging fire, hot and stingy and awakening.

I narrow my eyes at the burned fabric at my fingertips then hide my hands under my thighs, making sure no one questions me.

You have some horrific scraps of material for underwear. How does one even feel comfortable in these? The white ones are hot though. I think I'll keep them.

I stand abruptly. "May I go to the bathroom?"

"Can't you wait?"

Someone says, "She's a human, professor. She can't do anything but waste oxygen."

I grit my teeth, my nostrils flaring. I want to reach over and gouge their eyeballs out. When the teacher tells me to go, I grab my satchel and head to the door, wishing his chair would fly away from beneath him and—

A yelp comes from behind me, and I stop to see the person on the ground, their chair nonexistent. I freeze for a second but then inwardly groan that Dane evidently heard me.

When I reach my room, ready to give Dane an earful for going through my things, he's sitting on my bed, leaning back on one elbow while reading my notes on famous musicians and songwriters.

"If you have any of my underwear in your pockets, I want them back."

He doesn't look up from the book. "You better check for yourself, human. My hands are busy."

If he thinks for a second I'm taking a back seat, he has another think coming. I throw my bag off and shove his chest, so he's flat on the bed. The book slides to the side, and Dane watches as I search the pockets of his cotton shorts.

Why is he wearing mortal clothes again?

I narrow my gaze on him when I come up empty. "You're such an idiot. I left class because of you!"

My hand trembles as he captures it, studying the burn marks on my glove. "What happened?"

"Nothing." I try to yank away but fail.

"Don't lie to me. You were mad. I had to get you out of that classroom given how murderous you were becoming in your head. What happened?"

"Just some of the students commenting on me and how human I am, that's all." I manage to stand and free myself from his grasp. "Their comments are nothing compared to what you've thrown at me, so don't look so offended for me."

I rush to the bathroom, washing the burned fabric from my hands and binning the ruined gloves. I stare at my skin. When I was at breakfast, I could feel the curse growing, spreading up my palms, but right now, it's barely visible.

"Dane," I say, walking into the room while studying my hands. "Is it possible for the curse to... weaken? It was worse this morning."

He stays on the bed but gestures for me to come closer, and I listen. My skin prickles when he sits at the edge of the mattress, dragging me between his parted legs by gripping my hips. "It would only be possible to slow it down or weaken it through a release of energy." He pinches my fingertip, and I flinch. "Since you're human, that's not possible."

He sucks his bottom lip into his mouth, sliding his finger against my palm and sending waves of his own energy through me.

"Can you feel that?" he asks, pushing more energy into my palm, and I nod. It's tingly, and the pulse ricochets off each nerve and settles in my chest. "Keep your gloves on regardless of the state of your hands. I'll make new ones for you." He releases my hand, but neither of us moves. His eyes are a beautiful, dazzling shade of green as he keeps his gaze on me. "Do you feel okay?"

"Yeah." I nod, slowly stepping away. "You should go before your inspection. You don't need to siphon right now. I'll see you tonight?"

Dane doesn't respond right away. If anything, he seems to want to stay a little longer, but it's far too dangerous. If he's caught, this is done. Whatever this is. A friendship? A student-student bond over human relations? Enemies who like touching each other? I think, even after the way he treated me to begin with, I'd happily be his friend.

Dane blows out a breath and stands. "No offense, little mortal, but I don't want to be your friend."

I refuse to show how much that hurts me. "Good."

"Good," he counters. "I don't know of many friends who are tasked to fuck each other, let alone what we have to do for task ten."

I nod and look to the side. "It's nearly the end of day."

"I'll be back around eleven," he says, flattening my duvet, which was creased from him lying on it.

Before he can leave, I step towards him. "Thank you for what you did today. He was being a jerk, and I appreciate your help."

Dane looks confused. "I've no idea what the fuck you're talking about," he says then disappears, leaving me in silence.

I slowly blink a few times, staring at the spot he was in.

If he didn't do it, then who did?

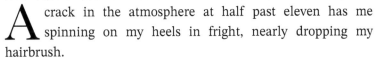

30

A crack in the atmosphere at half past eleven has me spinning on my heels in fright, nearly dropping my hairbrush.

"Good evening, mortal," Dane drawls, pulling lint from his cuff and flattening out his sleeves, making sure his sleeve garters at his biceps are perfectly in place. He regards me with a grimace. "Forever in your sleep clothes, aren't you?"

"It's nearly bedtime." I place a hand on my hip. "Why are you dressed up?"

Dane looks down at his waistcoat before pushing his hands slowly into his pockets. "Have I been so lazy that you seem to think this is me *dressed up*?"

"You've been wearing human clothes the last two days. I guess I was getting used to an immortal creature in cotton shorts and white tops." Then I pause. "How do you get clothes when you're in the dungeons?"

"One of my—"

"Powers. Yes, forget I asked."

He shakes his head. "We have to practice. We've missed three classes so far, and I refuse to dance with you at the ball if you fall over my feet. Plus, you're a terrible dancer."

I gape at him. "And how, pray tell, do you plan on attending? Your trial—for *murder*—is in a few days, and the ball is in two weeks. Poppy will find me another date."

"His name is Silas, and all he'll want to do is fuck you, which is not happening. Forget it."

I stifle a laugh. "Are you jealous, Dane Dalton?"

"Don't be ridiculous."

"Then I'm going with someone else. You're not going to see the light of day for a long time, according to the laws in this academy." I throw my hands out. "I need to go to the ball, Dane. I don't have a choice."

"Nothing will come of my trial," he says, inspecting my room like he hasn't spent the last nine days visiting it. "Do you have something that plays music? Or shall I conjure a piano?"

Of course he changes the subject. "Depends. Can you play?"

A smile tugs at Dane's lips, and he turns his back to me. "I had a great teacher. I was never as good as her, but I was fine with listening instead of playing."

"Sounds like you had a crush on your piano teacher."

"You could say that," he replies, turning to me. "She knew how to play every instrument beautifully. I was mesmerized by her."

I press my lips together. "Lovely."

"Who's the jealous one now?"

I grimace and move towards the small desk in the corner of my room, checking my phone for a reply from Poppy. She said she'd let me know tonight if she found me a date, and a part of me is glad my notification bar is empty.

"The curse hasn't spread much," I say, showing him my hands. "A little on my palms, but none of it hurts like usual. This is a good thing, right? You won't need to come here twice a day to siphon it if it stops. It's a win-win."

That sounds terrible, but the words are out before I can stop them.

Dane stares at me, emotionless.

"I just mean because you obviously risk a lot coming here. And it hurts you."

"Stop the backtracking. We both know you don't want me here."

"You don't exactly want to be here either," I reply quietly.

"Great. Can you get dressed? I can't dance with you while you're wearing..." He points at my sleep shorts, which barely hide my ass cheeks.

"You did teleport in here near midnight. I don't know why you expected me to be in my uniform. I'm about to go to bed. Can't we do this tomorrow?"

"No."

I wait for him to say something else, but all he does is lean against my dresser, staring me down.

I tut and head towards him. I see it the moment he thinks I'm closing the distance to him, and his breath hitches as he clears his throat. But then I move him with my shoulder, shifting him aside to get into my dresser.

I go into the bathroom with something more Dane appropriate. Once I fix my breasts into a bra and smooth down the dress that reaches mid-thigh, I finish brushing my hair and braid it to the side.

He patiently waits as I apply some mascara and lip balm. My cheeks are a little flush from... well, I guess because Dane looks the way he does. I hate that I'm attracted to him and my body has no idea how to not react to his close proximity.

And why does he need to smell so good? He sleeps in a dungeon, for crying out loud.

Hurry up, his voice comes.

Screw you, I fire back.

I check myself over once more before exiting the bathroom,

stopping in my tracks when I see Dane having a silent discussion with one of the shadows on my walls. He and the little girl seem to be staring at one another, and she jumps in the air in excitement as the corners of Dane's lips curl.

He chuckles as she shows him a stone she finds on the ground.

"Do you know her?" I ask, breaking his concentration.

Silence, and then Dane drops his head. "No," he says without looking at me. "She's alone, so I was keeping her company until her protector returned."

He lifts his head and nods to the large mass as it takes the girl's hand—then they both vanish into the crack of the wall.

"She's sweet," I say, fidgeting with my hair. "She always plays with the dog and waves at me."

"Hmm."

Crickets could fill the silence that stretches between us, if they existed on this island. Dane keeps his eyes on the wall, chewing on the inside of his cheek, seemingly lost in his head.

I try to listen, but he's sealed me out.

I stand here, kind of confused. "So...?"

He still doesn't look at me. "So?"

"You said you were here to practice."

He blinks a few times then rubs a hand down his face, which is filled with exhaustion. "Right."

When he turns, I watch him stride towards the dresser again and start playing music from a small wooden box. Chords strike on a piano, a soft voice in a different language fills the room, and then violins join in a beautiful symphony.

"You look tired," I say.

"Observant as ever, mortal."

"Are you not sleeping well?"

He frowns. "I sleep in a cell—what the fuck do you think?"

Good point. Although he better not snap at me like that again. But he looks different than usual—moodier.

"What happens down there?" I ask, sure he'll snap at me some more. "You hadn't healed yourself last night. You had a lot of bruising and cuts on you." I nod to his neck. "Especially there."

"Why do you care?"

I sigh. "Would it kill you to go a day without being such an asshole to me?"

"Yes." He runs his hand through his hair, messing it, yet still looking as dashing as ever. "Put heels on."

I cross my arms. "Excuse me?"

"I assume you will be wearing heels to the ball?"

Another good point.

Once I fasten a pair of stilettos, I walk to stand in front of him. He still towers over me. "How tall are you? I'm not considered short—I was taller than most of the kids in my year, but you're a skyscraper compared to me."

Instead of answering me, he goes for the one piece of information he took from that. "A skyscraper?"

I stare at him for a long moment, then my shoulders slump and I shake my head. "Never mind." I take his hand and place it on my hip. "Do you know the steps?"

"I've done this dance a thousand times. It's me here to teach you."

"How noble of you."

He leads us silently through the routine as he takes my other hand in his and pulls me around the room. "Probably the nicest thing you've said about me," he says, spinning me and capturing my hip again.

"Don't get used to it."

He dips me abruptly, and I yelp as my head nearly hits the floor. I gape at him as he smirks while tugging me back to stand straight. "Asshole."

He chuckles. "That's better."

There's a constant electrical current between us. It's...

comfortable, not something I need more or less of. My chest brushes against his as he pulls me closer, and I feel his breath on my cheek before he dips me again.

I swallow as his eyes clash with mine, holding my gaze. "Do we need to end the dance the same way we did before? Do we need to kiss?"

"No," he replies as he guides us in carefully coordinated steps. "I think that was just to help form a bond of sorts, so partners are more at ease with their pairing."

I let out a breath. "Good." Not good. I want a reason to kiss him without admitting to myself I actually do want a kiss—a real kiss.

His jaw clenches as he spins me and twirls me back to his chest. "Am I so undesirable, mortal?"

"Coming from the person who made my life hell and called me ugly and disgusting."

"The truth hurts," he says with amusement, and he fully grins when I smack his chest.

I seem to be smacking him a lot lately.

As before, I somehow know how to move, and Dane only needs to talk me through a few parts of the dance, and at one point, we smoothly sail through each step without missing a beat from start to finish. I giggle as he does the final dip, and I hear Dane's heart in my own ears.

"Not too bad," I say, grinning as I pant. "I bet Silas is better."

He lifts me. "Once more."

This time, he throws me around like he's trying to prove a point. I accidentally stand on his shoe, and he bumps my hip into the dresser intentionally. I stick out my tongue, and we start from the beginning again.

By the time we're done, it's nearly three in the morning. Dane has his sleeves rolled to his elbows, the top two buttons unfastened, and his hair disheveled. I'm in a worse condition. My hair is a mess, my dress clings to me, and my limbs ache.

We both drop on the bed after six billion run-throughs of the dance, breathing in sync. "You're worse than I thought," he says while filling his lungs. "Shockingly bad, to be brutally honest. There isn't a chance in hell Silas will want to fuck you after that."

"You know, it's sometimes better to not be honest." I roll onto my side, perching on my elbow with my hand to my head. "Which is why you withhold so much stuff from me, and I'm getting fed up with it."

"What do you mean? Like what?"

"Firstly, you won't tell me why Valin took me. Secondly, you won't tell me why you killed someone. Thirdly, you won't tell me why the tasks are made the way they are. Should I keep going? I'm sure I have another twelve to go through."

"Can you just settle on the fact you're better off not knowing?"

"No."

He sighs. "I'm starting to remember why I hate you."

"Good," I retort. "Because this nice version of you confuses me."

"Give me your hands, so I can leave."

I sit up and so does he, and I place my palms on top of his. I keep my eyes to the side, not looking at him as he mutters annoyances to himself while the burning begins.

But it doesn't come...

It should hurt, right?

It always hurts.

Why doesn't it hurt? I feel a slight heat, but that's all.

When I glance at Dane, he looks like he's in excruciating pain. His eyes are screwed shut, his teeth clenched, another trickle of black blood dripping from his nose.

His body is shaking while I stare at him.

Tightening his hold on my hands, he swears to himself as black tendrils claw up his neck as they always do, settling into his skin.

But I feel nothing.

He breaks away abruptly and falls off the bed, crouching down as he grabs his chest. "Fuck."

I go to him, dropping to my knees as I grab at his shoulders. "Are you okay?"

He shoves away from me, his eyes fully black, even the whites taken over, the dark veins climbing up one side of his face and into his hairline.

"I need to go."

"No. Wait."

But before he can materialize, I reach out to stop him, knowing he's too weak. But a sudden tug all over my body makes me dizzy, my room warping into nothing, and I drop onto a cold, hard floor with a stench that could burn my sense of smell to nothing.

Dane lands on top of me with a grunt, and he pushes himself up using his hands, blood gushing from his nose as his thighs bracket my hips.

"What the fuck did you do?"

I look around and feel myself paling more and more with each passing second. "Oh no. Is this your cell?"

"Yes, and I'm not strong enough to take you back. Are you insane?"

My eyes go wide. "No. You need to take me back."

He falls to the side, tensing all over. "I can't."

I get to my feet, gaping at the blood all over the bricks, the chains dangling from the ceiling, and the metal bed frame with no mattress. A wooden block sits to the side with food no one should ever be touching, never mind eating.

"I've seen this before," I say aloud. "This cell. There was a little boy in it."

Dane is still gasping in the corner, trying to settle his pain while I try not to panic at seeing all of this when I've already dreamed it and now being trapped here.

Think. Think, Sera.

"What was that thing you said immortals can do where they share power?"

Dane closes his eyes and mutters a curse under his breath. "Power linking."

I nod and crouch in front of him. "Yeah, that. Can I do that with you?"

He stares at me, the shivers wracking my body from both fear and how cold the cell is. Dane takes in our surroundings and then grimaces, as if contemplating and weighing other options. But there is no other option. Dane can use my body to get us out of here; he's too weak, but his power is not. He can sleep in my dorm room until he's fit enough to leave.

I grab his curse-covered hands. "Tell me what to do."

He groans and gives in. "This is dangerous—do you understand? Power linking isn't safe and should only be used under extreme circumstances."

Is he crazy? "This is extreme. I'm in your cell in the dungeons!"

"Fine," he snaps. "Picture your room, get a strong vision of it, and build up enough determination to get there."

"That's all?"

He nods. "I'll do the rest. You'll feel the need to travel there, so just do it. I'll try not to overwhelm you."

"Okay."

He squeezes his eyes shut with a rush of pain. "You owe me a fucking kiss for this."

My lips part. "You want to kiss me?"

His gaze levels on me, as if I've asked what color the sky is. "Haven't I made that obvious?"

I smile and nod with a blush to my cheeks despite our current misfortune. "Fine. If this works, I'll kiss you."

"Deal."

I picture my room as hard as I can, listening to Dane

muttering in another language as bolts of energy shift between us. I gasp from the intrusion of power I shouldn't feel, and my mind goes completely blank as my heart accelerates.

I feel like I'm waking up, lost but found, as if I'm reconciling with a part of me that's been missing for too long.

The smell of the cell vanishes, my vision warping once again, and Dane tells me to focus as he forces his power into me at full capacity. I manage to somehow materialize us out of the cell by focusing on my room like my life depends on it.

His hands are gripping me as everything around us ripples into a swirl of nothing. We land on a soft rug, his chest pressing to mine as we both gasp for air. He's crushing me until he pushes himself half up.

He grabs my face, and I see the curse has seeped into his skin already. "Talk to me. Tell me you're okay."

I blink. "I'm okay. Are y—"

I look up, the sound dying in my throat as all the blood drains from my face when I realize where I've brought him. The immortal creature who hates humans. Who hates my world and my people.

My eyes land on my bedside table—on my pink lamp and my electronic alarm clock, which is still working. My bed is still made from the morning I left for work, and a picture of me and Toodles sits on the bedside unit.

Dane frowns as he sits up and takes in our surroundings, his puzzled glare traveling around the bedroom I haven't been in for months.

"Where the fuck are we?"

To be continued...

ABOUT THE AUTHOR

Leigh Rivers is a Scottish Biomedical Scientist who has ventured into the world of writing dark, morally gray characters with rollercoaster storylines to drive her readers wild.
When she isn't reading, writing on her laptop, or gaming until ridiculous hours, she dances at the pole studio, goes to the gym, and walks her four dogs with her two sons and husband.

You can find Leigh on her socials here:

Made in the USA
Middletown, DE
03 January 2025

68747127R00155